"I grew up here, Miss Carr.

"Now your father and his partner want to destroy Santa Marta, level it, so they can turn it into paradise by the river, one of their exclusive developments. Expensive homes for extravagant people.

"Nobody worried about people living at the bend of the river when it flooded every time it rained all those years ago. Nobody gave a second thought to Santa Marta then. But now that the river's been dammed, Santa Marta has suddenly become prime real estate.

"Well, it just so happens I have my own plans for Santa Marta. Plans to build it up, not tear it down. Plans to improve conditions for the people who live here, not dispossess them."

Tori rose abruptly. "My father, Mr. Amorado, is not insensitive to other people's problems. I'm sorry you had a rough childhood. It seems to have left a chip on your shoulder the size of Coyote Mesa."

She turned to the doorway. He might think he'd won the first skirmish, but the battle wasn't over, not by a long shot.

Dear Reader,

Have you ever gone back to a favorite place—like the street where you grew up or the first house you bought after getting married—and found it completely changed? Maybe some of the buildings were still there, but somehow it all looked different.

A few years ago we took our young granddaughter to see the Christmas lights here in our city. There was one house in a certain part of town that had become so popular that the city included it on their nightly bus tour of holiday spectacles.

Kiki's joy and wide-eyed wonder melted my heart as we wandered through a magical wonderland set up on an oversized corner lot. Some of the figures were "store boughten," but there was nothing commercial about any of it. The spectacle was an elaborate labor of love, one proud family's generous gift to the community.

It got me thinking about the difference between a neighborhood and a development. What if this neighborhood's very existence were threatened? Who would be affected? How would they react? Would anyone be willing to do something about it?

Coyote Springs is fictitious, as is the Santa Marta district I portray in this story. But I suspect all of us have been to a place like it at one time or another. It's the place we call home—if only in our hearts.

K.N. Casper

A MAN CALLED JESSE
K.N. Casper

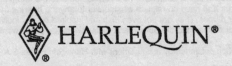

HARLEQUIN®

TORONTO • NEW YORK • LONDON
AMSTERDAM • PARIS • SYDNEY • HAMBURG
STOCKHOLM • ATHENS • TOKYO • MILAN • MADRID
PRAGUE • WARSAW • BUDAPEST • AUCKLAND

ISBN 0-373-70806-8

A MAN CALLED JESSE

To Roz, Jan and Connie,
who got me started and wouldn't let me stop.
And to Mary, who inspired me all along the way.

CHAPTER ONE

TORI CARR FLEW DUE WEST. The last leg of her journey home.

She clicked on her microphone. "Coyote tower. Twin Cessna, Romeo-Romeo-three-three-eight, ten miles east for landing."

A momentary pause, then a crackling response. She adjusted her altimeter and checked her heading indicator.

Without warning a violent lurch flipped her hard over to the left. As she glimpsed a T-38 military trainer jetting out from under her, Tori grabbed the control yoke with both hands and centered the wheel. Her right leg stiffened on the rudder to overcome the spin while her hands rammed the yoke sharply forward. Then came the hollow-stomach sensation of careening head-long into a nosedive. With calculated slowness, she pulled back on the yoke. The plane shuddered violently.

Her heart pounded. Her blood raced. Her ears buzzed from the engines' keening roar.

The rate of descent slowed.

She finally leveled off at a thousand feet, got her air speed under control. Sweat trickled down the back of her neck. She held extra pressure on the right rudder and adjusted the trim tab. Forcing a deep breath, she looked through the side window to assess the damage.

Jagged metal glittered like tinsel in the sunlight. The right wing fairing was clipped. Bad? Certainly. But manageable.

The Cessna regained three thousand feet.

"Situation under control," she told herself.

Then black smoke began ribboning from the amputated wing tip. The impact of the midair collision must have ruptured a fuel line.

Fire!

"Mayday, Mayday," she called on the radio. "This is twin Cessna three-three-eight. Mayday, Mayday. Right wing tip on fire. Repeat. I am on fire. Mayday, Mayday."

Tori clawed the yoke with one hand and reached with the other to turn off the fuel-boost pump to engine number two. She feathered the propeller, watched it stop. She'd practiced single-engine emergencies before. Plenty of times. She could do it. She had to.

Her fingers were steady as she adjusted the trim tab to maintain level flight of the crippled aircraft. The fire continued to burn.

There was a maneuver... It was a gamble, but one she had to take. Flight boots glued to the rudder pedals, she forced the plane into a slip to the left. Left wing down. Full right rudder. Gloved hands clamped in a death grip on the controls, she rammed the yoke forward into another deliberate nosedive. Her shoulders knotted as the Cessna screamed and fell from the sky, leaving her stomach behind once more.

Again the rusty brown earth zoomed toward her as the wind tore at the flames. "Go out, damn it. Go out!"

The savage land reached out to her like a magnet.

Fifteen hundred feet.

"I didn't resign my air force commission to die in

this little Cessna,'' she muttered to herself as the altimeter needle twirled counterclockwise.

A thousand feet.

Again the plane convulsed in bone-rattling tremors. She wasn't just tempting fate—she was daring it.

Five hundred feet.

At the last possible moment, the flames guttered out. Only the adrenaline of pure terror and relief gave her the superhuman strength to ease back on the yoke. G-forces plastered her to the seat as the aircraft swooped over a stand of pecan trees and began its upward swing above the cheated earth.

She surveyed the situation. The fire was out. Perspiration pooled between her breasts.

Clicking the mike button below her right thumb, she forced herself to speak calmly. ''Mayday, Mayday. Coyote tower. This is twin Cessna three-three-eight. I have an in-flight emergency. Request immediate landing instructions. Mayday, Mayday.''

''Twin Cessna three-three-eight. You are cleared to land at your discretion. Runway one-eight. Emergency crew standing by.''

''Roger, tower. Going for runway one-eight.''

She heard the tower advising all other aircraft in the area to clear the pattern. She wasn't home safe yet. Her life depended on keeping the plane straight and level in the glide path. The landing, less than a minute later, was a little rough, but with no more ballooning than she'd seen other pilots perform under much better conditions.

It wasn't until she'd come to a halt in the middle of the runway that her limbs began to tremble, all strength spent. Even lifting her hand to fumble with the last power switch demanded extraordinary concentration.

Emergency vehicles were already surrounding her. She yanked off her headset and moved quickly to the back of the four-passenger compartment. A wall of hot, dry Texas air assailed her when she opened the door. The searing stench of raw aviation fuel invaded her nostrils. Impulsively she ran her fingers through her short blond hair and skittered down the ladderlike steps into the brilliant summer sun. She was home.

Tori dashed on rubbery legs as far as possible from the plane while crash vehicles disgorged their crews. A foam truck stood by ready to douse the wing, or the whole craft, if necessary. Only heat waves radiated from the scorched metal.

A canvas-topped Jeep pulled up to within a few feet of her. A man, probably in his sixties, with parched, sun-wrinkled brown skin, smiled reassuringly at her.

"You must be Tori Carr. Name's Sam. Sam Hargis." He tipped his soiled baseball cap, which said Hargis Aviation. She'd arranged to moor her plane on his pad. "That was some flying you just did, lady. I haven't seen aerobatics like that since my daddy took me to see some barnstorming at a county fair." Fumbling in a cooler behind his seat, he extracted a frosty can of soda and offered it to her.

"Thanks." She accepted it gratefully and hoped he didn't notice her hands shaking as she popped the tab. She gulped. The cold drink burned the back of her throat.

"If you ever want to get a job crop-dusting or giving stunt-flying lessons, you just let me know," the old man said. "There's half a dozen outfits around here that could use you."

She gave him a wide grin. "Sam, you couldn't pay me enough to do that again, much less for a living."

He chuckled. "Anyway, that was mighty impressive. Jump in. Your folks are waiting for you at the hangar."

She climbed onto the hot canvas seat.

At the corner of the old wooden building, a tall, strapping man gave her a thumbs-up as they drove by, then tucked his big hands in the back pockets of snug jeans. The shadow of his white cowboy hat masked his features, but Tori could feel his eyes following her as the open vehicle pulled into the shade of the cavernous structure.

The Jeep drew to a stop, and Tori caught sight of her father and his secretary running toward her. His partner walked rapidly behind them. She jumped to the ground and was instantly swallowed up in a hearty bear hug. The familiar scent of her father's aftershave conjured up ghosts of love and sadness.

"Thank God you're safe," Winslow Carr whispered huskily in her ear. He released her quickly, as though embarrassed at his emotional display, and held her at arm's length. "I was listening to the tower chatter in Sam's office. You scared me out of a year's growth, young lady." The quaver in his voice stole even the pretense of harshness from his words.

"I'm fine, Dad," she assured him. "Really."

He offered her a small bouquet of cut flowers. Several of the stems were bent, the entire collection askew.

"I guess I got a little nervous watching you come in," he said sheepishly.

She paused for a second to get past the lump in her throat. "Thanks, Dad. They're lovely." She kissed him on the cheek.

His secretary, Lydia Anderson, was next. Her silver bracelets jangled as she threw her arms around Tori.

"You could have been killed up there," she said in a strained voice.

Tori was tempted to quip that it was all in a day's work, but the anxiety in the older woman's face told her this wasn't a time for levity. "I'm fine," she said, and gave her a loving kiss on the cheek.

Finally there was Burton, her father's business partner. Burton Hazlitt, with his big muscles and mischievous grin. She'd had an affair with him right after she was commissioned, the consummation of years of flirtation. But by her next visit home, she knew their relationship was over, on that level, at least. He'd tried several times to rekindle it, but his attempts were only halfhearted, more a game than passionate seduction. The repartee they'd fallen into since then was amusing and flattering, but neither of them took it seriously. Still, he'd been her first lover, and she couldn't help feeling a nostalgic affection for him.

He stood before her now, a fireplug of a man, his bulging arms bowed out from his stocky body, his hands by his sides. Obviously he was still pumping iron.

"You sure know how to make an entrance," he said, and gave her an openhanded salute. She chuckled softly when she realized she almost saluted back.

"At ease, Burton."

He dropped his hand and leaned forward, clutched her upper arms and gave her a stiff, formal kiss on the right cheek. She grinned at his mockery and decided not to tell him that even without heels on, she could see his brown hair was beginning to thin on top. As he repeated the gesture on her other cheek, she glanced over his shoulder to the side of the wide doorway. The cowboy in the snug jeans had turned his back and was walking away.

It took less than half an hour to file her mishap report with the Federal Aviation Administration. Then she stopped by the tower to thank the controller for his help. The T-38, she learned, had been from the air force base near the Mexican border. The pilot, on routine low-level maneuvers, had been practicing instrument approaches to the airfield but veered from his pattern and hadn't seen Tori's plane above him. He'd clipped his own vertical stabilizer in the midair collision but was able to get back to home base safely.

Tori returned to her waiting family.

Burton picked up the single piece of luggage she'd retrieved from the plane when Hargis towed it into the hangar. "Is this everything?"

"The air force is shipping the rest," she told him. Her father and Lydia were already walking across the shiny painted hangar floor to the parking lot. "It should be here in a day or two."

"You sure travel light—" he looked at her with the seductive little grin that used to send her pulse skittering "—for a woman."

She laughed. "Sounds like you've had a lot of experience traveling with women."

Judging from his not-so-coy leer, he regarded the put-down as a compliment.

Tori took a closer look at her father, a few steps ahead. He was only fifty, but his once-square build was beginning to appear more barrel-shaped. Obviously, he wasn't watching his diet. And Lydia had reported that he was also becoming obsessed with his real estate ventures.

Burton had parked his forest green Jaguar on the

shady side of the hangar. He deposited her flight bag in the trunk while Winslow and Lydia climbed into the back seat.

"I wondered how long you'd stick it out," Burton commented as he held open the front passenger door for Tori. "You lasted longer than I thought. But I knew eventually you'd quit."

"Quit?" she gasped as he slammed the door and walked around the front of the vehicle.

Her father reached forward from the back seat and placed his hand on her shoulder. "I hope you're not too disappointed about the air force not working out, sweetheart. Military life isn't for everyone."

She bit her lip. Listening to Burton and her father, one would think she hadn't accomplished anything since she'd graduated from the air force academy at the top of her class.

"The only reason I joined," she reminded him, "was to fly. Color blindness kept me from doing that for Uncle Sam, but I can still fly commercially. And in case you haven't noticed, I'm a damned good pilot."

"But why come back here?" Burton asked as he got in and buckled up. "This isn't exactly a mecca for jumbo jets."

The hint of condescension in his question annoyed her.

"I've applied to the airlines that fly into Coyote Springs," she told him. "In the meantime, I thought I'd spend some time with y'all. Lydia tells me you're up to your eyeteeth in this Riverbend project."

"Going to help us out, huh?" He started the engine. "Well, I'm sure we'll be very grateful."

"God, Burt, you're as chauvinistic as ever." She buckled her own seat belt, satisfied with the little tick of displeasure she'd provoked. He didn't mind being called a chauvinist, but he hated being called Burt. Lydia made a noise from the back seat that sounded suspiciously like a giggle.

"How's Riverbend coming?" Tori asked as they pulled out into the bright afternoon sunshine.

"Great," her father replied enthusiastically. "All the plans are drawn, most of the property has been bought or optioned and our contractors are standing by, ready to start development within thirty days."

One thing she'd learned from the military and diplomatic briefings she'd set up as an executive officer in the Pentagon was the judicious use of words.

"You said *most* of the property is accounted for."

"We've got one holdout," Burton explained.

"Tell me about it."

"Not much to tell. Jesse Amorado's a small-time builder who owns half a dozen rental houses in the barrio, and he's playing hard to get. Don't worry about him. It's just a matter of money. I'll bring him around."

THE MOVING VAN ARRIVED on Wednesday. The first thing unloaded was Tori's Corvette. She'd bought the red sports car for a good price from a fellow officer who'd gotten himself into a financial bind. Anticipating coming home, she'd registered it in Texas with her own personalized license plates—TORI. She checked it out after the long journey as carefully as she inspected her plane before a flight.

As for the rest of her possessions, there weren't many. She selected a few of her favorite treasures to decorate her father's guest room—an antique mantel clock from London, some delft from Amsterdam, crystal from Italy and an oil painting from Paris. The rest she stored in the garage until she could find a place of her own.

To her delight, a letter arrived the following morning from a major airline in Dallas, inviting her to come for an interview. She called them immediately and was pleased they were able to schedule her for Friday afternoon. She booked the last flight that night from Coyote Springs, then went to the airport early to check on her Cessna.

"Repair's not a problem," Sam Hargis told her, and showed her exactly what had been damaged. "The question is how long it'll take to get parts. Could be anywhere from ten days to ten weeks."

While they talked airplanes, she kept an eye peeled for the tall cowboy but didn't see him and couldn't think of an unobtrusive way to ask who he was.

"I run a charter service, too," Sam told her. "How about coming to work for me?"

Tori laughed and explained why she was on her way to Dallas.

"Well, you ever change your mind, you let me know. I can always use an experienced pilot, especially one who can keep her cool in a crisis."

LYDIA WAS ALONE Monday morning when Tori arrived at her father's office. Winslow and Burton had gone to an early city council meeting. There were half a dozen agents who worked out of offices down the hall, but they usually used the door at the other end of the building, so Tori didn't run into any of them.

"How did your job interview in Dallas go?" Lydia asked as she finished filling out a form on her computer screen.

Tori plopped into the chair next to her desk. "Overall, I guess it was positive. I'm not very comfortable blowing my own horn. I don't think I relaxed until we started talking airframes and performance characteristics. Now I wonder if I didn't come across as a little too opinionated."

In fact, the civilian world was a culture shock. She'd never had to look for a job before. In the military, work was assigned and pay was defined by law. Now she was faced with questions about how much "compensation" to ask for and what conditions of employment were negotiable.

"I'm sure you did fine. When will you find out?"

Tori got up restlessly and went to the credenza in the corner, poured herself some vanilla-flavored coffee, then brought the pot back and refilled Lydia's cup.

"It's decaf," Lydia pointed out. "What your father doesn't know won't hurt him."

"Sneaky." Smiling, Tori returned the carafe and resumed her seat. "They said they'd notify me within thirty days. Could be a hell of a month." She took a sip of the steaming brew. "I'm not very good at waiting."

Lydia pecked away at her keyboard as she talked. "Take some time off, go sightseeing, kick up your heels."

Tori shook her head. "I need to keep busy. Dad told me last night he's having some problems with this Riverbend project. I got the impression he's beginning to panic."

"Things have gone a lot slower than he expected."

"Maybe I can help. You know, check out the lay of the land. Can you give me a list of the properties Dad owns in Santa Marta?"

"That's easy." Lydia manipulated her computer mouse, changed the screen to a series of icons, then clicked on one of them to bring up a database. She asked over her shoulder, "Just the ones we own, or the ones we manage, too?"

Tori thought a moment. "Both."

"It's a pretty long list." Lydia poked at some keys. "Looking for anything in particular?"

"I just want to see what our holdings are."

Several sheets of paper rolled through the laser printer.

"These are the addresses of the properties we own," Lydia explained, pointing to the headings at the top, "and these are the ones we manage." She handed the sheets to Tori and settled back in her chair. "I'd better warn you, honey. Santa Marta doesn't look the way you remember it. A lot's happened in the past couple of years. You've got to understand that all those places are going to be torn down to make way for the Riverbend project."

Tori nodded absently as she browsed through the lists.

"Just a minute," the older woman said, and straightened up. Her ringed fingers skimmed deftly along the keyboard. The printer whirred and another list came spewing out. "Here are the properties we don't own or manage but have options on. As you can see, just about everybody's committed to Riverbend."

"Except Amorado."

"You got it. The last holdout."

IT DIDN'T TAKE LONG to get into the heart of Santa Marta. As a child, Tori had loved coming here after school to wait for one of her parents to pick her up on the way home from work. She'd been fascinated by the lilting speech and the wonderful vitality that seemed to permeate everything. The bakery and tortilla factory brought back happy childhood memories of warm fruit empanadas and honey-sweet sopapillas. There was heartbreak, too—the memory of her mother getting killed here. But she wasn't going to dwell on that now. She had a mission to accomplish.

As she meandered through the curbless streets, Tori understood why Lydia had warned her that things had changed. The old neighborhood had never boasted the lushness of Woodhill Terrace, where her father lived, but now it looked battered, run-down, neglected. A shiver of sadness rippled through her for a time that was no more.

Finally, she drove slowly down South Travis Street. Her eye caught blue-and-white ceramic tiles spelling out Amorado Construction on the left side of the road. The narrow, nondescript stucco building was in a sort of no-man's-land between cheap commercial structures and the heart of the barrio. Burton had said bringing around this last holdout was a matter of money. From the looks of the place, it shouldn't take much. So why hadn't he succeeded?

On an impulse she decided to find out what Jesse Amorado was like. Gruff and hard of hearing? Or would he be all Latin charm and cunning? For that matter, did he even speak English? Her fingernails drummed the leather-covered steering wheel as she watched several mud-caked pickup trucks go by in both directions.

When the coast was clear, she zipped into one of six empty parking spaces in front of the building. Climbing out of the sports car, she nervously checked her lipstick in the reflection of the driver's side window, adjusted her buff calf-length silk skirt and matching sleeveless vest and proceeded to the aged, wood-frame glass door in the middle of the single-story building.

As she opened it, a bell tinkled inside, reminding her of the sound of the bells they used during Sunday Mass at the old Spanish church a few blocks away. She resisted the temptation to close the door quietly in the silence of the tiny room.

"I'll be with you in a minute," a voice called out from somewhere in back, its male resonance filling the hollow space around her.

Her nervousness eased as she moved around. The reception room, if you wanted to call it that, was austere. Unadorned rough walls painted stark white, a battered oak desk that looked as if it might have come from a 1940s schoolhouse, a few equally ancient, stiff wooden chairs, a rag rug on the quarry-tile floor. Amorado Construction didn't make much of a first impression.

"How can I help you?" The deep masculine voice was close behind her this time, its richness compelling her to face its owner.

She turned and thought instantly of the cowboy she'd seen at the airport, the man standing in the shadows of the hangar.

"I'm Tori Carr."

He extended his hand. It was large, warm and rough with calluses. She was considered tall, but she still had to look up to meet his gaze. A smile tugged the corners of her mouth. No way would she see a bald spot on his head, even if she was wearing heels. And obviously this man's thick, shiny black hair wasn't thinning.

"I'm Jesse Amorado. What can I do for you?"

She looked around the room. "Is there someplace we can talk?"

"How about my private office?" He swept a hand toward the doorway he'd just come through.

"After you," she said.

She liked the way the creases beside his wide mouth intensified when he grinned back at her. He preceded her through the narrow passageway. She was vaguely aware of a little filing room to her left, but her attention was drawn to the broad back that tapered down like an arrowhead, pointing to Jesse's narrow waist and slender hips. Definitely not what she'd expected.

He motioned her to a worn, tapestry-upholstered wooden chair in front of a desk. "Please sit down. I was just fixing coffee. Would you like some?"

She looked up. He had high, wide cheekbones that hinted handsomely of Native American descent; his complexion was olive-toned. She also noticed he wasn't wearing a wedding ring. Didn't mean a thing, she told herself. A lot of pilots didn't, either. For safety reasons. Made playing around easier, too.

Now, what had he asked? Oh, yes, something about coffee. She'd already had two cups this morning. Her limit. Besides, this wasn't a social visit. But before she knew it, she was acquiescing, "Yes, thank you."

He disappeared into a small alcove, giving her a chance to examine the office more carefully. Larger than the outside room, its atmosphere was considerably warmer. The cherrywood desk was old but so well oiled that even the chips and cracks in its fine veneer took on a glowing nobility.

She noted, too, the homey display of framed photographs on the walls. One showed Jesse romping on the lawn with a youngster of five or six. The boy had

Jesse's big brown eyes and clearly loved the man he was playing with. Another captured a laughing Jesse tossing a toddler in a colorful dress high into the air. The little girl was giggling with glee, totally confident that Jesse's big strong hands would be there to catch her. In the third photo, Jesse was standing behind a pretty raven-haired woman who was sitting on a back-yard swing, his hands resting comfortably, assuringly, on her shoulders. The boy and girl stood on either side of her, their little fingers intertwined with hers. All of them were smiling contentedly into the camera.

That's what I'd like someday, Tori thought with an unexpected pang of longing. *A happy family with lots of kids.*

She almost jumped when Jesse reached in front of her and deposited a scarred but colorfully painted metal tray on the corner of the desk. The service was complete, if unconventional: sugar in an old tin canister and milk still in its plastic quart container. The spoons didn't match, nor did the two ceramic mugs. But the steam rising from them emitted an aroma that was rich and inviting.

"I hope you like strong coffee. This is my own blend. Colombian and French roast with a touch of cinnamon." He set the light blue mug in front of her and took the chipped brown one for himself. "I recommend milk and sugar unless you're particularly brave."

"Black is fine."

He shrugged almost imperceptibly and added milk and sugar generously to his own.

She took a sip and instantly wished she'd taken his advice. The concoction tasted like burned mud.

He didn't miss the shocked look on her face and barely managed to keep his expression neutral.

"It's delicious," she said with a slightly forced smile, "but..."

He chuckled softly and pushed the tray toward her.

Taking her cue from him, she added two heaping spoonfuls of sugar and filled the cup to nearly overflowing with milk.

"Much better," she said after tasting it. "Thanks."

"That was quite an exhibition you put on the other day," he said. "Are you home on leave from the air force, Captain?"

She raised an eyebrow, surprised he knew she had been in the service.

"Every time you moved to another assignment or got another medal," Jesse explained, "your name was in the paper announcing it."

The information startled her. She didn't know her father had publicized those details.

"I'm not a captain anymore. I resigned my commission. I'm looking into other career options now and thought I'd help my father out for a while."

He gazed at her for a long minute, took a deep breath, then exhaled. "What can I do for you?"

Behind his desk was a large map of Spring County with the city of Coyote Springs clearly outlined. She pointed to six properties prominently marked with colored pins.

"You own several houses in the barrio."

He leaned back in his swivel chair. "You mean the Santa Marta district? They're not for sale, Miss Carr."

"Oh, come, Mr. Amorado." She smiled ingratiatingly. His widely spaced eyes were as dark as Kahlúa. A woman could lose herself in those mysterious depths.

"Investment property is always for sale. It's simply a matter of the right price. My father's prepared to give you top dollar."

"They're still not for sale."

So he was going to play hardball. That didn't surprise her. She'd do the same thing in his place. "Of course they are. You can't live in all of them, and why would you want to, anyway?"

"I beg your pardon?"

"I'm just saying that from what I've seen of the barrio, most of the houses are pretty run-down. Some are little more than shacks, hardly habitable."

"But people do live in them. And my shacks are no worse than the ones around them that your father owns."

"That's exactly why we're planning to tear ours down and—"

"What about the people who live in them?" He leaned back in his chair.

Mirroring his action, she leaned back, too, then decided to go for broke. "Believe me, I know how unsettling moving can be. I've done a lot of it in the past few years. But it's not as if the residents would have to leave Coyote Springs. There are other places to live right here in town."

Places are like things, she wanted to tell him. *They can be changed. It's people we love who can never be replaced.*

She picked up her cup and took another small sip of coffee. It's richness was addictive. "As you probably know, the government offers several low-cost mortgage-assistance programs, and for people who can't afford to buy, there are other options."

"You mean the public housing over on the east side of town?"

Public housing. It wasn't a term she would have chosen to use. She'd seen so-called public housing in several large cities: rat-infested, crime-ridden hellholes in which human life was sometimes valued less than the price of a hit of crack or a line of cocaine. The idea of sentencing the people of Santa Marta to the environment of big-city tenements was totally abhorrent to her. But, of course, this wasn't a big city. This was Coyote Springs.

His next question was pointed, accusatory. "How much do you know about Coyote Springs, Miss Carr?"

"I was born and raised here, Mr. Amorado."

"So you call it home. But you haven't spent very much time here in the past few years, have you? And even when you did live here, how much did you get to know the place?"

"Perhaps more than you realize."

"Then you know public housing has the worst crime rate in the city, while Santa Marta—" he emphasized the last words "— has one of the lowest. Right behind Woodhill Terrace, where your father lives. Although I'm sure if white-collar crime were counted in the statistics, Woodhill would have an even higher crime rate than Santa Marta. There aren't too many white collars in this district."

The implied insult wasn't lost on Tori, but she held her tongue. Instead, she sized up the man in front of her...until she realized he was doing a reconnaissance of her, too, starting at the vee of her vest. She toyed nervously with her gold necklace, then self-consciously dropped her hand into her lap. The man behind the desk was positively disconcerting.

"I'll tell you why Santa Marta has such a low crime rate," he went on steadily. "We're family here. Sure, like any family, we have our disagreements from time to time. When we do, we take care of them among ourselves."

"Ah. That's very interesting." She couldn't resist indulging in a bit of sarcasm. "But it sounds like what you're saying is that there's just as much crime here as on the north side. You just keep it better hidden."

Jesse took a deep breath and tightened his grip on the arm of the chair. "I'm not saying that at all," he countered, then paused. "But I'm not going to argue with you about it, either. As I told you, my property is not for sale."

Tori wasn't pleased with her outburst. Trading barbs would accomplish nothing. The secret to successful negotiation was to take whatever he wanted to dish out, as long as in the end Carr Enterprises got his signature on a contract of sale. It rankled that she was losing control while he wasn't. Only the rhythmic throbbing of the vein in his neck beneath the smooth, strong jaw- line indicated any tension. His sensuous lips were smil- ing.

Maybe another approach.

"Look, Mr. Amorado, let's examine the financial an- gle for a moment. My father owns or has control of most of the property in the barrio."

Jesse opened his mouth to say something, but she raised a hand to keep him from interrupting. "Excuse me, Santa Marta."

His nod was almost imperceptible. She went on.

"I think you'll agree this is a great opportunity to develop it into something this entire city can be proud of. Riverbend will bring money and prestige to Coyote

Springs, and with it new jobs. That's going to help your people, as well as the rest of the city."

He frowned. "Miss Carr, I guess you haven't been listening. So let me say it again. My property is not for sale."

She pressed on anyway. "I'm not going to kid you. Your property is important to my father's venture. That's why I'm here—to open up dialogue. I'm sure if we try, we can find common ground and reach a mutually acceptable compromise. Look, name a price. Let's see if we can't use that as a starting point to work something out."

He shook his head, his eyes narrowed. "That's all you think about, isn't it? Money. Well, you're wrong. This isn't about money—it's about people. But you don't care about them, you and your father and his partner. All you see is a chance to make another killing at the expense of the same people you've been victimizing for years. I'm afraid, Miss Carr, we have a basic disagreement. I'm not interested in selling my property in Santa Marta to your father or anyone else." He leaned toward her, his chair squeaking slightly. "On the other hand, perhaps I can persuade you to sell me yours."

CHAPTER TWO

TORI CAUGHT A WHIFF of Jesse's woodsy aftershave. "You buy us out?" Her back stiffened. The idea was ridiculous, preposterous. "Impossible."

"Why? As you said, you aren't going to live in any of them. So you must own them for speculation." She winced as he threw her words back at her. "Why not let me buy you out?"

"They're not for sale."

"But you just told me investment property is always for sale. So what's your price?"

This was not going well. Somehow he'd reversed the tables, putting her on the defensive. She took a slow, deep breath and smiled.

"Touché, Mr. Amorado. But I'm here to buy, not to sell."

"Why not?" he persisted, his coolness adding further to her discomfort.

"Because we've got plans for—"

"Oh, I see," he interrupted, his words slow and dripping with scorn. "So they *are* for sale, but not to just anybody." He raised an eyebrow in a challenge. "Or perhaps you just don't want to sell to a Mexican?"

"I don't like your insinuation, Mr. Amorado. Whether you are Mexican or not has nothing to do with our willingness to sell."

"As a matter of fact, Miss Carr," he said quietly, "I'm not Mexican. I'm American."

She could feel her face growing hot. "That was your word, not mine. What you choose to call yourself doesn't make any difference. Carr Enterprises isn't going to sell to you or anyone else, because we have our own plans for Santa Marta."

"Well, it just so happens," he countered, "that I do, too. Plans to build it up, not tear it down. Plans to improve conditions for the people who live here, not dispossess them. You see, I've heard enough about your Riverbend project, Miss Carr, to know that your father and his partner want to destroy Santa Marta, level it, so they can turn it into paradise by the river, one of their exclusive developments with big lots, custom-built houses and professional landscaping. Expensive homes for extravagant people."

He was right, of course. There was no point denying it. But she didn't see any reason to apologize for it, either. "My father builds luxury homes, Mr. Amorado. But no one is forced to live in them. People buy them because they can afford to and because they appreciate quality."

"It's funny, Miss Carr," Amorado went on, his dark features taking on a determined hardness. "Nobody worried about people living at the bend of the river when it flooded every time it rained—unless their servants didn't show up for work on time or the mud kept the rent collector from the swift completion of his appointed rounds."

Tori shook her head in protest, but before she could speak, Amorado continued. "I know, Miss Carr, because I grew up here. I had to wade knee-deep in water along the only dirt roads in the city to get to the school bus up on the paved main road. Nobody gave a second thought to Santa Marta then." He brushed back the shock of hair that had fallen across his wide forehead. His deep voice was mocking. "But now that the river has been dammed, *mi barrio*—" He stopped abruptly, as if shaken by his slip into Spanish. "*Santa Marta* has suddenly become prime real estate, a charming little spot in the horseshoe of the Coyote River. And Winslow Carr, slumlord, wants to turn it into a high-class neighborhood." He picked up a glossy brochure from his desk and read, "A place suitable for sophisticated people who can truly appreciate its beauty and value."

The man was obviously inflexible. But Tori wasn't going to let his remarks about her father pass unchallenged.

"My father, Mr. Amorado, is not a slumlord, nor is he insensitive to other people's problems. I'm sorry you had a rough childhood. It seems to have left a chip on your shoulder the size of Coyote Mesa."

She rose with as much dignity as she could muster and turned to the doorway. He might think he'd won the first skirmish, she told herself, but the battle wasn't over, not by a long shot.

JESSE GOT UP AND WATCHED her stride purposefully through the narrow passageway. The spring-mounted bell jangled angrily as the front door slammed. A minute later, he heard the bass rumble of her car starting. It reverberated through him.

He got up from his desk and looked out the side window in time to catch a glimpse of the red Corvette as it squealed down the street.

"The joke, Miss Carr," he said out loud, "would have been on me if you'd taken me up on my offer."

There was no way he could buy out Winslow Carr. He was having enough trouble keeping up mortgage payments on the properties he already owned. His plan was to gradually upgrade each of them, then buy others and improve them, as well. Santa Marta would never be another Woodhill Terrace, but at least the word *barrio* in the mouth of a smug Anglo like Tori Carr wouldn't be synonymous with slum.

Of course, if old Mrs. Ramos's son got arrested again, she'd bail him out—again. Which meant she wouldn't be paying her rent this month, either, putting even more strain on his cash reserves.

He finished his coffee, which had suddenly grown bitter, and looked at the half-empty mug on the other side of the desk. He could still picture Tori's lips poised above its rim. He smiled crookedly as he picked it up and noticed the traces of her lipstick. If only she weren't the daughter of Winslow Carr.

TORI HAD TO FORCE HERSELF to control her speed along South Travis Street. Having to steer around the ubiquitous potholes helped. Suddenly she burst into laughter. Her father had written her about a program the city had inaugurated to finance repair of some of the streets. "Buy a pothole." He'd bought a dozen in their names. She wondered which of the ones she was maneuvering around belonged to her.

The momentary distraction at least gave her heart time to slow its wild pounding. But the emotional turmoil generated by her brief encounter with Jesse Amorado was still very much on her mind. Was it the hard stance he had taken that had her so agitated—or the man himself?

She turned onto San Jacinto Boulevard, the main

business artery of Coyote Springs, and a new kind of tension began to eat its way up from her stomach. Should she tell her father and Burton about her visit with Amorado?

There was no clattering bell when she opened the heavy plate-glass door of Carr Enterprises. No bare walls or scarred schoolhouse furniture to greet her here. Instead, across a wide expanse of plush vermilion carpet, Lydia stood at a row of filing cabinets, the gold bangles on her wrists jingling as she sorted through a pile of folders.

She looked up and greeted Tori with a broad smile. "I didn't expect you back so soon. I figured you'd be checking out the mall. There's a fresh pot of coffee if you want some."

Tori thought about the rich blend she'd sipped only a few minutes earlier and the man who had served it.

"No, thanks. I've had my quota for today. Is Dad available?"

"He's with Burt," Lydia said. "But there's no one else with them. Why don't you just go in?"

Lydia's desk was between two sets of double doors that faced each other. Tori walked to the pair on the right, gave two sharp raps in military fashion and entered the room without waiting for a response.

Burton was sitting behind his glass-topped desk, her father in the black leather chair across from him. Both men rose as she entered. She stifled the reflex to say, "As you were, gentlemen," and chuckled to herself. After nearly a decade of military protocol, civilian life was going to take some getting used to.

"Hi, sweetheart." Her father took her by the hand and led her to the other visitor's chair.

"Am I interrupting something?" she asked when everyone was seated again.

"Nope," Burton replied, a hint of mischief animating his still-boyish face. "But I bet your ears are burning."

Tori looked from one man to the other. Like two little boys, she thought with amusement, bursting to tell her a secret. She lifted an eyebrow slightly. "Oh?"

"Burton and I were just talking about you," her father explained, sounding very pleased with himself. "As you know, he owns one-third of Carr Enterprises and I own the other two-thirds. I've decided to give you half of my interest. That way the three of us will be equal partners."

Tori was flabbergasted. Her father knew she'd left a promising career in the air force because she wanted to fly for a commercial airline, preferably one that would allow her to make Coyote Springs her home base. She fully intended to help him with his business in the meantime, but not as a permanent occupation. She didn't even know if she'd like working in real estate. Besides, just last week both men had practically called her a failure, a quitter. It didn't seem like a very good basis for a partnership.

"I'll continue to handle current sales," her father went on happily. He had a reputation for being able to sell anything to anyone, which was one reason Tori was so surprised he hadn't been able to make any headway with Amorado.

"Burton will still take care of property management," he continued. "It's our major source of steady income."

"Santa Marta looks pretty bad," she remarked.

"There's no point in putting a lot of money into

places that are going to be torn down," Burton said a little defensively. "Santa Marta's only part of our investment."

She didn't want to get into a debate about business practices. "What about me?" she asked skeptically. "What would I do?"

"I...we...thought you could handle public relations," Burton offered. "You know, entertain prospective clients and investors, especially for Riverbend. Give them tours of the city, sell them on the advantages of getting in on the ground floor of the newest and biggest development this area has ever seen."

She looked to her father to get his reaction, but he only smiled back complacently.

"You want me to play tour guide?" Her heart sank. "I did that as a second lieutenant—for generals and admirals and members of Congress—when I worked at the Pentagon." She'd made sure their quarters were ready, their wet bars well stocked, their spouses suitably distracted—and she'd hated catering to whims rather than dealing with issues, watching while other people made meaningful decisions. At that point she'd realized she'd have to compete twice as hard to prove herself in this man's world. But she *had* proven herself and soon found herself in charge of multimillion-dollar defense contracts. Now Burton and her father wanted to hire her as a hostess!

Remembering her discussion with Jesse Amorado less than an hour earlier, she pictured how he'd looked at her. He'd seen a woman, too, but he'd respected her as an equal—enough to argue with her and not be afraid to win.

"That's not what I came home for, Dad," she said, unable to hide her disappointment.

Confusion clouded her father's eyes. "Honey... We just thought..."

"If that's what you need me to do while I'm here, of course I'll do it. But you don't have to make me a partner."

The discomfort on her father's face was palpable. The expression on Burton's was more complex. He looked puzzled, but she thought she also saw a note of approval in his quiet nod, as if she had passed some secret test.

"I tell you what," she said, lightening her tone. "I'll take on your PR campaign until I get an offer from one of the airlines. But why don't you also take advantage of some of the negotiating skills your tax dollars have paid for?"

She studied her father more closely, noted the lines of fatigue etched around his mouth, the expanding crow's-feet and the complexion that seemed more gray than pink.

"Tell me again about Riverbend," she said. "You mentioned the other evening that Jesse Amorado was the last holdout. Maybe I can get him to sell."

Burton brightened. "Do you know him?"

Tall, dark, with broad shoulders and narrow hips, long straight nose, perfect white teeth, and big strong hands. Her face grew warm when she realized Burton was staring at her. "Yeah," she said, "I met him once."

"Win," Burton said, turning to her father, "neither of us has been able to get anywhere with Amorado. Maybe we ought to give Tori a shot at this barrio baron. If anyone can persuade him to surrender—for a good price, of course—I bet she can." He winked wickedly at her.

She glared back.

"Hey," he chided with a soft chuckle. "What's happened to the sense of humor you used to have?"

For a moment she regretted not being in uniform. No one patronized her then. She gave Burton a withering glance. "Let's get on with it."

Winslow Carr stepped over to the side wall of the spacious office. It was covered from floor to ceiling with a framed board. One portion showed the same county map Amorado had tacked to his wall. This one was mounted on metal so color-coded magnetic markers could be used to indicate various properties. Next to the map was a blowup of their plans for the barrio.

Her father waved his hand across the board to half a dozen bright red dots. "Amorado's six plots are scattered all over the place and will interfere with every aspect of the project."

Burton rose from his chair, removed an engraved gold pencil from his breast pocket and used it as a pointer. Tori was instantly struck by the difference between his hands and Amorado's. Burton's were strong, but they had lost the coarseness and cobweb of axle grease and crankcase oil they'd had when he'd spent every spare moment working on his motorcycle. These days they were carefully manicured, more accustomed to holding fine crystal snifters and wineglasses than oil cans or torque wrenches. They were the hands of a weekend golfer, not a mechanic. Jesse's were larger, harder, with long, straight, tough-skinned fingers. She remembered their warmth when they'd held her own.

"This one—" Burton pointed to a red dot "—is right in the middle of the golf course. This other one's in the shopping mall. Those two are in prime residential areas. That one's in the schoolyard. And this one,

Amorado's place, sits right where we plan to build the clubhouse.''

"Amorado lives in Santa Marta?" Tori exclaimed, recalling the best-looking home in the barrio. "The house on Otero Street?"

"That's the one," her father said.

She wanted to kick herself. No wonder Amorado had turned hostile so quickly. She'd called his home a shack. *Do better research,* she resolved, *before the next time you meet him.*

"And there's no way to build around his properties," Burton concluded.

They discussed other aspects of the project, as well: the architects they had under contract, the builders they had under option, zoning waivers they were requesting, utility changes that would have to be negotiated. It was a complex undertaking, the kind Tori found absorbing.

"I commanded a logistics detachment for two years," she reminded them. "I know bureaucratic red tape. Why don't you let me take care of getting zoning waivers, permits and licenses downtown?"

"I've got a handle on that," Burton countered. "Developed the contacts, made the connections. No sense changing horses in midstream. Just see what you can do with Amorado."

After her father left Burton's office, Tori marched aimlessly about the expensively appointed room. The dull wood and shiny brass of his immense, Danish modern writing table was very different from the old polished desk Jesse used to fill the much smaller space he had available. Burton would undoubtedly scoff at his business opponent's taste for antiques. Burton never liked to look back.

"Let's go to the Manor tonight," he suggested in an apparent attempt to distract her from her restlessness.

The Manor was the most lavish restaurant in town. The food was rich, the wines exclusive, the service superb and the prices exorbitant. "They've got a band this evening."

"At the moment, Burton, I'm not interested in dancing." She gave him a commander-to-subordinate, dead-in-the-eye stare. "Was it your idea that I play chamber of commerce social coordinator?"

He balked. "I really don't understand what you're so worked up about. Your father said he wanted to bring you in as a partner and wondered what you could do. I suggested PR. What's wrong with that? It's a job that has to be done."

She turned her exasperation on Burton. "You act as if I were nothing but window dressing in the air force. I didn't get my promotions handed to me, Burton. I had to earn them. I controlled multimillion-dollar budgets and commanded dozens of men and women. But I'm not a salesperson and I don't want to be."

"Oh, I get it," Burton taunted, grinning. "You're worried about bagging Amorado." He turned serious. "Don't. You butter him up. I'll take care of the negotiations."

Anger flared as she faced him. "You just don't get it, do you? I suppose I should go home now and practice baking brownies. If I get that right, will you let me do fudge, too?"

She'd left Coyote Springs thinking the unconscious condescension of the "little woman syndrome" was unique to West Texas—a holdover of the cowboy code of chivalry that said it was a man's job to protect the women and children. The real world had taught her otherwise. Most men claimed they liked their women to be strong, yet they bristled whenever that strength competed with their own. Ultimately, men seemed to want women to be demure, domestic subordinates. And sexy as hell.

"Hey, chill out," Burton grumbled. "Boy, you really are uptight." He rested his hazel eyes on her and softened his tone. "What I'm suggesting is that we team up. Nobody expects you to arrive one day and conquer the world the next. You don't have any experience at this."

Forcing herself to calm down, she tried to analyze the situation dispassionately. On one level he was right. It was unrealistic to think she could move into his world of real estate and land development without training or experience. Still, his attitude rankled. She took a deep breath.

"Shall we call it a truce, then?" He approached as if to embrace her, but she sidestepped him. He shrugged resignedly. "So how about dinner tonight? I made reservations at the Manor for seven o'clock."

"A little presumptuous of you, wasn't it?" she inquired. "Don't you think you might have asked me first?"

He walked over to her and brought his hand up to her chin. Not only did she refuse to flinch, she locked onto his gaze.

"We've got some things to settle between us," she said. "We might as well do it over dinner. But you'd better change those reservations to seven-thirty. There's something I've got to do first."

"You've changed," he said quietly. "I'm not sure I know you anymore."

CHAPTER THREE

JESSE'S DAY WENT from bad to worse. Timing was everything, and right now his timing seemed to be syncopated. Bills were coming in faster than receipts. He'd had to transfer funds that afternoon from his personal account to make the minimum payments. As soon as he sold the house he had under construction in Oakdale, he'd be able to reimburse himself with interest. In the short term, however, it wasn't a very reassuring feeling.

Several times during the course of the day he asked himself if he might have been precipitous in rejecting the offer Tori Carr had made that morning. More than once he caught himself sitting motionless at his desk, picturing her in the chair opposite him. The smile she'd given him after she'd added milk and sugar to her coffee made him forget she was the daughter of his nemesis. The same smile had prompted him to wonder what it would be like to hear her laugh. Or better still, to share her laughter.

Then he'd replay their conversation—her talking about the "shacks" he owned in the "barrio," and how the residents would just have to find other places to live. Nevertheless, he found himself grinning at the memory of her reaction when he referred to Winslow Carr as a slumlord. At least he could admire the way she flew to her father's defense.

Was it possible she didn't know the reputation Carr Enterprises had in Santa Marta? Or the way her father's muscle-bound weasel of a partner treated people? Maybe not. As he himself had pointed out, she hadn't lived in Coyote Springs in a long time.

He heard the bell and the sound of heels hurrying down the hallway. "Jesse, Jesse, are you here?"

"In the back." He rose from his chair.

The arrival of Esperanza Mendez, bubbling over with good news, temporarily pushed aside thoughts of Tori Carr.

"I passed the SAT!" She waved the official notice in his face. "I'm going to TUCS!"

Texas University at Coyote Springs had started as a regional community college but a few years ago had been incorporated into the state university system.

"That's wonderful." It had been a long, difficult road for her to go back to school and pass her high school equivalency exam. Studying for the Scholastic Aptitude Test, the universal entrance test for admission to colleges and universities, had been even harder. But she'd stuck it out and he had to admire her for it.

"Henry Martin says he's going to get me a full scholarship."

In addition to working for Jesse part-time, she worked for Santa Marta's city council representative. Jesse hoped she wasn't making a mistake by counting on Martin's unqualified support. The councilman would probably get her the scholarship—he was a wheeler-dealer—but he was first and foremost a politician, and Jesse didn't trust him.

"I'm really proud of you," he said, putting his arms around her. Perversely, the closeness of her warm, voluptuous body made him think of the way the West

Texas wind had molded Tori's shirt to her breasts when she ran her hands through her hair at the airport. The erotic image stirred him uncomfortably. He backed away. "We'll have to celebrate. Where would you like to go?"

She smiled broadly, a childlike glee animating her face. "Can we go to the Manor?"

The fiscal manager in him groaned. A whopping bill at the most expensive restaurant in town wasn't exactly what his checkbook needed right now. Yet he was reluctant to deny her. He'd hired her to do typing and filing, but she'd done a lot more—like selling people on him for restoration and minor construction jobs, and dealing with the bureaucrats at city hall to get him the permits and licenses he needed. She'd even helped negotiate the sale of two of the Oakdale houses he'd built on speculation.

Besides, the prospect of spending the evening, perhaps the night, with a beautiful woman might be just what his restless body hungered for.

TORI GLANCED AT HER WATCH as she left Burton's office. The afternoon was getting late. She'd have to rush if she expected to catch anyone at the chamber of commerce before quitting time.

The familiar aroma of gardenia potpourri and stale cigar smoke greeted her when she pushed through the glass-paneled door of the building. The office manager, Evie Crump, was obviously still fighting a losing battle against secondhand smoke. Tori embraced the gray-haired lady as she greeted her. They'd met several summers before when Winslow Carr sat on the city council.

The slippers Evie wore around the office flapped on the tile floor as she scurried from desk to filing cabinet to copier and fax machine, picking things up from one spot and putting them down in another. "I wish they wouldn't have those late meetings here," the woman declared. "They could just as easily have them in Martin's office." She paused and looked up. "What can I do for you, Tori?"

"Can't I just stop by to say hello?"

"In your first week back?" Evie's mouth curved up at the corners. "I appreciate the thought," she said, "but you and I aren't *that* close. I reckon you want some sort of information. It's okay. That's what I'm here for."

Tori frowned with embarrassment, realizing she'd been patronizing. "What can you tell me about Amorado Construction?"

"Amorado Construction. Small business. Not a member of the chamber."

"Do you know anything about it?" Tori prompted as she lent a hand gathering the used plastic coffee cups that had been scattered around the small room.

Evie's brusqueness softened in appreciation of the help. "Old man Amorado, Fernando, had a small home-repair business. You know, handyman type of thing, for thirty years or so. When his older son, Jesse, finished school, he joined him and they started calling it Amorado Construction."

Started calling it. That didn't sound as if it were very successful. "How many houses have they built?"

"It's just Jesse now. The old man died a couple of years ago." Evie threw the soiled cups into a wastebasket, turned off the coffeemaker and held up the glass pot. "Want the last cup?"

Tori suppressed an urge to wrinkle her nose at the

acrid-smelling black residue. "No, thanks. So how is Amorado Construction doing?"

"He specializes in renovations and reconstruction work mostly. But he's also built and sold two houses in Oakdale and has a third one almost finished." Oakdale was a solid middle-class neighborhood. Tori decided she'd have to drive over there and see them.

"He has a reputation for high quality and dependability," Evie continued. "As I said, he's still small, but he seems to be doing well and growing."

So the offer to buy Carr Enterprises out of the barrio had been a bluff! She experienced a warm tickle of delight. Jesse Amorado had been testing her. She had to give the guy credit. He'd pulled it off beautifully. Thank heavens she hadn't told Burton or her father about his offer. They'd probably still be laughing. Well, worthy opponent, she mused. May the better person win.

"By the way," Tori asked casually as she was leaving, "is he married?"

Evie's face bloomed into a rare smile as she glanced at Tori. "Honey, no one's landed him yet."

THE MANOR WAS a pretentious structure designed to evoke the ambience of an antebellum Tara. The six Greek columns that spanned the front of the two-and-a-half-story building succeeded well enough, though the recent addition of aluminum siding spoiled the effect.

Burton had reserved a table by one of the wide, multipaned French windows that looked out onto a small garden separating the house from the parking lot. Tori settled into the plush brocade armchair held by a waiter while Burton ordered white wine for both of them.

She was starting to relax, allowing herself to be seduced by the gracious decor of the place, when she saw a couple stroll by on the brick walk leading to the main entrance. The man's head was bent down as he talked. The woman had a smile on her face as she gazed up at him. A minute later Jesse Amorado appeared at the velvet rope guarding the doorway to the dining room.

It was impossible not to notice him in his Havana brown Western-cut jacket and the white-on-white dress shirt. Was it the man who was causing her pulse to quicken or the business challenge he represented? She'd been contending with the property issue separating them all afternoon without her blood pressure rising, so...

Everyone else was looking at the woman hanging possessively on his arm, her generous curves elegantly emphasized by the empire-waisted emerald green dress that flared above her knees. There was no denying her beauty.

There was also something familiar about her. But who was she? Why was she here with Jesse? Alone. Together.

Jesse scanned the room, and before Tori could redirect her attention to the menu in her hands, his eyes fixed on hers.

He nodded in greeting and she smiled. Burton, who had his back to the doorway, noted her reaction, swiveled in his seat to see the source, then grinned at Tori approvingly. A moment later, Jesse passed alongside their table.

"Good evening, Miss Carr. How nice to see you again."

His eyes were playing with her, making her uncomfortable, and he was enjoying every bit of it. Was he going to mention their meeting that morning?

"Good evening, Mr. Amorado. May I introduce Burton Hazlitt?"

Burton had already risen from his chair and was giving the lovely young woman the once-over. Tori expected the two men to shake hands as a matter of form, but Jesse's impersonal nod made it clear he had no intention of touching Burton.

"Miss Carr, may I introduce my business associate, Esperanza Mend—"

"Espy!" Tori exclaimed. "Is it really you? I thought I recognized you."

Espy blinked slowly in acknowledgement. "Hello, Tori." The words came out hoarsely, a mixture of pleasure and…something else in her voice.

"It's been a long time." Tori smiled as she took Espy's hands in hers. "It's wonderful to see you."

There was a momentary lull, and Tori realized both men were looking at them with quizzical expressions on their faces. "Espy and I knew each other as kids."

"Really?" Burton asked.

"You never told me you knew Tori Carr," Jesse commented.

"Espy and I went to the same sitter every day after school," Tori explained.

Espy's confirming smile was polite but without warmth.

"Why don't you join us?" Tori suggested. "There's plenty of room at our table, and we have so much to catch up on."

She saw Jesse visibly stiffen as if the suggestion, like her offer to buy his property, were an affront.

"Thank you," he said with formal politeness, "but we wouldn't think of imposing. Perhaps another time."

Tori wanted to tell him it wouldn't be an imposition, but he didn't give her the opportunity.

"Enjoy your dinner," he said. "Now, if you'll excuse us—"

Tori put her hand out to delay their departure.

"Let's get together and talk sometime," she suggested to Espy. "Are you still living with your mother on Hidalgo Street?"

"Mom died years ago. I've got an apartment in the Spanish Arms on South Travis now."

"I'm sorry," Tori said, then tried to lighten the mood. "I'll call you soon," she promised.

"Sure, anytime," Espy replied, but the invitation didn't sound sincere.

Tori had an uneasy feeling about their chance meeting. She and Espy had played together as kids, dressing Tori's dolls, skipping rope and breaking open piñatas at birthday parties. It was inevitable, of course, that they would lose track of each other. But why this reserve bordering on unfriendliness?

Jesse ushered his "business associate"—whatever that meant—away. Then Tori saw Lydia and her father come through the door. They arrived at the table a moment later, followed by a couple Tori didn't recognize. Her father introduced Paul and Myra Triska, neighbors who'd taken up residence across the street a couple of months ago. Paul was tall and gangly, Myra short and round. What the two had in common—besides an obvious affection for each other—was a sense of humor that had everyone laughing even before another table was joined to theirs and the six of them were seated.

Tori had hoped to discuss the events of the day over

dinner with Burton and nail down the role she was
expected to play at Carr Enterprises. But she didn't
want to do it in the presence of her father, and certainly
not in front of strangers. It would have to wait until
later. For the moment, though, laughter was the tonic
Tori needed, and Paul and Myra did a wonderful job
of supplying it.

But every once in a while she would feel Jesse's
eyes on her from across the room, sometimes casually,
sometimes intensely. As she turned to look back at him,
she knew it definitely wasn't business affairs that had
set her nerves on edge.

JESSE WATCHED Espy's tongue lick salt from the edge
of her frosty glass and found himself picturing Tori
sipping coffee in his office.

"I had a visit from Carr Enterprises today," he announced after sampling his own margarita.

Espy practically slammed her drink down and nar-
rowly avoided spilling it. "You're not going to sell to
him, are you?"

Jesse thought about the bills that had passed across
his desk earlier that day. "At the rate things are going,
I may not have much choice."

The corners of her mouth turned down as she glared
at him. He knew what she was thinking. He'd made
the counterargument often enough—you always had a
choice. You might not like the alternatives, but there
was always a choice.

"Look," he said, "I can probably slow down their
damned project, maybe even ruin it. But what's the
point? Hell, all the other owners have either sold to
him already or agreed to."

"That's exactly why you can't. Have you forgotten Miguel?"

He should have known she'd bring up his kid brother. "No, damn it. I haven't forgotten."

"Then I don't see how you can even think of selling to that…that…bloodsucker," she sputtered. "I thought you had more pride."

"She wants to negotiate, that's all," he replied, and instantly regretted it.

"She? You mean he sent *her?*" Espy shot a jealous glance across the room to where Tori was warmly engaged in a conversation with an older man. "Didn't waste any time, did she?"

Espy was building up to a grand tirade. It was easy for a man to be seduced by her beauty and passion, but her fiery temper was one of the things that kept Jesse from considering a more permanent relationship. Taking a deep breath, he decided to change the subject.

"What are you planning to major in at TUCS?"

The diversion worked through dinner, until she caught him gazing over at the Carr table, at the slender woman in the long black dress. Then Espy's eyes flashed and the diatribe was renewed.

"You owe it to our people to stand up to Carr."

"I said no. What more do you want?"

Espy stabbed the starched white tablecloth with a long red fingernail. "I just wonder how long it'll take her to seduce you into giving her what she wants."

"What are you talking about?" he demanded.

"I can see the way she's been looking at you," Espy said with derision. "She has more on her mind than real estate."

"Don't be ridiculous." But he couldn't seem to keep

his attention from wandering to the laughing blonde half a room away.

Hazlitt was another matter. All charm and good manners here. In the barrio, he liked to twist arms and browbeat people. Only two weeks ago he would have physically assaulted one of Carr's own tenants, José García, if Jesse hadn't stepped in. José had complained because the broken windows from the hailstorm two months ago still hadn't been repaired and his little girl had cut herself when she tried to patch them with a piece of cardboard. Only two things had kept Hazlitt from taking a swing at Jesse when he took José's part: Jesse was bigger, and Hazlitt wanted something from him—his properties.

Jesse called for the check, smothered a groan at the amount and escorted Espy around the table of laughing people. Tori smiled pleasantly as they passed, and he thought he saw her lips wish him good-night.

The short trip in his truck to Espy's apartment passed in strained silence. When they got to her door, though, she invited him up for a glass of wine.

"No, thanks," he said. "I've got an early day tomorrow."

"Aw, come on, Jess." She slipped her hand seductively under his suit jacket and stroked his shirt. "Just for a few minutes."

His body couldn't help but react to the intimacy, and he might have been tempted had he not detected the gleam of spitefulness in her dark eyes. He gave her a simple brotherly peck on the cheek and started back to his truck, then turned around.

"Congratulations again on your test scores," he called out. "I'll see you tomorrow afternoon at the office."

THE NEXT MORNING, Tori decided to take a closer look at Santa Marta, especially at the properties Amorado owned—and at one of them in particular.

Her Corvette would have drawn little more than a passing glance in Woodhill Terrace—if there was even anyone outside to notice it. But people in Santa Marta lived more out-of-doors. A shiny red sports car passing through was an event, and a young Anglo woman with sassy blond hair a curiosity.

Since school hadn't yet started and the summer heat was stifling in houses with little or no air-conditioning, kids were in the streets playing ball or tag or huddled in little groups studying bugs or worms or other critters. They instantly interrupted their games to watch her pass. It took only one child to run toward her for an entourage of yelling kids and barking dogs to follow. Welcoming the distraction, Tori rolled down the window and greeted them.

She chuckled at the surprise on the faces of the older ones when she answered their questions in Spanish. They couldn't know she'd practically grown up here and that the language had once been as natural to her as it was to them. She'd been tempted to greet Espy in Spanish at the Manor the evening before. But Burton had never made an effort to learn even a few social phrases in Spanish, so speaking it in front of him would have been impolite. Besides, she wasn't sure how Jesse might have taken it. As showing off? Or as a put-down?

Finally an old man hobbled from one of the houses and shooed the children away. Tori smiled and called out to him in Spanish that they were no bother. She introduced herself, expecting him to come over and

pass the time of day. All she got in return was a tip of
his worn straw hat and a distant, *"Señorita."*

A large, stocky woman in a not-very-clean orange
dress came rumbling across the parched lawn from next
door. She looked at the personalized license plate on
the Corvette and grunted contemptuously.

"If you are looking for the Molinas," she said in
heavily accented English, "you can go away. They are
gone. God help them."

"The Molinas?" Tori asked. *"Qué hay de los Molinas?"*

"You are here to check up on them, right?" the
woman accused her, still speaking English. "Do not
worry. They did not trash your precious house, though
they should have. Little Paquito so sick, and you throw
them out just because they are a little late with the rent
again. Danilo, he is working three jobs just to pay for
all the medicine the baby needs, and now they have to
move in with relatives and send their other four children to live with friends."

"I don't understand," Tori said, her stomach tightening. "They have a sick baby and they were evicted?
When did this happen?"

"Last week."

"You are Carr's daughter, are you not?" another
woman called from behind her. "And you do not know
the papers your father sends us?" She didn't sound as
if she believed it was possible. "I suppose you do not
know about the Garcías or Dominguez, either."

"Oh," the first woman objected, falling into Spanish, "The Garcías' house was so bad it was a favor to
be thrown out. They got a much nicer place over on
Herradura Street. One of Jesse's places. At least—"

she reverted to English "—he don't threaten them with
the police if they are five minutes late with the rent."

"They only rented the Carr place because it was
close to José's mother," the second woman commented.

"I heard old man Dominguez got the money for the
rent from his son in California, but he refused to pay
it," the stocky woman added. "The hot water heater
busted for two weeks, and still it was not fixed. He is
living with his sister and her husband now."

"Aye. That won't work. Him and José, they don't
get along no way."

Before Tori knew it, several other women had joined
them. They seemed to forget she was there as they
gossiped in the mixture of languages called Tex-Mex.
Tori would have enjoyed listening to it if the message
hadn't been so ugly. People living in her father's
houses were apparently being constantly harassed for
rents. When pipes and refrigerators wore out, the residents were blamed for breaking them. They were told
they had to pay to have them fixed or be arrested for
destroying property. Everyone was blaming her father.

So this was why Jesse had called him a slumlord!

When Tori finally left the women, they stared at her,
their expressions varying from unmistakable enmity to
pity because she was a Carr. She didn't know which
was more unsettling.

Driving away quietly, she checked the rest of Jesse's
houses. They were small and basically like the ones
around them—Carr houses—but better cared for. The
outside of one had recently been painted. The old
wooden windows of another had been replaced with
burnished aluminum frames, and two others had new
shingle roofs.

She turned onto Otero Street. Jesse's address was in the middle of the block.

IT WAS AFTER ELEVEN when she returned to the office.

"Where is everyone?"

"At a meeting downtown," Lydia told her. "They'll be back around two."

Tori wasn't sure if she was relieved or disappointed. She wanted an explanation for what was going on in Santa Marta and had the feeling that getting answers to her questions wasn't going to be a pleasant experience.

"Do you have any plans for lunch?" she asked.

"I was going to call out for a sandwich."

"Why don't we go out somewhere? My treat."

Lydia's face lit up. "How about the Old Mesquite Grill?"

"You're on."

"I'd better leave these here, then." Lydia removed the rings on her fingers and dropped them into the desk drawer. At Tori's quizzical look, she said, "You'll see."

The Old Mesquite Grill on Main Street had been a saloon and dance hall—complete with "fancy ladies"—around the turn of the century and a speakeasy in the Roaring Twenties. Only the Depression finally put it out of business. There were several attempts to revive the landmark, but none was successful until five years ago, when two enterprising young men got some wealthy investors to back them in restoring it to its original splendor—minus the "fancy ladies," of course. They served a lavish lunch during the week. At night it was again the most popular dance hall in town.

While she and Lydia waited to be shown to a table,

Tori searched the noisy barroom with its high tin ceiling and electrified gas lights for familiar faces. No Jesse Amorado.

They filled their plates generously from the buffet spread out on the old mahogany bar and returned to their table.

"I drove through the barrio again this morning," Tori said as they sat down and arranged their dishes.

Lydia tucked a napkin unceremoniously into the front of her ruffled indigo blouse before picking up a huge, sticky beef rib. Tori smothered a chuckle. So that was why she'd left her rings behind.

"I wondered where you were," Lydia said after negotiating the first bite.

"It's in dreadful condition, and the properties we own are the worst. How could Dad let that happen?"

"Burt is in charge of property management," Lydia observed.

Tori nodded vaguely and buttered a piece of warm corn bread. "Doesn't Dad ever visit them, check them out?"

Lydia licked her fingertips and took another napkin from the dispenser at the end of the table. "He drives by the ones in other parts of town periodically, but he doesn't go through the barrio. Too many bad memories." Lydia wiped barbecue sauce from the corners of her mouth with the rounded fold of a clean paper napkin. "It's a place of guilt for your father. He's always felt he failed your mother, failed both of you."

"He didn't," Tori muttered as she cut a bite-size piece of brisket from the huge slice on her plate. "They both worked so hard, Dad selling real estate, Mom as a lawyer." Amusement crept into her voice. "Sort of role reversal, wasn't it?"

Lydia filled her fork with creamy potato salad but kept a close watch on her companion.

"Dad used to tease her about being the family mouthpiece," Tori reminisced. "I could always tell he was proud of her."

"Jean was a good lawyer," Lydia said. "She liked helping people. That's why she spent so much of her own time doing pro bono work in Santa Marta."

"Until it killed her."

CHAPTER FOUR

LYDIA LIFTED A BROW at the unusual note of rancor. "Is that what you think? That your mother's career was responsible for her death?"

Tori shrugged.

"Do you realize you've never talked about the day it happened?" Lydia asked quietly.

"Haven't I?" But Tori knew she hadn't. She'd tried so hard to put it all behind her. The shame, the guilt, the feeling of helplessness. She pushed her plate of half-eaten food aside. Maybe it was time, and with whom better than this dear, sweet lady whose calm sympathy had been such a soothing comfort those many years ago?

"Mom told me that morning she would be picking me up at Mrs. Gutierrez's day care because Daddy had a new client he needed to show around town. It was wintertime. A blue norther had come in earlier in the afternoon, dropping the temperature to near freezing, so the other kids and I were playing in the living room when Mom drove up. I saw her through the window and remember her looking around and watching a van stop at the curb. When she saw a big hulk of a man get out, her face turned pale and she came running to the house. She slammed the door and locked it behind her, then shouted for Mrs. Gutierrez. Something was terribly wrong. Mom never panicked. She always spoke quietly and talked to people patiently. But that day I could tell she was scared. She ordered Mrs. Gutierrez to take all of the children out the back to the neighbor's house.

"I didn't understand what was going on. I only knew I didn't want to leave Mom. When the others went out the kitchen door, I ducked into the back bedroom. Mrs. Gutierrez didn't realize I was missing until she got next door. Then she figured Mom had kept me behind."

Tori took a sip of her iced tea. Her insides were churning, just as they had that day nearly twenty years earlier.

"By then the man was pounding on the front door. Mom picked up a chair to put against it, but before she could get it in place, the man smashed through the glass panel. Mom dropped the chair and started to run, but he was too fast for her."

Lydia said nothing, but her gentle nod, her look of compassion urged Tori on.

"He didn't yell or shout at first, but I could still hear what he was saying—'You're trying to take my family away from me.' Mom said she wasn't, that she wanted him and his family to be happy. They just needed a little time apart to think things over. He was practically choking her, but she was still trying to calm him."

Tori stared at her mug of iced tea, her fingers cleaning away the condensation that formed like teardrops on its sides. She took a sip to ease the burning dryness in her throat.

"Lydia, I was so scared, more terrified than I've ever been in my life, before or since. By then the man was shouting, yelling at Mom that she was making people laugh at him."

Tori began picking at the edge of a paper napkin,

tearing little pieces from it. "I wanted to crawl under the bed, to get away from what was going on. And I did. But I took the phone with me. My hands were shaking but I held the receiver tight to my ear, hoping the man wouldn't be able to hear the dial tone. It seemed so loud. I called the operator. There wasn't any emergency number then. I told her I needed the police. I had to repeat it because she couldn't hear me. I told the policeman who answered to come quickly, that someone was hurting my mom. The policeman said to speak up, he couldn't hear me. I think I was crying. I told him I couldn't talk too loud, the man would hear me and then he would hurt me, too."

Tori closed her eyes to shut out the memory. But she couldn't. It was too real.

The waiter approached, observed the largely untouched food and began to ask, "Ladies, is everything—" But a dismissive wave from Lydia made him back away.

"I was so upset," Tori continued, "and the policeman was so calm. Instead of reassuring me, as I'm sure he meant to, it seemed as if he didn't care. I know I was crying by then, and that only made it harder for him to understand what I was saying. Finally he told me not to hang up and to stay where I was."

Lydia said nothing as she stroked Tori's fluttering hands.

"But I couldn't stay there. Not when that man was hurting Mom. I crawled out from under the bed and crept to the door."

Tori looked up. Her insides were trembling almost as much as they had been all those years ago. "Then I heard the sirens. Off in the distance. I thought maybe they were going somewhere else, but the wail was coming closer. As it did, the man got more excited. He kept yelling at Mom, blaming her for the police coming after him. I heard him hit her. She cried out and I started to run out to her. Then I heard her gasp. I thought she'd seen me and was trying to tell me not to come, so I ducked back behind the door."

Tears were streaming down Tori's face now, tears she was shedding for the first time. "But when I didn't hear anything, I got even more scared. I thought maybe he'd taken Mom somewhere. So I stuck my head out into the hall just in time to see the man dash out the front door. I was so relieved to see him go, and that he wasn't dragging Mom with him, I ran into the living room.

"Mom was lying on the floor. Perfectly still. I could see blood was oozing out in little rivulets from a wound in her chest."

Tori tried to swallow, but the lump in her throat wouldn't let her. She wanted to speak, but it took several minutes before she was able to. Lydia continued to hold her hands across the table.

"Go on," she finally urged when Tori had gotten better command of herself. "You've been holding it in long enough."

Tori shook her head and attempted to pat her cheeks dry with a fresh napkin, then glanced around the room to see if anyone had noticed.

"I tried to stop the bleeding, you know. I pressed on the hole, trying to keep the blood from seeping out. All the time I kept telling Mom not to worry. The man was gone and I was going to stop the bleeding. I promised I'd take good care of her."

Tori bit her lip and was grateful for the gentle companionship of the woman holding her hand. There was

a pang of embarrassment, a grown woman crying like
a child. But after so many years of grieving in solitude,
she felt a wave of relief at being able to recount the
events that had haunted her.

"There was nothing you could have done, honey,"
Lydia said softly. "He'd stabbed her in the heart. She
was already gone."

"I guess I knew that, but I wouldn't give up. I kept
trying to push the blood back in, kept telling her she
was going to be okay." Tori took a deep breath and
gave herself a moment to regain control of her voice.
"I have only a vague recollection of someone pulling
me off her."

"You did everything you could," Lydia assured her,
"all the right things, far more than anyone would expect of a ten-year-old. You were very brave."

"That's what everyone said. But I knew it wasn't
true. It was my fault she was dead. If I'd done what
she told me…if I'd left with the others and not stayed
behind, not called the police, the man wouldn't have
panicked when he heard the sirens, and maybe he
wouldn't have stabbed her."

"Stop," Lydia ordered with sudden firmness, compelling Tori to look at her. "Stop torturing yourself.
You and your father have been doing it for years. He
blames himself for not being there to protect his family,
for not picking you up at the sitter's himself that day
instead of asking your mother to do it. You blame yourself for being there and not being able to save her."

"It wasn't Dad's fault," Tori objected. "The man
was obsessed, deranged. He would have found her
somewhere else."

Lydia stroked her hand gently over Tori's and smiled

softly. "His mind knows that, honey. Just as yours does. But your hearts won't listen."

Tori regarded the woman sitting across from her. Lydia Anderson understood love and heartbreak and loss.

"I've never even thanked you for everything you did for me," Tori told her. "You didn't try to replace Mom, but you were always there, always willing to listen and give me a hug when I needed it most. I can't tell you how much that's meant to me."

"I only wish I could have helped you more," Lydia replied. "I've been blessed, you know. I had a man who loved me, two wonderful sons, and you've been the daughter I never had."

"I wish I had your strength," Tori said. "Those years of taking care of Jake after he was diagnosed with Lou Gehrig's disease...it must have been torture watching him fade away."

This time it was Lydia's eyes that misted. "It wasn't always easy," she admitted, then brightened. "But in a way it wasn't that hard, either. Watching him lose control was difficult, but even in the end, when he couldn't communicate, he still managed to let me know he loved me, and that kept me going."

Will I ever find someone like that? Tori wondered. *Will there be a man I can give myself to with all my heart and know he loves me, too, no matter what happens?*

Lydia dabbed at the teardrops poised at the edges of her long eyelashes. "We make quite a pair, don't we?" she commented wryly, then regained control with a steely resolve Tori couldn't help but admire.

"Your father helped, too. You probably don't know it, but during those years when Jake was declining, he kept me on the payroll, even though he couldn't really afford to, so we would have the medical insurance coverage we lost when Jake's firm had to let him go.''

Tori nodded, thinking her father was just that sort of man.

Lydia helped Tori clean up the confetti she'd made of her napkin and push their soiled dishes to the end of the table. Immediately, the waiter was there to remove them. He returned a moment later with two large bowls of hot peach cobbler topped with generous scoops of homemade vanilla ice cream.

When they were alone again, Tori picked up the thread of the earlier conversation.

''So you think Burton's to blame for the state of our properties in the barrio. You've never liked him, have you?''

Lydia shook her head. ''He's handsome and intelligent and full of boyish charm, but sometimes the charm wears thin. I admit he's a good businessman. I've just never been able to warm up to him.''

Tori gathered ice cream on her spoon and sampled it, grateful for its silky coldness in her burning throat.

''Why didn't you ever tell me?'' Tori asked. But before Lydia could answer, Tori chuckled. ''But then how could you? I was lovesick.''

It felt good to laugh again, even if it was at herself. ''I was, what, fifteen the summer Burton came from Chicago on that big Harley looking for work. He was so different from any boy I'd ever met.'' She smiled. ''Of course, he wasn't exactly a boy, either. He's ten years older than me—an older man!''

He'd exuded a sort of toughness under a veneer of social polish, like the bulging muscle beneath the tattoo of a leopard on his left biceps. There was a second tattoo, as well—the one she'd eventually gotten to see in private. "I was sure I was in love."

"Along with half the other girls in town," Lydia teased. "I tried more than once to suggest he wasn't suitable, you know."

Tori grinned back. "I can be pretty stubborn." Even now it embarrassed her to think how she must have looked trailing after him, hanging on to his every word.

"You were a teenager," Lydia pointed out, as if that explained everything. "Besides, having a mind of your own is an asset."

"Sometimes," Tori agreed. After all, it had been determination and perseverance that got her through the academy. She sampled a spoonful of warm peach, then changed the subject.

"I don't like what's going on in the barrio," she commented. Jesse's words came back to her. *I have plans to build it up, not tear it down. Improve conditions for the people who live there, not dispossess them.*

Lydia plunged her spoon into the rich dessert. "It's just that the project has taken longer than we expected. Amorado's been a real stumbling block. Now the barrio's suffering for it. If your father had realized—"

"Do you know what Jesse calls Dad? A slumlord."

Lydia winced. "That's not fair."

"No," Tori agreed, feeling strangely defensive about the lone holdout, "but can you blame him? What Burton's done has been in Dad's name."

Lydia looked up at Tori quizzically. "By the way, how do you know what he calls your father?"

Oops. "I went to see him yesterday morning," she confessed.

"Ah, that explains it."

"Explains what?"

"You said you'd met him once. I wondered when that could have been."

The light went on. "You were listening," Tori accused, feigning indignation. She was rewarded by the sudden pinkness rising to her companion's cheeks.

"The door wasn't completely closed and I just happened to be passing by—"

"Uh-huh. What else did you just happen to overhear?"

"I understand why you turned down your father's partnership offer," Lydia said, growing more serious. "You're right, of course...."

"But..."

Lydia reached across the table and placed her hand on Tori's. "Your father really loves you, honey. He can be an insensitive jerk sometimes—"

"He's a man."

"Yes, he's a man," the older woman agreed lightly. "But he needs your help more than he's willing to admit."

"He doesn't sound as if he thinks I have much to offer."

"You're going to have to forgive him, you know," Lydia said. "He doesn't know he's being unkind." She snorted. "But don't expect him to change. No matter where you've been or what you've done, he still sees you as his little girl in pigtails and party dresses."

The waiter brought the bill. Tori paid it in cash and left a generous tip.

"I was wondering," she said offhandedly as they left the restaurant, "if you might have time to do some shopping with me later this afternoon?"

"Shopping?" Lydia stopped beside Tori's sports car. "Shopping for what?"

"I need clothes for the office. One advantage of being in uniform was that I didn't have to think about what to wear when I got up in the morning. I've got plenty of casual stuff and a few nice things for evenings, but my wardrobe is a bit limited when it comes to dressing for business." Then she added, "But I don't want to keep you from anything you have to do."

"Honey, does the sun rise in the east and settle on Coyote Mesa? Of course I have time. You're looking at the shoppingest grandma in Coyote Springs."

WINSLOW CARR WAS still downtown at a meeting when they got back to the office, but Burton was in.

Tori paused a moment, fingering the gold chain that scooped gently from beneath the crisp pointed collar of her tailored blouse, then walked straight into his office without knocking. Her heart was pounding but she ignored it.

"We need to talk."

Burton shoved some papers off to the side of his desk and came over to greet her. "What's up?"

"I drove through Santa Marta this morning."

Burton raised one eyebrow. "The barrio?"

For the first time Tori noticed the way he said the word. Not as an innocuous Spanish expression meaning neighborhood or district, but with careless condescension. A put-down. Is that how Jesse had heard her say it? The thought made her mentally cringe.

"I was checking out the properties we own. Burton, they're in worse condition than I thought."

He shrugged. "We've already talked about this, Tori. Why put a lot of money into shacks that're going to be leveled?"

Shacks. The very word she'd used to describe them

to Jesse. *I'm getting an awful lot of my own words thrown back at me lately,* she thought. *First Jesse. Then Lydia. And now Burton.*

"They're people's homes," she reminded him. "We still have an obligation to maintain them in a reasonable manner as long as people are living in them."

"I don't disagree with you," he said. "I guess the question is what, in your estimation, constitutes maintenance, and how do you define reasonable?"

"Don't play games with me, Burton," she snapped back. "I think you know the answers to those questions as well as I do."

"No, I don't think I do. Otherwise we wouldn't be having this conversation." He rubbed his hands together and rolled his lips between his teeth. "I told you yesterday, you're embarking in an area you know nothing about. It would be a complete waste of money—"

"What about the Molinas?"

He raised an eyebrow. "The Molinas? What about them?"

"They have a sick child and you evicted them."

For a moment he looked as if he were going to lose his temper, but then his features softened. "The Molinas were evicted, Tori, because they hadn't paid the rent in three months, not because they have a sick child. As a matter of fact, I checked around to make sure they had a place to go. I understand they moved in with relatives."

Tori remembered one of the women saying the Molinas had been late with the rent more than once.

"I don't throw people out on the street because they're down on their luck," Burton assured her, clearly disturbed she might think he would. "You don't have to tell me about being poor. I've been there, done that, and I have the scars to show for it.''

He ran a hand through his thinning hair, and she knew by the gesture that he was uncomfortable with the admission. He'd rarely talked about himself, even in their most intimate moments. It was perhaps one of the reasons they'd broken up. She'd never felt close to him emotionally. Maybe she was being too critical of him after hearing only one side of the story.

"Look,'' he said patiently, settling into the executive chair behind his desk, putting space between them. "If you're going to take an active interest in this business, you might as well learn how things are done. No one has been evicted illegally. I've been very careful about that. I've violated no law, no code and, under the circumstances, no reasonable expectation. I have to admit, though, that I've only done minimum upkeep on those houses.''

He swept a hand toward the map across the room. "The Riverbend project is going to make us a lot of money, Tori. Millions. If you want to become a philanthropist, by all means do so. But frankly, right now, we can't afford it. We're stretched to the max. Everything we've got is in Riverbend. If it fails, we go bankrupt. I don't know about you, but I have no intention of letting that happen.''

He rose from his seat, approached her and placed his hands on her shoulders. It wasn't a display of intimacy, though she thought she detected a genuine fondness in his expression.

"If you really want to help your father,'' he said, "talk to Amorado and get him to sell. The sooner we get this thing resolved, the better.''

Tori left the meeting with Burton feeling drained.

Everything he said made sense. He'd neither denied evicting people who hadn't paid their rent nor apologized for letting superficial maintenance slip. So why this gnawing sense that she wasn't seeing the entire picture?

Jesse Amorado was the one tilting at windmills. Everyone else in Santa Marta had accepted the inevitability of the Riverbend project. Why was he being so stubborn?

His words kept echoing though her mind. *I want to build it up, not tear it down.*

Time to pay him another visit.

LATE AFTERNOON in the old Hispanic community was hectic. But it was also exciting. Working people came home to kids playing boisterously in the streets. Lively Mexican music blared through open windows, and there was a general atmosphere of festivity.

Her Corvette wasn't quite as much of a curiosity as it had been earlier, but she still drew stares. Some of the kids who'd greeted her that morning waved to her now as if she were an old friend.

She turned a corner a few blocks from Jesse's place and immediately encountered a crowd. Men, women and children were standing in the street, more or less facing a white clapboard house. Tori recognized it as one of Jesse's rentals.

She slowed her car to a crawl some distance away and watched a minute to gauge the mood of the crowd. There didn't seem to be anything threatening about the assembly. In fact, people were already parting to let her get by. She drew closer and opened her window to a woman standing on the edge of a sun-parched lawn.

"What's going on?"

The woman glanced at her warily and said nothing.

"House got flooded," said the little girl by her side.

"Was anyone hurt?"

"Nah. Just messed up the house real bad."

"Ruint all the furniture," a boy nearby offered with the fascination children often show with disaster. "Pipe busted."

Tori pulled the car to the side of the road and got out. As she approached the house, she felt the stares. Suspicious stares, wondering what the Anglo wanted.

Several men, mostly in baggy work pants and sweaty T-shirts, hovered around the door of the railless porch, some looking in, some talking.

"The plumbing is completely shot," one of the men said.

"I warned Jesse about the leaky pipe just the other day," someone else said. "I told him *en esa cañería, hay un escape.*"

"Everybody knows those old lead pipes are no good," a third man offered. "But Jesse said he couldn't get anyone to work on it until next week. He figured that would be time enough."

"What are we going to do?" a woman asked in Spanish. "My new couch is ruined, and I haven't even finished paying for it yet."

Tori could see only a little of the inside of the house through the curtainless front window and the open doorway. The room was very small and painted hot pink. A black velvet painting of Our Lady of Guadalupe hung on the wall behind the waterlogged couch. In the corner, Tori glimpsed a statue of the Madonna atop a TV set.

She heard movement inside, and a moment later Jesse appeared at the doorway. He was soaked, his jeans molded to his thighs and hips. The red cotton shirt was plastered to the contours of his chest and belly.

"Insurance will pay for your couch, Carmelita," he answered in Spanish. He pulled up the bottom of his shirt and wiped the grime from his sweaty face, revealing a fascinating washboard of stomach muscles. "Or I will."

"But they won't fix the plumbing," one of the men reminded him. "Same thing happened to my cousin's brother-in-law last year. They pay for some of the damage, or say they will, but not for what caused it."

"I know," Jesse replied sympathetically.

His eyes collided with Tori's and he stopped in his tracks. For a split second she felt the warmth of welcome in their soft caress, but shock quickly turned to embarrassment, then anger.

"What are you doing here?" he challenged her in English. The others instinctively pulled back, giving them space.

"I was passing by—"

"Sure. The barrio—" he snapped out the word, trilling the double *r* violently "—just happens to be on your way home to Woodhill."

"Well, no..."

The others around them were silent, listening, their steady glares focused on her.

"Are you going to be able to fix whatever is broken?" she inquired.

He ignored her and turned to the woman he'd called Carmelita and spoke to her in rapid Spanish. "Have you got someone to stay with tonight?"

"*Sí,* my sister."

"Good," he said in English, then reverted to Spanish. "Maybe you can stay at her house for a while. There's no way we can get this place dried and cleaned up tonight, and I'm not sure how long the plumbing work will take."

"But what about my clothes? That broken pipe shot right into the closet. I have to go to work in three hours and I don't have anything to wear or for the children to sleep in. There's no time to go to the Laundromat."

He managed to extract his wallet from his wet, clinging jeans and removed several large bills. He handed them to her. "This should be enough to buy some clothes for tonight."

"Please let me help," Tori said, opening her purse. Feeling the people around her stir, she regretted her sudden impulse. She should have gone more slowly, inquired how many children the woman had, what their names and ages were, and then asked if she could help.

"Keep your money, Miss Carr," Jesse snarled, while Carmelita stared longingly at the billfold in Tori's hand. "I told you before, we take care of our own here."

She felt the people around her stiffen. A minute ago she'd been merely an outsider. Now she was the enemy, and for a moment she was afraid. Could their hostility turn violent?

She bit her lower lip. "I'm trying to help, Mr. Amorado."

"I think you and your father have done quite enough in Santa Marta. We don't need any more of your kind of help."

"I know what you think of my father," she replied as evenly as she could. "But you've got it all wrong. He's not what you think. At least let me do this to—"

Someone in the crowd behind her laughed harshly.

"It will take more than a few bucks to make up for what he's done here, lady."

"Jesse's right," a woman shouted defiantly in an emotional mixture of English and Spanish. "We can take care of ourselves. We don't need no *gringa* giving us charity. I've got some clothes that will fit your Ramón and Ernesto, Carmelita."

"It's not charity," Tori insisted. "I just want to help."

"Then leave," another woman shouted. "We don't want you here."

An overpowering feeling of loneliness and isolation gripped her. When her mother was killed a few blocks from here, the residents of Santa Marta had offered warmth, love and tears for *la pobre niña*. The last thing she wanted was to hurt or offend these generous people.

"Jesse, please. I—"

"You heard them. We don't need your help."

"Well, you need someone's," she retorted, anger finally overcoming forbearance. "The plumbing in this house is bad, and from the look of things—" she pointed to a bare lightbulb dangling by two wires under the eaves by the porch "—the wiring isn't any better."

"Goodbye, Miss Carr," Jesse said, placing his hand firmly on her elbow.

CHAPTER FIVE

TORI PULLED OUT of Jesse's grasp and started back to her car, but he followed, his presence looming behind her. Seeing the contempt on the faces around her, she found his closeness oddly reassuring. Despite his obvious displeasure, she felt safe with him, protected.

They reached her Corvette. With one hand opening the door, he clasped her arm with the other, releasing his grip only after she'd lowered herself into the bucket seat.

Jesse's gaze, black with fury, sliced into her. The raw power emanating from him was frightening, yet unexpectedly exciting.

She looked at his sodden shirt and remembered the rippled flesh under it. *It's all distraction,* she told herself, *not attraction.*

"You called my father a slumlord the other day. Well, look around you, Mr. Amorado. You're no better."

Hardly noticing the people staring at her, she started the car and slowly moved forward. In a moment, she knew, she'd begin to shake from the tension of the encounter.

She'd gone to Santa Marta with an idea to reconcile their business interests. She'd felt genuine sympathy for the plight of the woman whose house had been

flooded. Her offer to help had been sincere and uncon-
ditional. Yet she'd come off looking vain and arrogant.

What was it about the man that disturbed her so
much that everything she did and said came out in the
worst possible light?

THE DISASTER at Carmelita's house was only one of
many problems that plagued Jesse over the next few
days and into the weekend. He hadn't finished his first
cup of coffee Saturday morning, when he got a call
from Mrs. Perez. Her thirty-year-old refrigerator had
finally given up the ghost. There was a broken back
door at the Rodriguez house and an electrical short at
the Rosario place. To cap it all off, old Feliciano called
to say he'd found termites around the back porch. By
that night Jesse was exhausted from running from one
crisis to another.

"She's right," he told Espy late that evening. They
were at his house having dinner. He'd marinated strips
of skirt steak in lime juice, grilled them with onions
and peppers and served it with *pico de gallo* on flour
tortillas. "I am a slumlord."

"No, you're not," she consoled him. "It's not your
fault those houses weren't maintained right for years.
That's the reason you were able to buy them. You're
doing the best you can."

"Well, my best right now isn't good enough.
There's far more work to be done than I have either
the time or money to do."

"What are you saying, Jesse?" Her musical inflection had taken on an all-too-familiar edge, making him
feel even more exhausted.

"I'm saying maybe I should sell. As desperate as
Carr is to get his hands on my properties, I should be

able to demand a high price, higher than I ever could otherwise.''

"So you just want the *dinero*."

He knew she was taunting him, but he wouldn't be insulted, not in his own house.

"Damn it. You know that isn't true. But with the kind of profit I'll be able to get from the sale of these places, maybe I can do some real good somewhere else.''

"And abandon Santa Marta?"

He wanted to tell her it was just a bunch of houses. But that wasn't true, and that was the problem. He would be deserting the old Hispanic district that had given him and his family a home for generations. Santa Marta was the heritage of his parents and grandparents, the place that had nurtured his people, seen them born and laid to rest, witnessed their marriages and watched their children grow. Some had prospered and moved away. A few had gone to prison and come back. But most of them had stayed and contributed to the rich tapestry of life there, given it *alma*, soul. Every street had its cache of joys and tragedies. Sometimes Jesse was convinced no farmer could feel closer to the land than he did to the river-rimmed plat called Santa Marta.

"I'm not abandoning it," he retorted, not convinced that what he was saying was indeed the truth. "I'm facing reality. I'm the only holdout. Everybody else has given up.''

"That's why you can't," Espy insisted vehemently.

The argument went on for another hour. Jesse saw her home but didn't accept her invitation to come in. She rested her hands on his shoulders, drew him down to her level and kissed him softly on the cheek.

"Buenas noches, mi amigo," she whispered, and was gone.

He turned and walked back to his own house. He needed to savor the barrio tonight, to be intoxicated by its *fantasmas*. He knew it couldn't stay the same. Nothing could. But he didn't want it destroyed, either, and he certainly didn't want to play a part in its destruction. There was so much good here, the *espíritu de la familia*. There was a lot of pain, too. He thought sometimes the pain had fashioned his people more than the joy, but it was those elusive moments of joy that made it all worth enduring.

He was bone-weary when he finally went to bed around midnight. Still, he couldn't sleep. He was a man on a tightrope. A thin wire without end.

What would be gained if he continued to resist Carr? Would Santa Marta be saved? For whom and for what? The longer he waited, the worse conditions would get. And what about the people who had already sold their homes? Either Carr would continue to rent the houses out until they completely collapsed or he would tear them down. In which case people would have sold out for nothing. As for Jesse's properties, in his current financial condition they'd continue to deteriorate, their values plummeting, as well. In the end he might lose them, anyway.

He recollected the smug satisfaction Tori had shown when she'd turned his words against him the other night. Slumlord.

But he'd sensed immediate contrition, too, in the way she fumbled with her keys to start the car. Or was it simply the situation that made her nervous? In that instant he'd wanted to hold her, feel the silky skin of her arm under his hand, calm her trembling body the way he would a frightened child.

He turned on his side, uncomfortable with the heat his body was generating.

No. Not a child. She was a woman...and he was a man.

SATURDAY MORNING Tori resisted the temptation to drive through the barrio to see what work was being done on Jesse's flooded rental house. He'd made it clear that he and his people didn't want either sympathy or support from her.

She had no difficulty picturing the face of Jesse Amorado. Seeing his anger. And something else. Hurt? Shame? Humiliation? Those emotions were there, but there was more. She searched for a word. *Pride.* Not the arrogance she'd often encountered in Burton or the bravado that was so often stereotyped as Latin machismo. Jesse's pride was an underlying self-assurance in himself as a man. What was it Burton had called him? The baron of the barrio.

Tori smiled to herself. The title fit the proud man with the work-hardened hands.

By Sunday afternoon she could stand it no longer. She had to try to resolve the issue of Santa Marta. She had to see him.

It was after six when she drove through the old Hispanic neighborhood, fast enough this time not to draw a following of kids, though a dog or two still barked as she went by. The rental house with the disastrous plumbing looked deserted. She drove the few blocks over to Jesse's house.

The lawn was bright green with cheerful zinnias skirting the small porch in front. She pulled into the driveway just as Jesse came around the side of the building. He was bare-chested, pushing a wheelbarrow weighed down with bags of steer manure. Halfway across the front yard, he saw her car and stopped, settled the ponderous load and stood up, flexing his big hands.

For a moment they stared at each other, and in that silent span of time she wondered if he was going to order her off his property. But then his deeply bronzed face creased into a polite, if somewhat forced, smile.

"To what do I owe the honor of this visit, Miss Carr?" His tone was guarded.

"I came to apologize," she said.

"For what?"

"For my lack of tact the other night."

He reached for the checkered red handkerchief dangling from his hip pocket and wiped the sweat from his hands, face and the back of his neck. Walking over to her car, he opened the door. She looked up at the mesh of coarse black hair on his bare chest.

"Apology accepted. But only if you'll accept mine for the same reason."

He put his right hand out to seal the deal, and there was an unexpected gentleness in his touch. Then he tightened his grip and pulled to help her out of the car. Releasing her hand, he turned around and went to the porch rail. She leaned against the car and watched him pick up his T-shirt and put it on.

"Your house is charming, Mr. Amorado," she said, tearing her eyes away from him long enough to take in the surroundings.

He chuckled, a deep rumble. "Mr. Amorado?" His tone was teasing now. "Not only did the air force take the girl out of West Texas, but they seem to have taken the West Texan out of the woman." His smile showed even, sparkling white teeth. "Why don't you just call me Jesse?"

"If you'll call me Tori."

"It's a deal, Tori."

Their glances met, acknowledging a mutual awareness, and quickly separated again. He stood beside her, and together they examined the white clapboard building.

"My father built it for my mother right after they were married," he said. "It's nothing spectacular, nothing like what you're used to, but Dad was always proud of it."

Was the statement a casual comment or a provocation?

"Is that why you still live here?" she asked.

"I stay here during the week," he said. "On weekends I usually go out to the ranch."

"You own a ranch?"

He chuckled. "Actually, the bank owns it. Just a few hundred acres. Insignificant by Texas standards."

He moved the wheelbarrow off the lawn to the edge of the concrete driveway.

"Where did you go to school?" she asked, trying very hard not to fixate on the graceful lines of his arched back.

"Texas A and M."

He turned to her, grinning. There was that pride again.

"An Aggie!" she exclaimed.

Texas Agriculture and Mining was one of the finest schools in the state and the constant butt of jokes, as if the people who attended it were dim-witted klutzes.

The ultimate joke, however, was, What do you call an Aggie after graduation? Answer: Boss.

She chuckled nervously. "No Aggie jokes. I promise."

He laughed, unconcerned. "Don't worry. I've heard them all and made up my share of them, to boot."

He took the steps of the porch two at a time and opened the screen door for her. "I'm about ready for a break. How about a cold drink?"

As she approached the doorway, a cool draft of humid air from the evaporative cooler greeted her. Stepping into a room that ran the full width of the house, she felt instantly at home. This was the Santa Marta she remembered. There was none of the staid formality of her father's house in Woodhill. This comfort was more casual, spontaneous, warm and colorful.

"I'll just be a minute." He strode down the hall. "Make yourself at home," he sang out in the same deep baritone that had initially captivated her in his office.

She studied the clay-potted houseplants under the window beside an overstuffed armchair. The chair looked so inviting she wanted to sink into the comfort of its sagging upholstery and soak in the ambience of the room. Jesse came back with a tray, which he placed on top of an old Victrola. He handed her one of the two large blue plastic glasses filled with iced tea.

"It's unsweetened." He moved the sugar bowl toward her.

She grinned at the cautious smirk he offered and the memory of his rich but bitter coffee. "This is fine."

He leaned against the doorway.

"This is a comfortable room," she commented, unnerved by the way he was watching her. Not ogling. Appraising.

"It used to be a living and dining room. I knocked out a wall here." He waved an upraised arm at an imaginary line in the ceiling on the far side of the front door. "I did the same thing at the other end of the house. Come take a look."

She followed him through a narrow passageway, past a kitchen and bathroom on one side of the hallway and a closed door opposite them. The room at the far end stretched across the back of the house, equaling in size the one in front. To the right was a combination sitting-and-dressing area and a big rolltop desk.

"You like antiques," she noted, stroking its polished sheen, trying to ignore the big double bed at the other end of the room.

"They're our continuity with the past."

"And the future?"

He paused a moment as though weighing his next move, then crooked a finger. "Come with me."

He opened the door to the room they had passed. Standing in the doorway, his hand still grasping the knob, he beckoned her in with a nod. Tori entered the small room and stopped. Old-fashioned flowered wallpaper, torn and stained in a few places, suggested it might once have been a bedroom. It wasn't now. A sheet of plywood on sawhorses dominated the center of the limited space, and displayed on it was a model village, reminding her of the model villages set up at holiday time under Christmas trees and in store windows.

She was very much aware of Jesse standing behind her as she leaned forward and inspected the tiny houses and buildings, the flawlessly paved streets, the miniature shrubs and trees, all neatly trimmed and idyllically tidy. No flaking paint or crumbling porches in this pristine world.

"This is what I want to do with Santa Marta," Jesse commented. He was so close she could feel his breath on her ear.

The tips of his fingers were featherlight on her shoulders as he sidestepped behind her. His body heat warmed her and the electricity between them made the hair on the back of her neck stand up. He stood beside her and she had to control the sudden urge to lean into his side.

Biting her lip and clasping her arms against the fluttering in her belly, she tried to concentrate on the aerial view before her. She recognized enough of the houses—upgraded, painted, shuttered, more stylishly roofed—to know she was looking at the old Mexican quarter. A few buildings had been removed and replaced with parks and playgrounds, a swimming pool and tennis courts.

"It's beautiful," she murmured. "It's a wonderful dream."

The buzzing of cicadas wended its way through the partially opened window opposite them. A cardinal called, *what-cheer, cheer, cheer.*

She reached out and pointed to a large residence. "That's your house, this house." He'd enlarged the back, added a wing on one side, replaced the wooden clapboard with stylish brick and wrapped the entire building with a wide-columned porch. "It's charming."

He moved around to the side of the board and pointed out other houses, as well. The one that had been flooded, for example, was bigger, its roof of silvery gray shingles replaced with Spanish tile.

"How do you propose to accomplish all this?"

He settled his weight on his right hip. She tried not to dwell on the way his snug jeans shifted, accommodating themselves to his rugged build.

"You mean, where's the money going to come from?" he asked.

"You're not going to get anywhere," she said, "if you haven't got capital, backing and connections."

He folded his arms across his chest, the hands tucked under his biceps. God, he was sexy.

"Do you?" she asked, not knowing what part of him to look at that wouldn't make her heart skip a beat. She took his silence as confirmation that he didn't. Yet even his lack of reply spoke of strength, not weakness.

"What about grants?" she asked. "There are all sorts of state and federal programs—"

He shook his head, then threaded his fingers through a raven's wing of shiny black hair that had fallen over his brow.

"They're just another form of welfare," he responded. "We'll use our own sweat equity."

That pride again.

"What you want to do here is admirable," she continued. "It's also impractical. Santa Marta has hundreds of houses that need a lot more than new roofs or siding. At the rate you're going about it, fixing up half a dozen places at a time, you'll never come close to rescuing more than a fraction of the total."

He stared at her for what seemed an endless minute. She fiddled self-consciously with the gold stud in her left ear and wondered if the sunlight coming in the side window was making her blouse translucent. The idea should be disconcerting, yet the thought disturbed her in a way that had nothing to do with modesty.

"Look," she concluded, "my father's told me he's willing to give you twenty-five percent over appraised value. You can make enough profit on your investments here to get a fresh start."

He laughed ironically. "If I sell, you'll destroy Santa Marta and I won't have anything to put the money into."

"The people who live here can move to other parts of town." She wasn't going to mention the east side again. She'd checked. He was right. The crime rate there was appalling.

"You don't understand," he said. "We've lived here, side by side, for generations. We share a common heritage. We're not a bunch of strangers who just happen to live in the same part of town, like the people in Woodhill Terrace. Take us out of Santa Marta, and you take something out of us, too."

She heard his words. Even more, she felt their intensity and the implacable truth beneath his frustration. He'd shared something with her. Not just a dream, but his pain and disappointment. She lifted her gaze from his curled hands to his high cheekbones and the long, straight nose that lent his face a regal dignity. Peering into the black pools of his eyes, she expected to see passion, the passion of hostility. Instead what she found was desire. It jolted her, then washed over her like a warm spring rain.

The room had suddenly grown uncomfortably small. Too intimate, too full of implications. Too full of a man who was stirring her imagination far beyond real estate ventures. She risked another quick glance at him, only long enough to confirm the danger she felt, a danger whose allure frightened her because she wanted to taste more of it.

Silently, she edged out of the room.

"Thank you for the tea and the tour," she muttered nervously over her shoulder while she made her way slowly toward the front door, hearing his footsteps behind her. She waited until she was on the porch before daring to face him. He smiled and she recognized the want in his eyes. How could she tell him she understood, shared his yearnings?

"Thank you for coming," he said in a murmur so low and lonely it brought a flutter to her chest.

He placed his hand on the small of her back and guided her to the porch steps, then slipped his hold to the outside of her hip. Together they descended to the walk. For one rapturous moment she imagined her whole body being surrounded by his arms. The notion brought a fresh wave of heat.

"I think you underestimate the quality of your people, Jesse." Head bent, engrossed in the path that lay before her, she dared not glance up at him for fear of tripping on the uneven path. "And their resilience. They're stronger than you're giving them credit for."

He walked her to her car in silence, his hand slipping up to her waist. *Any higher,* she thought, *and I'll melt.*

"Your goals for Santa Marta are lofty." Her chin came up defiantly, as if she could quell the magpies fluttering in her stomach. "But they're unrealistic." She took a deep breath. "I suspect you know that. I hope you'll reconsider my father's offer."

He opened the car door and handed her in. Again the gentle strength of his fingers closed around hers. They held her captive a little longer than necessary, yet not long enough.

"Thank you for coming," he said warmly, then added, "but my properties are not for sale."

Her hand shook as she turned the key in the ignition, the reverberation of the engine producing loud barks from a neighbor's dog.

She drove away in turmoil. She'd apologized for her insensitivity and gotten him to recognize his own. What happened after that had been completely unexpected. He'd shown her a carefully crafted model of Santa Marta that, unfortunately, could only be realized at the expense of Carr Enterprises.

But there was a bigger rub. Deep down, she wished he could succeed. And almost irrationally, she wanted to be part of that success.

MONDAY MORNING Tori's father called a strategy meeting in his office. Burton had arrived only a few minutes before.

The mood as they sat around the conference table at the far end of Winslow's office was sober and businesslike. Tori noticed her father looked tired, like a man who had just returned from a rough weekend, though she knew he wasn't a drinker.

They sipped their coffee while Tori told them about her latest encounters with Amorado, about the small but disastrous flood at one of Jesse's rental houses last week and her follow-up visit to his house Sunday afternoon. She didn't go into detail, of course, didn't tell them that his ideas were beginning to tweak her imagination. She just said he was still adamant in his refusal to sell.

"Maybe if we sweeten the pot," her father suggested. "Tori offered him twenty-five percent over appraisal. Maybe we should go higher."

Burton had been quiet until then. He, too, looked drawn, haggard. He'd left Friday afternoon to spend the weekend in Austin visiting friends. Tori wondered if one of those friends might be a woman. It didn't matter, of course. They had no claims on each other. But as she recounted the circumstances under which she'd met Jesse on Sunday evening, she couldn't help noticing the intense expression on his face. Was it disapproval of her tactics or was it jealousy? The first alternative irritated her; the latter she found amusing.

"We can go to fifty percent easily," Burton said. "No appraisal is going to be very high in that neighborhood. We can afford to be generous."

"Or look like we are," she shot back, knowing there was no generosity in the gesture. The unfortunate deterioration of Santa Marta was working in their favor.

Her father waived her comments aside. "Whatever works. We've got everything tied up in Riverbend. It's do or die."

Tori had always done her best under pressure, whether competing for honors at the academy or playing intercollegiate tennis tournaments. Except this wasn't a test or a game. This was real life. Not only did the destiny of Carr Enterprises ride on Jesse's decision, so did the fate of his beloved barrio. And what about her and Jesse? The possibilities were tantalizing. There was no mistaking the attraction she'd felt while in his house. No denying he'd felt it, too.

"If you still think you can bring Amorado around," Burton continued, "that's great. But if not, please say so. I've had a little bit of experience handling situations like this."

She sensed that her father was becoming increasingly uncomfortable. He poured them more coffee from the carafe in the middle of the table.

"Have you got any specific suggestions on how we might approach him?" he asked her.

"What he wants is to preserve something of the old Mexican quarter. He showed me a mock-up of what he thinks it should look like."

"His etchings?" Burton quipped.

Winslow's steel blue eyes shot daggers at Burton, who exhaled sharply and settled back into the plush leather armchair.

Tori ignored the body language between the two men. "So maybe we can help him."

"How?" they asked simultaneously.

Tori was in a quandary. How could she reasonably present Jesse's position without appearing to advocate it?

"Jesse wants to upgrade the existing houses in the barrio," she said, trying to sound detached, objective. "At least the ones that can be improved. He wants to tear down those that can't and put in parks and other recreational facilities. It's a good plan." She saw a subtle smile on Burton's face. "But unrealistic, since he no longer has access to other properties and the price would be prohibitive."

"Damn right," Burton interjected.

"So what's your idea?" her father asked calmly.

Tori pushed her chair back, grateful for the opportunity to flex her tensed muscles. She'd been toying with a strategy all night. She pointed to the map on her father's office wall. "This spur of Santa Marta where Jesse lives will end up behind the park as a sort of separate enclave. We own the other six houses there in addition to a couple of vacant lots. Why not offer them to him in exchange for the six houses he has scattered all over the district?''

Winslow Carr studied the map. ''You mean reduce his barrio to that one little area? From what you've said, I don't think that's what he has in mind.''

''We're going to build the clubhouse and three of our most expensive residences there!'' Burton objected.

''Build them here instead.'' Tori indicated an adjacent area where less expensive houses were planned.

''Hmm. Yes. It has possibilities,'' her father said. ''What do you propose, an even trade?''

''I think we'll still have to pay him something for his Santa Marta properties. For one thing, he'll need capital to fix up the ones he'll be getting from us.''

''That's a pretty expensive compromise,'' Burton muttered as he studied the map. He addressed Winslow Carr. ''We'd be giving up a quarter of a million dollars in potential profit even before paying him for those shacks of his. Still, since it means he could keep his own house, it might work. What do you think, Win?''

Her father still looked unconvinced. His hesitation worried her, not because it suggested lack of confidence in her judgment, but because it betrayed an uncharacteristic distrust of his own. It was Burton who finally made the decision.

''Okay, Tori. You seem to be developing some rapport with this guy. Go ahead and set up a meeting and let's see how he responds.''

CHAPTER SIX

ESPY MUST HAVE SENSED Jesse's ambivalence on Saturday night, because she arrived at the office earlier than usual Monday.

"What have you decided to do?" she demanded.

He continued examining the blueprints he'd laid out on a drafting table near the window. "I'm going to make a deal with Carr."

He wasn't surprised when she exploded and called him a traitor. He let her rave on for some time while he fixed coffee and gave her a cup—which, at one point, he seriously thought she was going to throw at him.

"Are you finished now?" he asked with stoic patience when she finally stopped to catch her breath. "If you are, perhaps you'll give me a chance to explain what my conditions with Carr are going to be."

Grudgingly she plopped down in the seat Tori had occupied a week before, added an exorbitant amount of sugar to his special blend, poured milk and glared at him. "Well?"

He spent the next half hour going over the strategy he'd spent most of his sleepless night working out. It was a gamble, but it might work.

Espy's temper was as quick to subside as it was to flare. She sat quietly listening to him, admiring his approach but ultimately doubting that Winslow Carr would go along with it.

"He has no choice," Jesse told her. "If he doesn't agree to my conditions, he'll end up losing Riverbend altogether—unless he thinks he can build around my houses." He laughed. "Can't you just see Rosario's place between two mansions? I'm sure his broken-down Ford and old Chevy pickup will make quite a fashion statement."

Espy remained dubious. Jesse wasn't sure whether it was over the conditions of his plan or his sincerity.

"I'm going to make an appointment with Carr for ten o'clock this morning," he told her. "Come along with me." She brightened. "But keep your mouth shut. I do the talking. *Comprende?*"

"Yes, Jesse," she said demurely.

LYDIA WAS AWAY from her desk when the phone rang. Tori picked it up on the third ring and was surprised to hear the deep masculine voice that would have been familiar even if the caller hadn't introduced himself. Jesse didn't waste time on amenities.

"I'd like to stop by to meet with you and your father at ten."

It was remarkably short notice, and the appointment book on Lydia's desk showed a prospective buyer coming in at that time, but a meeting with the competition at this point was far more important than a meeting with a client. The other appointment would have to be rescheduled.

"Ten o'clock will be fine, Mr. Amorado...Jesse."

She thought she detected a smile in his inflection as he thanked her and rang off.

Her father was standing at the coffee bar helping himself to a second cup of decaf when Tori hung up.

"What do you think he has in mind?" he asked.

Burton stepped out of his office, obviously pleased. "Sounds like Amorado's ready to sell. Nice work, Tori."

"Don't compliment me yet," she warned. "We've yet to have a meeting of the minds. Let's see what he has to say when he gets here."

The prospect of seeing Jesse Amorado again stirred contrary emotions in Tori. His strength was captivating, his determination intimidating. Which made him a formidable opponent. Those qualities also made her apprehensive—which she found stimulating as well.

What she wasn't prepared for was the presence of his business associate. Espy was dressed more modestly than she had been at the Manor, but the teal-and-burgundy pantsuit she now wore was no less chic. The long string of wooden beads didn't seem to know if they should surround her generous breasts or slink between them. The calm submissiveness with which she followed Jesse's lead seemed to Tori only a facade.

"Good morning again," Tori said to Jesse, and felt her hand engulfed in his. She turned brightly to Espy. "I'm glad you could make it. You met Mr. Hazlitt the other evening."

Tori watched Burton with amusement. Did he know his mouth was open and he was staring? Well, only for a moment. But it was comical.

"This is my father. Dad, this is Espy Mendez. We knew each other as kids."

"Thank you for coming, Mr. Amorado," said Winslow, as if he'd invited them. "I'm pleased to meet you, Miss Mendez. Didn't I see you at the Manor the other evening?''

Espy cocked an eyebrow, clearly surprised he'd noticed her.

After they were seated at the conference table in his office, Winslow seized the initiative. "I think we've come up with a compromise that may interest you, Mr. Amorado.''

Glancing at Tori, Jesse said, "Your daughter indicated you're willing to pay twenty-five percent over appraisal.''

"Yes, but under this new proposal—"

"I'm afraid that won't do." He turned to Winslow. "The deterioration of your holdings in Santa Marta has severely depressed everyone else's real property values there, as well. Any appraisal at this time would grossly underestimate the fair market value of my property.''

Burton interrupted. "The depressed state of the barrio—" Tori shuddered at the word and wished he hadn't used it "—is precisely why we're willing to pay a premium.''

"You're the ones who've wrecked Santa Marta," Espy said hotly. "If it weren't for you—"

"Miss Mendez," Burton broke in, "we are not solely responsible for conditions in Santa Marta. We are, in fact, only minority holders.''

"Minority holders!" Espy exploded. Jesse signaled her to silence with the wave of his hand. She fumed openly but held her tongue.

"I'm not interested in playing a game of semantics, Mr. Carr." He deliberately ignored Burton Hazlitt. "I am fully aware your company owns forty-five percent of the property in Santa Marta. I also know you are the active agents for another thirty percent. Except for my six properties, you've bought options on all the rest—options that you must exercise within thirty days."

Tori was impressed. He'd done his homework.

"I also know," Jesse continued, "you intend to demolish all of them for this Riverbend project of yours."

Burton was about to say something else, but this time Winslow cut him short. "What do you suggest, Mr. Amorado?"

"Not suggest—demand!" Espy blurted out.

Jesse cast a stabbing look at her, forcing her again into unwilling silence.

"Considering what not getting my properties could cost you, Mr. Carr, I want seventy thousand dollars apiece for my five rental houses and one hundred and fifty thousand for my own house."

The only sound was the moan of the air-conditioning. Tori looked at her father. He seemed momentarily stunned, then mildly amused.

"Five hundred thousand dollars for less than two acres of land?" Burton finally muttered, amazement mixed with awe at the boldness of the proposal. "That's absolutely out of the question."

The shock effect of his demand obviously pleased Jesse.

"Well, that part's negotiable," he conceded offhandedly. Then his tone hardened. "The rest isn't."

Winslow and his daughter exchanged glances.

"The rest?" she asked.

"By destroying Santa Marta, you are destroying the homes and neighborhood of a lot of people who, in spite of what you might think, take great pride in their community. In exchange for the land you'll be taking from the people there, I want you to contribute an equal amount of land in the Coyote Mesa area."

Tori had a sinking feeling in the pit of her stomach. She'd been prepared for an outrageous sale price. She could have negotiated that. But this demand went far beyond anything imaginable, and the expressions on the faces of her father and Burton reflected the same shock.

"Mr. Amorado," her father said patiently, "Coyote Mesa is a newly platted subdivision only recently incorporated by the city. No one has even registered building plans there yet."

"That's preposterous," Burton sputtered, something Tori had never seen him do before. She found it perversely gratifying. "Next you'll want us to put in housing for your people there, too."

"No, Mr. Hazlitt. I'll build the housing. You need only guarantee my loan for seed capital in the amount of five million dollars."

Espy smiled smugly.

Tori had to stop herself from laughing. Her own words coming home to haunt her again. Hadn't she been the one yesterday who pointed out the need for venture capital?

Burton looked as if he were about to slam his fist on the table until Winslow shot him a stern warning glance. Patiently, he addressed their visitor.

"Mr. Amorado, we don't own any land there, and purchasing it... Well, such an undertaking in itself would be cost-prohibitive. As for guaranteeing your loan—"

"What you pay me for my property is negotiable," Jesse countered, "but unless you are willing to cede as much land as you are taking and support its development, there won't be any deal. As for ownership," he added, "you may not personally own any property on

the mesa, but your associates, the people who are bank-
rolling this venture, do. I suggest you discuss it with
them. I think the alternatives are quite plain. Either you
accept my offer or you give up Riverbend. Because,"
he concluded ominously, "I'm also prepared to legally
contest every move you make, every petition for zoning
variance you file, every request for public utilities you
submit."

"Is there no room for compromise?" Tori asked.

"No, Miss Carr," Jesse said coldly. "There will be
no compromise."

"Mr. Amorado, I understand why you want land for
the people of Santa Marta," Winslow stated politely.
"But to expect us to purchase land, back you to build
on it and then just give it up…it's unreasonable."

Until that point, Jesse's manner had been firm but
businesslike. Now it turned positively frigid.

"Would it have been unreasonable to expect you to
maintain the properties you bought in Santa Marta to
the same standards you maintain in other parts of
town?" He cast a contemptuous glance at Burton, who
remained defiantly passive, then looked back at the senior partner. "Would it have been unreasonable for you
to ensure basic standards of safety were being met?"

Winslow blanched and looked over at Burton, who
seemed intent on examining his fingernails.

Jesse Amorado rose from the leather chair. Espy
jumped instantly to her feet.

"Those are my terms, Mr. Carr," Jesse concluded
casually. "Take 'em or leave 'em."

Winslow Carr, struggling to control his temper,
stood up, as did Tori. "I'm not sure we can meet all
your conditions," he said. "You're right about one
thing. Without your properties, Riverbend, as presently

conceived, cannot happen. I sincerely do want it to happen, Mr. Amorado. So give me some time to see how I can satisfy your requirements.''

Jesse faced him, his demeanor implacable. ''You can reach me at my office during the day or at my home in the evening. Both numbers are in the book. If I'm not there, leave a message.''

Winslow moved from the head of the conference table and offered his hand. Jesse accepted it politely.

''Thank you for coming by, Mr. Amorado. Miss Mendez.''

Jesse moved leisurely to the door, totally ignoring Burton, who'd also gotten to his feet. Espy was right behind Jesse, her eyes hard, gleaming. Tori moved into the doorway just enough to block her easy exit.

''It's been nice seeing you again, Espy.''

Espy stared blankly for a moment, as if she didn't quite know what to say, then accepted Tori's outstretched hand. ''Yeah, me, too,'' she mumbled, and fled.

The door was firmly shut before Winslow turned to his partner. ''I know we're letting cosmetics slip, but what's this about our failing to maintain minimum safety standards in Santa Marta?''

Burton plopped down in the chair he'd previously occupied, his legs outstretched in a casual pose of indifference. ''Words, Win. Perceptions. He's got no proof that our houses are any less safe than anybody else's.''

Tori watched with concern as her father's face flushed with anger. ''We're not talking about other people's houses,'' he rebuked him in a hard voice. ''We're talking about ours.'' He ran his fingers through his graying hair. ''Peeling paint is one thing, but I will not risk the safety and welfare of families to save a few dollars.''

Burton sat up straight, drawing his short, thick legs under him. ''Check the records if you don't believe me.'' He shifted his defiance to Tori. ''We use the same licensed plumbers and electricians in the barrio as we do in other parts of town, and we pass all our safety inspections.''

Tori was more concerned about her father than she was about responding to Burton's challenge. She poured him a glass of water from the carafe on the table and handed it to him.

He smiled but avoided looking her in the eye. His hand, she noticed, wasn't quite steady as he accepted the drink. ''I guess I'm going to have to drive through the barrio more often,'' he muttered, and took a sip.

A minute passed. The atmosphere cooled.

''You're not serious about trying to meet those ridiculous demands?'' Burton questioned his partner. Tori could sense the temper, the outrage in his voice. He'd been called to task and didn't like it.

Winslow Carr slid back in his seat, apparently unaware of his associate's lingering emotions. ''I'm serious about trying to find a way to appease him,'' he observed. ''I know there's no way we can meet his conditions as they stand. But at least we've got him talking to us.''

He took another swallow of water and explained to his daughter, ''There's always private investment money available to develop middle- and upper-income housing. But not for low-income housing. The only source for that kind of financing is the government, and frankly, I don't think we have a chance of getting any,

at least not for Coyote Mesa, and certainly not in time
for us to proceed on Riverbend.''

WHEN TORI CAME into the office the next morning,
Burton was telling her father he'd called a buddy of
his at city hall and arranged everything.

"What's been arranged?" she asked. Burton seemed
very pleased with himself.

He sipped from the coffee mug hooked in his right
hand. "Amorado put on a good show yesterday, but I
suspect that's all it was, a show. His girlfriend was
pretty quick to blame us for the deterioration of the
barrio, but if you look around, his houses aren't in exactly showcase condition. If he's so damned proud of
his neighborhood, why isn't he maintaining his places
better?''

A fair question, Tori thought, one that had been
bothering her ever since she'd called him a slumlord.

"He's building houses over in Oakdale on spec,''
she ventured. "Maybe he's got the same kind of cash-
flow problems we have.''

"That's exactly how I see it,'' Burton said, nodding
approval of her analysis. "So let's turn up the pressure.
Let's give him a little more of an incentive to sell to
us.''

"How?" Tori asked, suddenly afraid to hear the answer.

"I've arranged for a building inspector to go out and
take a look at Amorado's flooded house. If the water
damage is only half as bad as you say, it'll be condemned on the spot. As soon as that happens, the bank
will have no choice but to call in his loans, not just on
that house but on his others, too, in order to protect
their investments.'' Burton gave her a vicious grin.

"All we have to do is wait for the foreclosure sales and gobble up his properties, all of them, probably at less than appraised value."

Tori's insides tightened. "You can do that?"

"I've got connections downtown." He smiled complacently. "All's fair in love and war. This is the war part."

Was he telling her he'd seen through her attempt at poised detachment from Jesse the day before? The amused gleam in his hazel eyes said just that. She stared at him without flinching until he squirmed.

"Look, I'm not suggesting we do anything illegal," he insisted. "Just using the weapons we have at our disposal."

"And I'm just wondering," she responded, "if our houses in Santa Marta can withstand the same scrutiny. Isn't turnaround fair play? Won't the inspectors inevitably have to look at our houses in Santa Marta, as well—if not at Jesse's insistence, then at his lawyer's?"

Her father, who had been quietly sipping coffee, sat up in his chair. "She's right. We have a lot more to lose if this gambit backfires."

"It won't," Burton assured them both. "We've got enough clout downtown to make sure it doesn't."

"What about our reputation when word gets out?" Tori countered. "And it will." She turned to her father. "Is that how you want Carr Enterprises to be known?"

Winslow rose heavily to his feet, his face red. "Call off the dogs, Burton," he ordered, and marched from the room.

Tori was decidedly unhappy with the way things were going. She didn't consider herself naive, but she had to admit she was surprised by the tactics Burton was proposing to use against a business rival. Technically not illegal, perhaps, but certainly unethical. Her father's reaction disturbed her, too. Had his anger been aimed at Burton for his unscrupulous scheme, or at her for putting him on the spot? Would he have backed Burton if she hadn't goaded him into rejecting the idea?

The other question that kept coming to mind was what Jesse's reaction would be if he learned that they'd schemed to have his property condemned. She knew he would fight back. His pride wouldn't let him do otherwise. But how? She couldn't imagine him stooping to the same kind of underhanded tactics, but he'd have to do something.

IT WAS AFTER FIVE when Tori drove over to the Spanish Arms on South Travis Street. Espy's apartment was on the second floor of a long barrackslike building of rough-cut vertical siding, up an outside flight of steel-and-concrete stairs that rang and vibrated with each step. Tori pressed the button under the tarnished brass nameplate to the apartment on the left and heard a muffled buzz inside. A moment later the door opened the length of a security chain.

There was no mistaking the look of surprise on Espy's face, followed by what Tori interpreted as annoyance, though it could have been anger or even hostility.

"Hello, Espy," Tori said pleasantly. "I thought I'd take a chance and drop by." Espy's full mouth turned down slightly at the corners, and Tori felt distinctly unwelcome. "I hope this isn't an inconvenient time. Maybe I should have called first."

Wordlessly Espy shut the door, released the chain

and swung the door open wide. "Come in," she said tightly.

Tori stood in the small, dark entry while Espy resecured the chain, then followed her into the living room, where miniblinds were drawn up, filling the room with brilliant summer light.

"Sit down," Espy invited without making any move to sit herself. "You want some sun tea?"

Tori remained standing and forced a pleasant smile. "Thanks," she said. "That'd be great."

While Espy made domestic noises in the kitchenette, Tori strolled over to the entertainment center, her eye caught by a collection of framed photos clustered above a shelf of hardcover and paperback books. She couldn't miss the picture of Jesse Amorado, snug jeans and T-shirt provocatively shadowed by streaks of sunlight. A wave of black hair arched over one eye, giving him a rakish look.

Espy handed her a sweaty glass of iced tea. "Leave him alone, Tori. He's not your type."

Tori's ire flared. *What is my type?* she wanted to demand. *And who are you to decide it?*

Instead she insisted tersely, "My only interest in Jesse is business. He owns some property my father wants to buy."

"Yeah, sure, right," Espy snorted. "Who do you think you're kidding? I saw the two of you gawking at each other over dinner the other night and at your office yesterday."

Tori's palms grew damp. She didn't like being called a liar or getting caught in equivocation. "Is that what this is about— Jesse?"

Espy's eyes narrowed suspiciously. "What do you mean?"

"Espy, we haven't seen each other in years. We were friends once, and now you treat me as if I've offended you in some way. I'd like to know why. If it's about Jesse... Are the two of you going together? Are you afraid I'll try to take him away from you?"

Espy laughed, then sighed. "I'd like to marry Jesse, or someone like him. *Este es muy macho.* He's the one who insists on keeping it only a friendship."

A surge of relief rippled through her. "Well, if it's not Jesse, what is it?"

The sentimental Mexican ballad that had been playing softly on the radio was abruptly replaced with a brassy rock number. Espy shut it off violently.

"You really don't have a clue, do you?"

Even as a little girl, Espy seemed always on the point of crying or having a fit of temper. Tori never quite understood why. The woman's glower now was so harsh Tori was forced to back away.

"Friends, huh? Don't make me laugh. Friends are supposed to have things in common. What do we have?"

"Our childhood. We grew up together."

"Grew up together?" Espy repeated, her low voice sharp at the edges. "What do you know about how I grew up? You never came to my house, and you sure as hell never invited me to yours. So tell me, what did we have in common? You, the beautiful Victoria Carr, with an educated mama and a rich daddy, and me, just another Mexican brat."

Tori was taken aback by the bitterness in her words.

"No, Tori," Espy snarled, "we have nothing in common. While your daddy was making killings in real estate, mine was either home beating my mother or getting thrown in jail for being drunk and disorderly."

She glared at Tori with large, hostile eyes. "Well, he finally had the fight of his life. He got stabbed to death in a bar over some stupid game. Didn't know that, did you? Of course not. Who cared? Not me. At least he wasn't beating up on Mama and me anymore."

Tori reached out for her hand but Espy turned her back.

"Espy, I'm sorry," Tori said, knowing the words were totally inadequate. "I had no idea."

"While you were going to your fancy academy," Espy continued as if she hadn't heard, "I had to work full-time to put food on the table for my kid brothers and sisters…and buy my mother medicine so the cancer wouldn't hurt so much."

"I didn't know," Tori repeated, shocked by what she was hearing.

"No—" Espy spun around and shouted back at her "—you didn't care."

"That's not true. If you'd told me what was going on, I would have helped."

Espy laughed, an ugly, hysterical sound, full of terrible pain. "How?"

"There are laws against wife and child abuse. My mother—"

Espy's lips curled in a cruel parody of a smile. "After what happened to your mama, you must know laws don't work."

Tori felt a sudden surge of outrage. She didn't want to be reminded of her mother lying on the floor, her life's blood oozing away. She fought to control the pain of the memory.

"Why didn't you ever answer my letters?" she managed to ask.

For a moment, Espy's temper seemed suspended. "Letters? What letters?"

"After my mother…died…and my father made me stay home with a sitter after school, I wrote to you. Long letters, telling you how much I missed you. But you never answered me."

Sudden tears welled in Espy's eyes, and for a moment her voice became soft, pleading—the hurt sound of a little girl abandoned. "Did you really write me, or are you just saying that?"

"I did write, Espy, many times."

Espy turned away and faced the picture window overlooking the pool, arms crossed under her breasts as she hugged herself. The fire in her eyes was gone when she spoke, her words now low, thoughtful and mournfully sad.

"So that's what Mama was so mad at him about. I remember Papa ranting and raving about something, then tearing up papers and flushing them down the toilet." She looked at Tori, her eyes moist and red-rimmed. "It must have been your letters he was tearing up."

The sense of irretrievable loss was overwhelming, and for the first time since coming here, Tori felt they were sharing something together.

"The filthy bastard," Espy muttered, then spun around and hurled her next words out rebelliously. "I'm glad he's dead."

Tori watched the play of emotions on Espy's face. What kind of love-hate relationship had she had with her father? Tori remembered Mr. Mendez picking up Espy at the Gutierrez house only once. Espy had hesitated, pulling back, evaluating the man when he called. Then she'd run to him and been swallowed up in his thick brown arms and cuddled against his chest. Now Tori was hearing he also beat her and her mother. A cold shiver went down her spine.

"I'm sorry he hurt you and your mom," she said, and watched Espy's eyes grow cold.

Espy sank into an overstuffed chair. "It was a long time ago," she murmured.

Tori needed to steer the conversation away from such ugly memories. She glanced back at the cluster of photos on the wall. Among them, holding prominence, was a certificate in an oversize document frame. A graduation equivalency diploma. It was odd seeing this lowest of educational awards prestigiously displayed the way doctors and lawyers presented their credentials. The achievement was obviously important to Espy. Tori looked more closely. The date above the stamped signature showed it was less than a year old.

"You managed to finish school, I see. Congratulations."

Espy said nothing. Tori could feel the tension emanating again from her old playmate. Perhaps she was suspicious that Tori might be laughing at her.

"Are you planning to go on to college?" She sat on the couch and reached for her tea. The ice was nearly melted.

"If I can get tuition assistance. Henry Martin, our councilman, says he's going to get me a Bennett scholarship."

The Bennett scholarship fund was a private endowment earmarked for high school minority graduates who couldn't afford to go to college. Competition for it was high.

"What will you study?"

She felt Espy gauging her, trying to decide if the

question was sincere or some sort of trick to make fun of her. Tori held her gaze.

"I'd like to go into medical research so I can help find a cure for the cancer that killed my mother. She shouldn't have had to die."

Tori didn't doubt Espy's sincerity for a moment. "Then do it."

Espy shook her head. "I haven't got the money and I'm not smart enough. I didn't even finish high school."

"Because your mother and the family came first." Tori pointed to the framed certificate on the wall. "You're not stupid, Espy. You got your diploma. You can do whatever you set out to do. Go for it."

Espy rose from the chair and began pacing like an animal in a cage, which, Tori thought, was probably how she felt.

"Maybe I can help, if you'll let me," Tori offered.

"What? How? Give me money?"

"No," she replied evenly. "But there are scholarships and grant programs that go begging every year because people don't know about them or how to apply for them. Let me help you find them. I can give you a hand with the applications. Believe me, I can fill out paperwork in triplicate with the best of them."

"You would do that for me?"

"Isn't that what friends are for, helping each other?"

Espy's face brightened. There was something not only beautiful but magical about her expression. Then suddenly it turned glum.

"I can't...won't give you what you want in exchange."

Tori's head jerked up. "What I want?"

"For me to convince Jesse to sell to your father."

So Espy thought this visit was to get something from her. The idea of so much distrust, so much suspicion of always being used was heartbreaking.

"There are no conditions, Espy. As far as Riverbend is concerned…Jesse showed me the model at his house of what he wants Santa Marta to look like."

"You were in his house?" She blinked in surprise and perhaps with a flicker of jealousy in her eyes. "Then he told you about his brother?"

"His brother?"

"About Miguel."

"No," Tori admitted, and licked her lips against a sudden dryness. Intuition told her that what she was about to hear wouldn't make things easier.

"Jesse didn't tell you Miguel built that model?"

"No. He only showed it to me." He was damned proud of it, too, she almost added. "What about Miguel?" She needed all the facts if she was going to deal with the situation effectively— deal with Jesse honestly.

Espy dropped back into a chair, her feet flat on the floor, her hands dangling over the armrests. "Miguel was five years younger than Jesse and idolized him. Their papa, Fernando, did a lot of repair work in the barrio, among our people. He worked cheap. Knew people didn't have much money.

"Jesse expanded the business in other parts of town. Got into construction. Miguel joined them when he graduated from high school."

Espy reached over to the coffee table and picked up her glass of tea. She took a slow sip and went on. "When Jesse started making decent money, he began renovating his parents' house. After the old man dropped dead of a heart attack a few years ago, Miguel came up with the idea of fixing up the rest of Santa Marta the way they had their own house.'' Espy rested her head back on the chair.

''What happened to Miguel?'' Tori asked.

''Killed in a drive-by shooting last year. It was stupid. Gangs. We never used to have gangs in Santa Marta before. We do now. Maybe killing Miguel was part of some initiation ritual. Who knows? He'd just stopped off at the Quickie Mart to pick up some milk and bread and ice cream for the kids. God, he loved Lupe and those kids. He was getting back into his car when the gangbangers wheeled by and shot him.''

Tori shivered. ''Did they catch whoever did it?''

''The police picked up a couple of teenagers, but their buddies gave them an alibi and they were released.'' Espy scowled. ''So if you think Jesse's going to let you tear down Santa Marta, you're wrong. He'll never let you destroy his brother's dream.''

CHAPTER SEVEN

On Wednesday morning, Jesse drove to Oakdale, where the last of the three family residences he was building on speculation was nearing completion. His father had supervised the construction of the first one. Then, after he died, Jesse had let Miguel oversee the second one. The two brothers had gotten together every morning at the building site to share a thermos of coffee and breakfast burritos, talk about their plans for rebuilding Santa Marta and laugh at the latest antics of Miguel's kids.

Jesse thought about Tori standing over the make-believe community he'd shown her Sunday afternoon. She didn't understand how much his barrio meant to him, didn't realize he couldn't abandon it without feeling he was betraying Miguel.

He left his cell phone in the cab of the truck and walked around to the back door. Kitchen cabinets were being installed this morning, and he took extra time to make sure the finishing touches, the details by which clients judged the quality of a house, were as meticulously executed as the structural components.

Satisfied his crew was productively on the job, he headed for the airport. Sam Hargis wanted him to do a relatively minor renovation job—partition off a corner of his old hangar to use as office space. It wouldn't be a big moneymaker, but the wily old aircraft mechanic had business interests all over town, and Jesse had the feeling Hargis was testing him. If he did this job right, he'd intimated, there'd be more work coming. That had been the day Tori had flown in on a wing and a prayer.

Jesse still remembered the fascination he'd felt as he watched the crippled Cessna touch down and glide to a stop in the middle of the runway and the way his gut had tightened when he saw the cool blonde emerge from the side door of the plane. He hadn't realized who she was until he'd seen her embrace Winslow Carr.

AN HOUR AND A HALF LATER, Jesse and Sam were shaking hands in the corner of the huge wooden structure, sealing their deal, when a bright flash of color streaked by the side door from the parking lot. The red Corvette might as well have been a flag waved in front of a bull. When Tori came around the corner of the hangar, his heartbeat went up a few notches. Her step seemed lighter, her expression more cheerful, her golden hair less disciplined than any other time he'd seen her.

She stepped into the shadowy structure, removed her aviator sunglasses and paused long enough to let her vision adjust to the gloom. Then she brightened perceptibly and strode toward them.

"Hello, Sam," she said easily. "I hear my plane's ready."

"Yes, ma'am. Test-flew it myself yesterday. It's all set." They exchanged a few technical questions and answers and Sam moved on.

She replaced her glasses and turned to Jesse. "What brings you out here? You fly?"

"The usual airlines," he said.

He imagined her eyes twinkling behind the dark green lenses.

"I'm going up for an hour or so," she said. "The wild blue is great for clearing out cobwebs. Would you like to come along?"

"Cobwebs, huh? I don't think I've ever looked at them from the sky."

This time she graced him with a quick, amused grin.

"If you don't fly," she said as they walked out onto the broiling tarmac, "why are you here?"

"Hargis has a renovation job he wants me to do for him."

"Ah."

But already Jesse could tell her mind was on other things. He stood by while she talked to the ground crew, then he followed her as she went through her preflight inspection. He certainly admired the view. Her worn jeans fitted perfectly. She wasn't wearing any of the gold bracelets or chain necklaces he'd seen her wear on other occasions, but the two top buttons on her daffodil yellow shirt were open, exposing a creamy smooth hint of generous cleavage.

It was a strange feeling to be standing in the glaring sun next to an airplane that suddenly didn't look very big and not quite understand what was going on. He definitely wasn't used to following a woman's lead, no matter how bewitching she was.

"What kind of plane did you fly in the air force?" he asked as they climbed into the roasting fuselage and made their way to the cockpit.

"I wasn't a pilot in the air force. That's why I resigned."

She put no particular emphasis on the words, but they weren't casually spoken, either, and he could sense disappointment hidden in them. Had it been her dream to fly jet fighters? To break sound barriers? Gender barriers?

She slipped into the left seat. "I couldn't pass the physical," she explained as she slid the small side window open.

He raised an eyebrow. She would certainly pass any physical he could imagine.

Her eyes laughed at him, practically daring him to pursue the subject. She motioned him into the right seat. He bent toward her as he folded himself into it. She smelled like wildflowers on a spring morning. He watched her feet work the rudder pedals in and out.

"Height obviously wasn't a problem," he noted. "Not with those long legs."

She gave no overt indication she'd heard him, but he could tell by a delicate tilt of her head as she pulled the yoke back and forth, testing it, that she had. He brought his gaze up to her full breasts.

"There doesn't seem to be a question of adequate upper body strength, either," he added. "You want to arm wrestle?"

That did get a reaction. She stopped fiddling with knobs, turned slowly toward him, her brows lowered. "I may not be as strong as you, wise guy, but I'll match reflexes with you anytime." She went back to her tasks. "I spent a ton of quarters playing arcade games to sharpen them."

Yes, he thought, *I'd love to play games and match reflexes with you.* "So what's the problem?"

"I have a slight color acuity condition."

"You're color-blind? Pretty rare for a woman, isn't it?"

"About one-tenth as likely as it is for a man." She

flipped switches and tapped gauges. "Mine's very subtle. I can tell you that the bright colors in your plaid shirt are red, green, tan, gray and brown. But I can't tell you if this dark stripe is titian or malachite."

He looked down at his chest, at her finger barely touching a line in the cloth of his breast pocket. The sensation was unnervingly erotic, and for a moment he stopped breathing. The bucket seat threatened to become uncomfortably snug.

"Hell," he said with a chuckle as she withdrew her hand, "I'm not sure I can tell you, either."

"I passed all the other tests, then the flight surgeon's office flunked me. Their chromatic parameters are more stringent because of the requirement to read military maps."

"But you can still fly?"

"Privately and commercially, I'm qualified. But not for the air force. I interviewed to fly with a commercial airline in Dallas. I should hear something in a few weeks."

Engine start-up effectively terminated their discussion. She made sure he was properly buckled in, helped him don his headset and showed him how to adjust the radio so he could follow the air traffic chatter. The instrument panel in front of him was bewildering.

They taxied out to the runway, and he listened in as she checked with the tower requesting clearance for takeoff. He became uneasy only when she revved up the engines, making the plane shudder as if with pent-up energy. Then she released the brake and they shot down the runway like a stock car. He wasn't actually aware of them lifting off. One minute he was watching airport buildings speed by, the next he was looking down at them.

"Where are we going?" he asked when they reached their altitude and leveled off, and the resonance of the engines faded to a tolerable drone.

"How about a tour of the city?"

"Sounds good."

He'd seen Coyote Springs from the air when he'd flown in on commercial airlines from Dallas. But those flights had never given him a chance to really examine particular parts of the city. Tori now did a complete circle of the town, with both of them pointing out various landmarks.

The pilot fascinated him as much as the flight itself. Her movements as she checked switches and adjusted controls were crisp and efficient. No hesitation. She was in her element here. He could tell she was acutely alert, yet her self-assurance seemed to dispel tension and relax her. This was a different Tori Carr from the businesswoman on the ground.

He looked down at the corrugated sun-drenched land surrounding Coyote Springs, at the checkerboard of modestly tall buildings. Not a metropolis, but it didn't want to be. The townspeople and city fathers made that abundantly clear every time they rejected bond issues and referendums that would allow the community to grow.

As she banked into a gentle turn, he spied the new dam on the river. Farther to the south, tucked into the horseshoe bend, was Santa Marta.

"There's your house," she announced as she dipped to give him a better view from his side of the plane. "It stands out like a green thumb."

It was a compliment, Jesse knew, but it also pointed out another truth. Santa Marta was a disaster area. As bad as it looked from ground level, it looked worse from up here. *Shabby* was too mild a word.

"Where do you live?" he asked.

She gave him a quick sidelong glance. "I'll show you."

The G-force on her power turn reminded him of the exhilaration of downhill skiing or a ride on the roller coaster at Six Flags. He was beginning to appreciate more fully the lure of flying.

The compass needle swung and they headed due north. The green belt where she lived with her father came into view. Woodhill Terrace was the most prestigious address in Coyote Springs, a country club enclave built around a luxuriously maintained, championship-quality golf course.

The Carr residence wasn't the biggest house in the sumptuous development, but it wasn't the most modest, either. Jesse nodded when Tori pointed it out.

"Let's take a look at Coyote Mesa," Tori suggested as she pulled away from the green swath of golf course and well-watered landscaping.

The mesa was on the northwest end of town, a high bluff of scant vegetation and rocky outcroppings. Tori circled it.

"Pretty desolate," she commented through the interphone.

"But it's got a great view. You can see the whole city from up there. At night it's really romantic."

"Romantic?"

"See that road?" He pointed to a ribbon of white caliche hugging the rim of the rugged plateau. "Lovers' lane."

Had she ever been there? he wondered. Judging from the rapt expression on her face, she hadn't. *What kind of teenager were you?* he wanted to ask. *Did you go steady with anyone? Did you neck? Or were you the serious student type?*

"This won't be an easy place to develop," she noted. "Bringing in water and utilities is going to be expensive."

"As I recall, there were no water or utilities in Woodhill Terrace ten years ago, either. Now there's a golf course that probably drinks more water in a month than Santa Marta does in a year. These things can be done if the right people want to do them badly enough."

He watched her face, saw the wistful look of a minute earlier close up and the practical professional woman take over. The truth hurt. He could forgive himself for being the bearer of bad news, but did he have to take satisfaction in dishing it out? A moment ago his question had been, "What kind of woman are you, Tori Carr?" Now he wondered if it shouldn't be, "What kind of man are you, Jesse Amorado?"

Tori gave a small sigh. "We really need to sit down and discuss your offer. I've come up with an idea that might work, but I have to talk it over with my father and Burton first. Can I call you in a couple of days so we can get together?"

He looked over at her. The set chin said one thing; the way she kept her eyes straight ahead, unwilling to meet his, said something else. "We can get together anytime you want, Tori."

The engines droned, white noise in the silence between them.

She turned south on the western edge of the city. "Where's your ranch?"

"On the river, a couple of miles off the intersection of Farm-to-Market Road 1080 and Highway 24."

"You want to see it?"

"That would be great."

She veered west. The sun, high in the sky, turned the Coyote River into a sparkling strand of molten silver. It blinked and twinkled between the branches of the native nut trees that lined its banks.

Jesse peered down, orienting himself in the vast openness of cross-fenced rangeland. When they flew over a single rail line, he asked her to turn a little to the north.

"There!"

The house looked like a tiny cabin nestled among live oak trees. Tori scanned the sky for traffic, then descended to a thousand feet and circled the small clearing. He pointed to the two children who darted out from the shade of the house and the gray-haired woman trailing behind them. Tori rocked her wings. They waved, though they couldn't possibly recognize who was in the aircraft.

"Your niece and nephew?" Tori asked, making another pass.

"And my mother."

"Nice family," she said. Did he detect a note of envy?

A half hour later they landed in smooth silence. Tori taxied the plane back to its mooring by Hargis Aviation. Ground heat rose in shimmering waves and smothered them as they climbed out. This time he insisted on helping her secure the aircraft—chocks in place, ground wire clipped to its metal ring in the concrete pad.

Sam Hargis met them as they reentered the cool shade of the hangar.

"I was able to keep the repair cost within the ten thousand your insurance allowed," he boasted, "although the air force will probably pick up the tab." He returned her maintenance log. "You've taken good care of that baby," he said. "You know it's due for a complete overhaul in another forty hours. Run you roughly twenty thousand. Standard for a twin engine."

Jesse gave a low whistle and glanced at Tori's face. Her lips were slightly compressed in displeasure, but she didn't seem surprised at the dollar figure.

"Let me get back to you," she said.

"Give me a call when you're ready."

Hargis said goodbye and crossed the hangar floor to a crew of mechanics working on an old biplane. Jesse walked with Tori out to the parking lot. His pickup appeared derelict beside Tori's shiny sports car.

"Thanks for taking me along, Tori. I didn't realize flying could be so much fun." He held her car door open for her. "Do you do this very often? Go out and fly around for an hour or so?"

She climbed behind the wheel. "Depends."

He had an urge to close the first and second buttons on her shirt—or open the third and fourth. He licked his lips. "On what?"

"Having the time and the money."

He nodded. "Yeah, a Corvette and a private plane. I'd call them very expensive toys." And totally out of his league.

WHEN TORI RETURNED to the office with her idea for a compromise with Jesse, there was no one available to discuss it with. Burton was meeting with various city employees to coordinate permits and waivers required for demolition and construction. After that he had a dinner engagement with contractor reps to make sure equipment and skilled workmen would be available in the right mix and numbers as soon as they got the go-ahead. Her father was at the bank all afternoon, doing his best, according to Lydia, to convince the loan department that his cash-flow problem was temporary and wouldn't affect the Riverbend project.

Tori would have talked with him later at home, but he was on the phone until nearly midnight assuring nervous investors the project was still on track—though deadlines were getting close.

Thursday morning wasn't any less hectic. Tori herself was tied up, reviewing photographs for brochures and news releases and conferring with the radio and TV station directors and their advertising departments. The PR campaign she was designing was going to be the biggest media blitz Coyote Springs had ever seen. It was a new challenge for her, one she found herself thoroughly enjoying.

Finally, around noon, she was able to get her father and Burton together for a strategy session in the conference room.

"I hope you called this meeting to announce you've convinced Amorado to sell," Burton told her.

She held her chin up. "We need to change our approach."

Burton stiffened in his seat. "You must be kidding. It's too late for changes."

"What do you have in mind?" her father asked.

She took a deep breath. "Scale back. It'll still be an ambitious project. We just have to refocus it."

Burton glowered.

Her father nodded. "Go on."

"Instead of making Riverbend exclusively high income, broaden its base, make it a family-centered community with a wider range of homes. We'll still build high-value residences, but we can also upgrade some of the better ones that are already there. Does Coyote Springs need another full-size eighteen-hole championship golf course? Probably not. We've already got three. Make this one a nine-holer or an 'executive' par-three. Expand the clubhouse, make it more of a community center—"

Burton slammed his palm down on the conference table. "Is this how you've been spending your time?" He leaned toward her across the polished walnut table. "Instead of building up Riverbend, you're tearing it down." His voice was low, mocking.

She laughed. "You sound just like Jesse Amorado describing what we're doing to Santa Marta."

Burton clenched his jaw tight. He stared over at the map wall, then glared at her. Tori wasn't sure if he was incensed by her ideas or by her laughing at him. "There's no point in discussing this fur—"

"Let's listen," Winslow interrupted quietly. "She's got some good ideas." He gave Tori a sympathetic smile.

"For the Land of Oz maybe," Burton exploded. He jumped to his feet, took a couple of steps and turned around to face Tori. "We've got less than one month before the options we have for the sale of the Santa Marta properties expire."

"There are provisions for renewal," she pointed out.

"After renegotiation. If we have to sit down at the bargaining table with those people again, you can kiss Riverbend goodbye. First, it'll take time. Second, just on the basis of the publicity you've put out so far, they'll demand bigger payoffs. Damn it, Tori, we can't afford the time and we haven't got the money.''

She resented his implication that her doing the job he'd suggested in the first place was going to be the cause of the project's failure. ''Are you suggesting now I shouldn't be promoting Riverbend?''

''No, of course not,'' he relented with a huff.

''Good, because I'd hate to think I wasted my time and your money on PR that isn't necessary. Don't try to make it sound as if it's my fault you haven't been able to cut a deal, Burton. You haven't exactly been a public relations asset.''

''Calm down, you two,'' Winslow broke in. ''Let's see if we can reach a compromise.''

''We can't,'' Burton declared. ''Not if we're going to change course.''

''Actually,'' Winslow told his daughter, ''what you're proposing is what I originally wanted to do in Santa Marta.''

''You did?'' Tori asked breathlessly. ''You never told me—''

''It's too late, Win,'' Burton interrupted. ''Our contractors aren't interested in building low- and middle-income housing. They're into high-value construction. God knows, we're not going to make the profit margins our investors were promised on cheaper housing. In fact,'' he said ominously, ''we may not be able to re-coup what we've already invested.''

Winslow stroked his chin thoughtfully.

''Then change contractors,'' Tori interjected.

''What?'' Burton looked outraged.

''Change contractors,'' she repeated. ''Nothing's

signed. If the ones you're dealing with now can't meet your requirements, find others who can."

Burton threw up his hands. "This is ridiculous. It's taken me months to work out these details. Now you want me to just scrap them." He shifted his address to her father. "Win, we're too far down this road to turn back."

"Dad, someone's going to have to bend."

Winslow Carr swiveled his head from his daughter to his partner and back again, then ran a hand down his face in exasperation. "Let me think about it," he said morosely.

AN HOUR LATER, TORI WAS returning a stack of contract folders to Lydia for filing when the sheriff arrived.

She'd known Rudy Kraus since she was a little girl. Her mother had introduced him as a "nice policeman," and Tori had never had any reason to think of him any other way. He'd come to her school every fall and talked more like a big brother than a contemporary of her father about protecting themselves, watching out for each other and not using drugs or alcohol. He'd spent many a social evening at their house, as well. A few years ago he was elected sheriff. Tori hadn't seen much of him since joining the air force, but she still considered him a good family friend.

She greeted him enthusiastically now, feeling a bit guilty for not having stopped by to say hello since she'd gotten back. She was about to invite him to the house for dinner, but the troubled expression on his face stopped her.

"I best get this over with, Tori," he said uncomfortably. "I'm afraid this isn't a social call. I need to see your dad."

The realization that he was there as a lawman rather than a friend brought her heart to a standstill, and for just a moment she felt light-headed. Lydia bolted to her boss's door.

"Hello, Rudy," Winslow said as he emerged from his office. He offered his hand. "What can we do for you?"

The outstretched hand was ignored. "I'm sorry about this," Rudy announced with businesslike efficiency. "I have a warrant here for your arrest."

"What?" Tori and Lydia cried simultaneously.

"Arrest?" Tori demanded. "For what?"

The sheriff's unhappy expression came as close to an apology, Tori supposed, as his official duties would allow. He faced his old friend. "You're charged with bribing a city inspector."

Tori rushed to her father's side and pressed her hand in his. His face had gone pale. "There must be some mistake."

"I hope so." Rudy sounded like a man who'd heard every excuse and didn't believe any of them anymore. "But that's not for me to decide. I just carry out the orders of the court."

"Call Dad's lawyer," Tori told Lydia, who already had the phone to her ear and was furiously pressing buttons. "This has to be a terrible mistake. Who brought these charges?"

Kraus took no offense at her demanding tone. "The charge is criminal, not civil," he told her. "It was brought by the city attorney in the name of Coyote Springs."

Carr's lawyer, Nelson Spooner, arrived within minutes. He was a trim man in his early forties. Tori had met him at the country club on her last visit home but knew little about him except that he was an aggressive, if not particularly competent, weekend tennis player. At the moment, however, he looked every bit the successful lawyer in his slate gray three-piece suit, blue silk tie with monogrammed gold tie tack and highly polished Italian loafers. He confidently assured his client that the matter would be straightened out in no time.

Winslow Carr was driven to the sheriff's office, where he was formally charged and fingerprinted. The experience was all the more humiliating because everyone there pretended not to recognize him. People he'd known on a first-name basis for years were suddenly addressing him gruffly as Mr. Carr—or just plain Carr. He was reduced to the status of another criminal being booked. At least Rudy didn't put him in one of the cells in back while they waited for Spooner to arrange bail. But there was no doubt Winslow Carr wasn't going anywhere, not for a while, anyway.

The attorney didn't return for nearly two hours. Tori stayed with her father in the small room Rudy allowed them to use.

"I don't understand this," Winslow said. "Burton assured me last evening he'd gotten the inspections called off."

"Is it possible he didn't?"

Her father shook his head. "He can be pretty crafty with clients and contractors, Tori. But he's never lied— not to me." He threw up his hands. "None of this makes any sense."

He sank into a chair against the wall, his shoulders slouched. The humiliation reflected in his eyes almost brought his daughter to tears. When her mother died, he'd been so strong for her. Now it was her turn to be strong for him.

"Our first priority is to get you out of here. We'll sort the rest out later." She walked up to him and placed a hand firmly on his shoulder. "There's a logical explanation for all this. As soon as we get to the bottom of it, the sooner we can fight it—and we will."

He put a hand over hers and smiled. "You bet we will."

He got up and ambled to the window. How strange, Tori thought, that there were no bars on it. They could just climb out and walk away. Except they couldn't. In any case, her father wouldn't. Winslow Carr was down but he wasn't out. He was a fighter, and he'd taught his daughter to be a fighter, as well.

"I've certainly made quite a mess of all this. I've broken rules now and then, played a few tricks and taken advantage of some opportunities. Hell, I've even used the system when it was convenient."

Tori listened, saying nothing, regretting that this man, whom she revered, felt obligated to explain himself to her.

At last Spooner arrived with a paper for Winslow's release. They drove directly to the lawyer's office, where the three of them went over the facts of the case and Spooner started working on a defense.

"Defense?" Winslow shouted in outrage. "Hell, I've been set up!"

"Of course you have," Spooner said with a patronizing calmness he probably thought was reassuring but which in reality was infuriating. "That's going to be our public and legal stance. You're completely innocent and you're going to fight these groundless charges. We'll make it clear that certain parties opposed to your project are conspiring against you. That various other people, who shall remain nameless, are the ones who are really guilty of the offenses they're charging you with, and that they're striking out at you to cover up for their own malfeasance.''

Winslow fidgeted, clearly unhappy with Spooner's approach. Tori wasn't exactly thrilled with it, either. It sounded as if her father's lawyer didn't have much confidence in his client's innocence or in the intelligence of juries. The strategy smelled of lawyers' tricks, when it seemed to Tori the truth would have served them better.

"Did you find out who's behind these charges?'' she asked.

"I tried to. That's one reason I was gone so long. No one's talking. We might learn something during the discovery phase of the process.''

"Would the accuser have to identify himself?''

Spooner shook his head. "Not necessarily. It could have been an anonymous tip.''

Tori didn't think so. She again considered the possibility that Burton hadn't called off the dogs as her father had ordered. But he'd said he had and, like her father, she'd never known Burton to flat out lie. Besides, what would he gain by having his partner publicly disgraced? Then she remembered a comment Espy made—that she handled Jesse's paperwork downtown. Her sympathies and loyalties were definitely with Jesse, in spite of any promises of assistance Tori might have offered. Could Espy have heard rumors about the impending inspection and passed them on to Jesse? Could he be behind this?

CHAPTER EIGHT

EVEN WITH the air conditioner set on max and the fan blowing full blast in her face, Tori couldn't seem to cool off as she drove down South Travis Street. It was midafternoon. The daytime routine of commercial traffic was in full swing.

She'd called Lydia from Spooner's office and let her know Winslow had been released. Lydia insisted he come over to her house. Her father objected, but his protests were mild, and Tori sensed his gratitude when she said his going over there would be a favor to her, put her mind at ease that he was all right. When they arrived, Tori politely declined the invitation to come in.

Once again she had to wait for trucks and cars to pass before she could make a left turn to Amorado Construction. Her fingers drummed the steering wheel and she glared at the empty parking spaces in front of the building. Did he ever have any clients? He had a reputation as a successful builder, so why the hell didn't he ever seem to be doing any business?

Her stomach roiled as she climbed out of her Corvette and strode to the modest stucco building. This time the clamor of the bell on the door wasn't the pleasant tinkling it had been when she'd first entered the reception room. Nor did she wait for Jesse to come out and lead her down the hallway to the office in the back.

Jesse swung around on his stool at the drafting table by the window at the bell's sharp jangle when the outer door slammed. He'd only gotten to his feet by the time his visitor came storming into the room.

She stopped in front of him, her eyes blazing, her lips compressed.

"Tori," he said in surprise. "What's the matter?"

It had been three days since he'd proposed conditions for selling to Carr. Tori had told him yesterday in the plane that she thought she'd worked out a compromise but needed time to discuss it with her father and Hazlitt. Hah!

"Is Espy here?" she demanded.

"No," he assured her quietly. "She only works a couple of days a week."

Tori faced him squarely, her chin high, determined. "When was the last time you saw her?"

"Monday, after our meeting. Why? What's going on?"

"My father was arrested." Her lips twitched and she bit them for control. "They claim he bribed a city inspector."

Jesse seemed surprised, but he said only, "Did he?"

Her eyes flashed. "No, he didn't."

"Then he has nothing to worry about. What was he supposed to have bribed this inspector to do?"

She lowered her chin and pivoted around, suddenly unwilling to face him, to meet his eyes. *Maybe he doesn't know,* she told herself. *Maybe I've been wrong.* The thought pleased her, even if it didn't solve the mystery of who did.

"Tori?" Jesse's tone took on the same hardness

she'd heard when he'd talked to her at the flooded house, an "I'm in charge here" quality. "What was he bribing someone to do?"

She couldn't lie to him, no matter how much the truth hurt. "I just told you he wasn't bribing anyone to do anything." Her retort was too loud. Too strident. She made an effort to moderate it. "What he's charged with is bribing a city inspector to have your flooded house inspected and condemned."

She saw the skin under his smooth olive complexion blanch, saw his square jaw tense. He lifted a hand, then dropped it and spread his fingers as if he had to fight them from tightening into a fist. For a brief minute, she was sure he was going to strike out. The sheer power of his stance sent a shock wave through her. What surprised her was that she felt in no danger. He might be in a rage, might crush something in the room. But he would never hurt her, not physically.

"Please let me explain," she said, her own temper spent.

His eyes were hard, unflinching, wounded as he faced her. "So that's why you were in the barrio the other night—looking for a soft spot. How lucky that you just happened to be in the right place at the right time. That's why you came to my house over the weekend—to see just how vulnerable I might be." He dropped into the chair behind his desk. "And I, like a damned fool, was taken in by your..." He took a deep breath and looked up at her. "I actually thought you might have some sympathy for the people in Santa Marta, when, in fact, you were just sizing me up for the kill."

"No," she protested weakly. Did he know he'd just put a knife in her heart? "It wasn't like that—"

"You had this whole thing planned when I went to see you Monday," he seethed. "You let me make my demands and you sat there laughing at me, knowing that whatever I did or said was of no avail. You had already worked out your dirty little deal under the counter."

He shook his head from side to side, his voice becoming sad and scornful. "The plane ride yesterday...just a diversion to get me out of the way while the inspectors..."

She stood there, stung by the harshness of his judgment, feeling he'd pushed the blade in deeper, then twisted it. "That's absolutely not true. How could I have known you'd be at the airport? Your house wasn't inspected or condemned yesterday, was it?"

"And you dare accuse me of double-crossing," he went on, ignoring her question.

"Jesse, we're talking across each other." She sat in the chair opposite him, wishing there wasn't a desk between them, no Riverbend, no barrio.

"So you're denying it all." His words, spoken quietly, still rent the air. "Are you saying the charges are completely unfounded, that Carr Enterprises never discussed getting the city to condemn my houses?"

"Not exactly," she said. "Some of it's true."

He looked at her, obviously startled. "Well, which is it going to be? I'll wait while you make up your mind. This ought to be good."

He slouched down in his seat, his large hands hanging loosely off the arms of the chair, but she could see the calmness was false. She didn't doubt his anger.

"Have you got anything here to drink?" she asked. "A soda or something?"

The quick change of subject threw him for a moment.

"What? Yeah. In the fridge." He nodded to the alcove where a few days ago he had made them coffee. He remained behind his desk, unconsciously flexing his long fingers.

Tori got up and found the small refrigerator under the counter, took out two cans of cola and stepped back into the office. Jesse was standing in the middle of the room now, moving toward her. He took one of the cans, his hand briefly touching hers, a warm contact that might as well have been a branding iron scorching her skin.

"Please excuse my poor hospitality."

She wasn't sure if he was sincere or still being sarcastic.

He popped the lid and took a deep draft, motioned her to her chair, then resumed his seat behind the antique desk. "You were telling me," he prompted.

She tried to take a deep breath, but her chest seemed constricted. "Monday, after you made your demands, Burton took it upon himself to talk to some of his friends downtown about doing a safety and welfare inspection of your flooded house." Jesse cast her a withering look, but she refused to flinch. "If your properties were condemned by the city, the bank would be forced to call in your loans."

"You figured I wouldn't be able to pay them off." She nodded.

"The bank would foreclose and you'd be able to buy my places."

She nodded again.

"Cheap."

This time she did look away.

He rose from his chair, paced the short width of the room, caught himself, stopped and spun around to face her.

"I must congratulate you on a very slick maneuver, Miss Carr."

So we're back to formalities again, she thought.

"First, your father neglects his properties in Santa Marta until the district's turned into a slum. Then he gets what's left there condemned because it *is* in a slum. Clever, Miss Carr. Very clever."

She started to object, but he cut her off. "Of course you just happened to find one of my places flooded. Good timing. Or did you arrange that, too?"

"What?" Her jaw dropped.

"Why not? You're a member of Carr Enterprises."

She straightened on the edge of her chair, then fell back. "You think I'd sneak into somebody's house and break a water pipe? Destroy a family's home, their possessions? You think I'd do that?"

He lowered his head and looked at her from under black eyebrows, apparently amused by her indignant reaction.

"No," he said. "You probably wouldn't do it personally—"

"Neither would my father. You've got this all wrong."

"You might get a smudge on your pretty designer clothes."

She suppressed an urge to scream. "Listen, Jesse, as soon as Burton told us what he was planning, Dad ordered him to cancel the inspections, stop the condemnations."

"Uh-huh."

"Not only that, we were just discussing a compromise I proposed, an idea very close to your dream of Santa Marta.'' She didn't like the pleading tone she was taking, but at least he was listening. ''Burton isn't too happy with it, because it means scaling back Riverbend, but he'll come around, especially since Dad's probably going to agree.''

''How magnanimous of him,'' Jesse said, lounging back in his chair. ''So why was your father arrested for bribery?''

''You tell me.''

That had him sitting upright again. ''Me? What the hell are you suggesting?''

She put the soda can down firmly.

''I imagine you have contacts downtown, too, Mr. Amorado. You and Espy Mendez. Isn't it just possible one of you found out about the inspection and got desperate?''

''I thought you said it was called off.''

''Oh, it was,'' she drawled sarcastically. ''But maybe you didn't get the word in time. Or maybe—'' she paused dramatically ''—you thought this would make a good preemptive strike.''

She could see by the thoughtful narrowing of his eyes that she had his full attention now, but there was still doubt and distrust on his face.

''As long as we're being honest,'' he said, his demeanor resuming its earlier gruffness, ''let me tell you a few things. Yes, I do have contacts downtown who try to keep me informed about what's going on. No, I wasn't told about this raid against me. No, I didn't squeal on your father or have him arrested.''

He crossed his hands in front of him and bent forward so they were at eye level. ''But if we're going to be perfectly honest,'' he added in little more than a whisper, "I have to tell you that if I *had* known what your father was up to, I certainly would have had him arrested."

Tori fumed. Why had he told her that? He didn't have to. God, how she wished he hadn't. It was as though, for a moment, he'd held out friendship with one hand, then slapped her with the other. The worst part was that she believed him.

"You've got a blind spot when it comes to your father," he continued. "Loyalty is fine. Family is important. But so is objectivity. He's your father. Love him in spite of his faults. But don't try to fool yourself into denying them."

Spoken harshly, the words could have been accusatory, hurtful. But he offered them with sympathy and forgiveness.

"Do you know who Henry Martin is?" he asked.

The question took her by surprise. "Yes, the city councilman for District Seven, Santa Marta. Why?"

Jesse nodded. "He was Enrique Martinez until about twenty years ago, when he developed political ambitions. He's been on the council for fifteen years now, longer than anyone else. That's given him power, lots of power, and he knows how to use it."

Tori found herself staring at Jesse's hands, remembering their roughness and warmth. They were perfectly still now, the violent tension gone from them. And the warmth?

"Martinez, or Martin," he went on conversationally, "controls the permits department in city hall, not technically or by ordinance, but by virtue of his longevity. He's also their champion on the city council. If the department needs a new computer, more staff, extra space, raises—talk to Henry. He'll get it.

"As a result," he continued, "some of the employees are willing to help him out—conveniently lose applications for a week, maybe permanently, insist on every *i* being dotted, every *t* crossed, just generally be obstinate bureaucrats. Mayors and city managers come and go, but Martin is always there. You want to build a house, you get a permit. You want to add a garage, get another permit. In the past couple of years the list of things that need permits has grown astronomically. New roof? Permit. New siding? Permit. Toolshed? Permit. Sprinkler system? Permit. And on and on."

"What's this got to do with my father?"

"Martin is corrupt."

Tori curbed an impulse to laugh. "So are a lot of politicians. That's not exactly earth-shattering news."

"Corruption's a two-way street," he said. "There wouldn't be a bribee without a briber."

"Jesse, if you're saying my father's been paying bribes to Martin, you're wrong. My father wouldn't—"

"He's doing more than that."

Suddenly she was frightened. The confidence with which he spoke, the searching look he gave her twisted like barbed wire inside her. "What do you mean?"

"Martin isn't just taking bribes to give people permits, Tori. He's taking them not to give permits."

It took a moment for the implications to sink in. "Are you suggesting my father has been paying Martin to deny permits to the people in Santa Marta?"

He nodded. "Permits to improve, add on to or even maintain their homes."

Tori was speechless.

"It's a neat little setup," he explained. "A home owner wants to do something to his house, but either he can't get a permit or he has to pay an exorbitant bribe he can't afford. So what happens? After a while your father's little bulldog comes along and suggests to the owner that since he's having such a hard time maintaining the place, he ought to sell it to Carr Enterprises and rent it back. That way he doesn't have to worry about those pesky little permits and repairs.''

"Have you got any proof of this?''

"That'll stand up in court? No. If I did, your father would have been behind bars a long time ago, I assure you. But isn't it strange that the properties he owns in other parts of town get their permits without delays and get decent maintenance?''

"You're saying my father is involved in a conspiracy with Martin to dominate the barrio?''

Jesse nodded. "Then he came up with the Riverbend project, which will destroy it.''

TORI USED THE SPARE KEY Lydia had given her to let herself into the office the next morning. She made coffee and put the half-dozen Danish pastries she'd bought at Kramer's on the credenza they used for a coffee bar.

The stimulating aroma filled the room, reminding her of the coffee Jesse had offered her on their first meeting. That simple gesture had been a dare. In fact, everything about him seemed to be a challenge.

His obstinacy was threatening the Riverbend project and the continued success of Carr Enterprises. Now he was contesting the image she had of her father, threatening to destroy the esteem she'd always had for him.

She'd spent a restless night, bouncing from uncertainty to fantasy, forced to reassess her father's integrity and motives in Santa Marta, haunted by images of Jesse condemning him as a slumlord, a bigot and a corrupt conspirator. She imagined Jesse, eyes cold, knuckles white, standing over the grave of his brother, promising to keep faith with their dream. In the background she saw the barrio, a decayed ruin.

"My, aren't you the early bird?" Lydia said as she stepped through the front door.

"Good morning," Tori replied. "Is Dad with you?" Her father hadn't come home last night.

"I ordered him to get some rest, told him not to come in before noon."

Tori smiled. Lydia's carefully applied smoke gray mascara only partially succeeded in distracting attention from the lines of worry and fatigue around her pale blue eyes.

"Of course you expect him to follow orders."

"Hell, no." Lydia chuckled. "But if he doesn't come in till ten, I've gained a small victory." She deposited her purse in the top left desk drawer and nervously straightened her lilac skirt. "He's awfully tired, you know. I'm worried about him."

"Well," Tori suggested, "maybe when this is all over we can talk him into taking you on a nice long Caribbean cruise."

Lydia perked up for a moment. "Sounds like a wonderful idea. But it's going to be several more months before this project settles down enough for him to take time off. I'm not really sure he should wait that long."

Tori realized this wasn't just idle talk about the pressure of the job. She'd experienced days of burnout in the air force, days when she didn't think she could possibly survive another briefing or put up with the vanity and turf battles that seemed to preoccupy ambitious senior officers. Usually it took only a good night's sleep and breakfast with a friend to clear away the shadows of exasperation and exhaustion. But she didn't have to remind herself that her father was no longer twenty-eight years old and hadn't been for a very long time. She'd seen the fatigue tugging at the corners of his mouth when he thought he was alone.

"That bad?"

"He's running in overdrive, Tori. This past year has been pure hell. He's invested so heavily that he has the kind of cash-flow problems we haven't experienced in years."

"Because of Riverbend?"

"It's taken so much longer than he planned. The delays are eating into his capital reserves."

Maybe Jesse would get his revenge after all.

"It's really got your father worried. He isn't sleeping well, and he's not eating right. You've probably noticed I'm putting out no-fat cookies instead of the doughnuts we used to have, and fruit in the afternoon."

Lydia turned on her computer terminal, apparently lost in thought as she watched it boot up. Tori brought her a cup of coffee, then opened the bag of Danish. "I guess you don't want these then."

"Mmm, naughty, naughty." Lydia chuckled and took a small tray from one drawer, a paper doily from another and arranged the sweet rolls on them. "I guess we'll just have to eat them all before your father gets here."

There was a bond in the smile the two women exchanged. Tori was glad her father had found an ally, an intimate in this woman.

"He used to go golfing every weekend with friends," Lydia went on after taking a generous bite of Danish and wiping her mouth with a paper napkin, "but he never has time anymore."

Tori took a tentative sip of hot coffee and sat on the

chair next to her desk. "If I'm going to be part of this outfit, even if it's only temporary or part-time, you're going to have to let me know what's going on. Every time I try to get somewhere with Jesse, I find another piece of the puzzle I didn't even know existed."

"I should have told you what was going on from the beginning," a familiar voice said behind her. If she hadn't already put down her coffee cup, it would have spilled. She hadn't heard the door open, hadn't heard her father's quiet tread into the room.

"Hmm, Kramer's Danish. Something I can really sink my sweet tooth into." He grinned. "I'm glad I skipped breakfast."

Lydia frowned as he put one of the gooey pastries on a napkin.

He was wearing a suit and tie even though the temperature outside was already on the rise and would probably break the century mark by late afternoon. But the business apparel didn't disguise the weariness of his step, the creases in his cheeks or the worry in his piercing blue eyes. The threads of silver in his brown hair seemed to have multiplied overnight.

"Grab your coffees, ladies, and come on into the office. It's time we had a long talk."

He stood back while they gathered up their cups and preceded him into his richly appointed office with its thick oriental carpet, shiny brass lamps and romantic oil paintings.

As soon as they were seated, Tori began, "Dad, I went to see Jesse yesterday. I thought he might have been behind your arrest."

"What was his reaction?" he asked after a cautious sip of steaming coffee.

She bit her lip, remembering the look of bewilderment on Jesse's face, followed by outrage when he realized what she was talking about.

"He made some pretty wild accusations of his own. He said you've been intentionally destroying Santa Marta. That you've not only refused to maintain your own properties but have been paying Martin to deny permits to other people to keep them from maintaining theirs."

Winslow's face grew bright red. He slammed down his fist on his desk. "That's absolutely not true," he exploded.

"Calm down, Win," Lydia urged him softly, and shot a warning glance at Tori.

Win took a deep breath. "Look, I take full responsibility for what this business does. But intentionally run down a whole section of town where I have major investments? There's no profit in that. I'm not claiming I'm innocent of what's happened in the barrio." He looked blindly across the room, then concentrated on his daughter. "But your friend Jesse has it backward."

Winslow started to take another bite of his Danish, lost interest and put it down on his desk. "I guess in hindsight I should have seen this coming. Burton never wanted me to buy houses in the barrio to begin with. Said they were all losers."

Tori wondered if he was referring to the buildings or the people.

"Then we came up with the Riverbend project," Winslow said. "Well, that put things in a completely different light. There was no reason to do anything more than minimum maintenance. But, damn it, I never intended for the area to turn into a slum, and I certainly didn't interfere with other people taking care of their homes."

He took a deep swallow of coffee. "I should never have allowed things to get as bad as they are."

"Jesse also told me you've been paying off Martin," she said. "Bribing him."

Winslow leaned back in his chair. Reluctantly, he said, "Well, let's just say greasing his palm."

God, what next? This wasn't the response she'd expected. She'd had visions of absolute, categorical denial, anger that she would consider him capable of such unethical behavior. Perhaps even a suggestion that Burton had gone too far and acted unilaterally.

"But yesterday...you denied..."

"I didn't lie to you or the police," he countered immediately. "The charges yesterday were for trying to have Amorado's property condemned. You heard me tell Burton to call it off. I talked to him late yesterday and he insisted he had. He was miffed that I'd think differently. Or that you would."

She didn't want to deal with the subject of Burton's ego at the moment. "But now you're telling me you've been bribing Martin all along?" she questioned, still not wanting to believe she'd heard right.

"Yes."

The response was so straightforward it rattled her even more. Was bribing public officials such an ordinary business practice?

She watched her father closely. His eyes were sharp, defiant, but the hand holding the coffee cup was shaking. He lowered his gaze. She felt his shame and wanted to weep.

She folded her arms across her stomach and the hollow feeling inside her. It seemed as if the world were tumbling down around her. Maybe Burton was right. Maybe she didn't know enough about the real business world. But she knew her father. Lydia had told her about the times he lowered his commission, or even waived it altogether, to help people in need. Sometimes he was insensitive, but she never knew him to be intentionally cruel or mean-spirited. There had to be more.

"I'm sure it's not that simple, Dad," she said. "How about filling in the details?"

Winslow rewarded her with a wan smile, obviously pleased she wasn't taken in by simplistic answers. "It started innocently enough years ago," he began. "Martin was in a position to help us and it seemed reasonable to support him."

"Just good politics," Tori observed.

Her father nodded and went on. "He would send us regular accounts of how many and what kinds of permits we were submitting and getting approved. We sent regular contributions to his reelection fund. It wasn't until last year that I realized the extent to which it had gone."

"That's when your father stopped making the payments," Lydia pointed out. She had been quietly observing the exchange between father and daughter. Tori had not been unaware of her presence. She just wished the older woman had been more forthcoming from the beginning.

"You stopped?" she asked.

"Of course I stopped. I'm willing to scratch other people's backs, Tori. That's good business. But I stop short at wholesale bribery."

CHAPTER NINE

"So HOW DID THIS 'wholesale bribery' get started?" Tori asked.

Winslow exhaled through his nose and pursed his lips in disgust. It was Lydia who answered the question.

"Over the past couple of years Martin's become pretty bold. When he sent the lists of permits and approvals he started adding notes suggesting amounts to contribute to his fund. The implication was clear enough. Pay up or you won't get your permits approved."

"But you're still getting permits approved, aren't you? Jesse says your...our...properties in other parts of the city are well maintained."

"Martin controls Santa Marta but not the other districts. Hell, if he tried to turn down permits in those areas, their councilmen would be all over him."

A redeeming thought struck her. If Martin had refused Carr Enterprises the necessary permits to maintain their properties in the barrio because they'd stopped paying graft, it wasn't her father's fault that the houses had fallen into such disrepair.

"That means," Tori said aloud, "that the deterioration in Santa Marta isn't because you wouldn't maintain the houses there, but because you couldn't."

This put a completely different complexion on the

whole situation. Her father hadn't intentionally neglected the barrio; he'd been denied the ability to
improve it because he refused to be dishonest. She
wondered how many people in town knew that. Jesse
obviously didn't.

But Winslow Carr shook his head in disagreement.
"Ordinary repairs don't need permits."

He rose heavily from his chair and turned to face
the window behind him. His speech, slow, abject,
bounced off the plate glass. "Amorado's right. When
we started the Riverbend project, we lowered our standards for Santa Marta properties. We might repair a
roof, which doesn't require a permit, but not replace it,
which does. If a toolshed got too shaky, we simply tore
it down rather than build a new one. We certainly
didn't build new carports or garages the way we did in
other parts of town to increase the properties' market-
ability, either for rent or resale."

He turned to face his daughter again. "That's why I
could afford to just stop paying the graft," he concluded. "Not because I'm so self-righteous."

Tori's heart sank.

"Look, I never set out to destroy the barrio," Winslow pleaded. "I'm sorry about what's happened there.
I don't know how things got so out of control. But
you've got to understand that the real problem in Santa
Marta has been Martin's willingness to hold his own
people hostage. He wasn't counting on the Riverbend
project taking off the way it did."

"Why didn't either of you tell me about this?"

"Lydia wanted to, but I asked her not to. I hoped I
could straighten things out so you would never have to
know."

"I should have told you, anyway," Lydia protested.

She looked down at her hands and twirled the rings on her fingers.

Winslow concentrated for a moment on the coffee cup on his desk. Then, steeling himself, he looked Tori in the eye.

"It's not easy telling your daughter you're not the paragon of virtue she likes to believe you are."

Tori saw something in her father's countenance at that moment, an insight that explained the lukewarm reception he'd given her, his ambivalence about her coming home. He didn't want her to learn his secrets, his shame.

It had been almost ten years since she'd lived here. She'd visited over holidays and sometimes for longer stays during the summers when she was attending the academy. But the physical separation from her father and their completely different life-styles and interests had driven them apart psychologically and emotionally, broken the special bond that had only begun to develop after her mother died. In its place she'd created an icon of her father, seen him as a model of virtue and moral rectitude, an ideal probably no one could achieve. But he'd been wise enough to understand the position she'd put him in and, consciously or not, had tried to nudge her away before she discovered the truth about him.

"I know you did the best you could," she offered, trying to be upbeat, forgiving. "No one can ask more than that."

"Nice thought," her father said with a faint smile. "The fact is, I failed the people in the barrio because I avoided going there whenever possible. Too many memories and associations. You'd think after all these years—"

Tori's heart melted. "I understand, Dad. Believe me, I understand."

He waved the comment away. "I've let you down, Tori. Just like I did after your mother was killed."

"You didn't," she objected.

"Let me finish. I should have said this years ago."

She started to get up and go to him, but Lydia put her hand on her wrist. Tori looked over at her, ready to protest. But the gentle woman's eyes counseled the same compassion Tori had seen at the Mesquite Grill. Tori rested back in the chair and waited for her father's catharsis.

"After your mother died," Winslow said in a drone, "I knew I wasn't taking care of you the way I should." He still faced the window, though Tori doubted he saw anything but his own reflection in the glass. "I worked a crazy schedule, between sixteen and eighteen hours a day, to get the new business started. It was a rough market then. A lot of Realtors were going under. I was practically broke. Your mother's income as a lawyer paid most of the bills."

"Dad—"

"I was determined to become successful so I could give you the things your mother and I had planned for you. So you'd be proud of me."

"I've always been proud of you, Dad."

She could tell by the set of his shoulders and the pause before he went on that he'd heard her. How long had she wanted to say just those words? How long had he wanted to hear them? She ached for him, for affection left unspoken too long.

"The irony," he went on, his monotone remote and throaty, "is that by the time I was able to give you the material things I thought you deserved, you'd gone off and made a life of your own and didn't need me. In a crazy way, it made the sacrifices all worth it.''

Tori bit her lip to stanch the flow of tears. She couldn't swallow past the burning in her throat.

Her father finally turned to face her. ''I can't tell you what it's been like seeing you grow and blossom, knowing I had nothing to do with it.''

''You had everything to do with it,'' Tori objected quietly. Though she ached to console him, some instinct told her he wasn't ready yet. She forced herself to brighten. ''Are you forgetting the summers and holidays we spent together? I've always been able to count on you to listen, Dad, even when I called you from the academy at two o'clock in the morning to complain about some chauvinist classman's prank or a training officer's stupid demands.'' Tori tilted her head and smiled. ''You reminded me I was strong enough to handle whatever they cared to dish out, that I could grow from the experience and be a better person. You always listened. You always encouraged.''

''I didn't tell you how much I love you.''

''You're wrong there, too,'' she argued mildly, not sure she could trust herself to get the words out. ''You told me every time we were together, when you sent me silly little gifts or a card for no reason.''

The room grew quiet. Even outside noises seemed reluctant to intrude. The stillness was no longer charged with tension, only the peace that comes with honesty. But Tori knew there was something more she had to do. She hesitated. It meant giving up her dream of flying for a while longer, but what was more important than family?

''You made a proposal the other day,'' she said,

breaking the silence. "To make me a partner. Is the offer still open?"

He looked shocked, but amazement quickly changed to disbelieving hope. "After what I just told you, you want to—"

She stood up and circled the end of the desk. He rose to his feet and faced her, his back hunched in uncertainty, his eyes gleaming. Gently she placed a hand on his shoulder and drew him toward her. "I love you, Dad."

Their embrace was long and heartfelt, one whose intensity had been held back for too many years.

TORI AND LYDIA BROKE for lunch late that afternoon. Winslow declined the invitation, insisting he had to catch up on phone calls. Tori suspected he needed the time alone to recover from the draining emotions of the morning. He assured them he wouldn't go hungry. After all, there was the fruit basket Lydia was always urging on him.

Over peppered ham and baby Swiss cheese croissants at the Cowboy Café, Lydia and Tori talked business. Lydia promised to push Nelson Spooner on the legal paperwork to formally make Tori a partner in Carr Enterprises.

"With your father's proxy," Lydia commented, "you can take a lot of the workload off his shoulders. I know you still want to fly, honey, and after we get over this Riverbend hurdle, you'll be able to. But right now your father needs you. I'm so glad you're doing this. It means so much to him."

Tori smiled and secretly wished she felt as good about this as everyone else seemed to.

They were pulling into the parking lot at Carr Enterprises when she spotted a pickup truck and the man slouched against its front fender.

Lydia grinned. "It looks like your dueling partner is back. I must say, I like the looks of the competition."

Jesse's jeans, though neatly pressed, still molded his lithe body. His boots, scuffed and battered, were crossed at the ankles. A blue chambray shirt stretched across his thick chest and broad shoulders.

The two ladies got out of the sports car.

"Good afternoon, Ms. Anderson," Jesse said cordially, and tipped the perfectly shaped straw hat on his head.

"Mr. Amorado." Lydia nodded and excused herself.

Jesse crossed his arms and smiled as she retreated into the building.

"Ms. Carr," he said, tipping the brim of his hat up slightly with a forefinger. "Nice to see you again."

He was, oh, so cool, but she had no doubt he had an agenda. Her office was no more in his neighborhood than the barrio had been in Tori's on the evening of the flood.

"Good afternoon, Mr. Amorado. Is there something I can do for you?" She made motions with the keys in her hand to lock the car, but her fingers for some reason turned to butter. The key ring fell to the ground.

He moved to her side with the speed and agility of a cat, bent over, picked up the fallen keys and dangled them within a few inches of her.

"Do you think we can call a truce?" he asked.

She reached for the ring, paused and caught the faintest hint of a woodsy aroma. "We can try," she conceded. She relieved him of the keys, but not so fast that their fingers didn't touch.

"Can I make a suggestion?" Jesse ventured.

"What?" Her single-word response wasn't hostile, just curious.

"I have to go out to the ranch to take care of some chores. It's not too far. There are rolling hills and cattle. A few chickens and goats. It's peaceful. City problems take on completely different dimensions out there. It's a good place to clear the cobwebs," he said with a smile. "Why don't you follow me. You can meet my family and we can talk."

Meet his family? Was that his way of assuring her they wouldn't be alone? She had already been alone with him in his office and his house. She remembered the way he smoothed back the lock of hair that fell across his face when he was showing her his model of a rejuvenated Santa Marta, the happy pride when he talked about his parents. And the way he stood in the doorway, half blocking her entry into the tiny room so that she had to brush past him to enter. And the electricity created when his skin rubbed against hers.

Yes, she muttered silently, *I'd like to meet your family. But I wouldn't mind being alone with you, either.*

"Let me tell Lydia where I'm going," she said.

She followed Jesse's ten-year-old pickup, laden with two-by-fours and other building materials, out Highway 24 west of town. He took the twenty-minute drive conservatively, glancing at her periodically in his rearview mirror. They would make brief eye contact before each of them had to concentrate on the road ahead again.

About ten miles outside city limits Jesse turned off the highway onto a narrow road, blacktopped once, mostly caliche now. Wild mesquite, its tiny willowlike leaves swaying gently in the breeze, and thick clusters of prickly pear cactus were the dominant forms of vegetation. Thistles dotted the uneven ground, as well, their delicate white blossoms totally out of character with their untouchable thorny stems.

He drove another mile or so and stopped. Tori waited while he crossed the dusty road on foot and opened a gate on the left. She noticed it was latched, but not locked or chained. He pulled his truck far enough forward for her to follow him inside the fence line, then walked back to her.

"I have to get the gate," he explained as he leaned down to her open car window. "When you leave, please make sure it's closed behind you. We don't have much livestock here, but what we do have likes to wander."

"Of course." She smiled and watched in her rearview mirror as he sauntered to the gate.

The house wasn't far, but small hills and boulders and stands of Chinese elm and hackberry trees hid it from the road. She remembered the building from the air. It wasn't big or fancy, no rustic Ponderosa, and certainly no mansion. Just a simple, single-story, tin-roofed cabin nestled in the soothing coolness of sprawling live oak trees, its vertical siding weathered to a silvery gray.

Two children were playing in the area near the house. They looked up at the sound of the vehicles. Tori recognized them at once from the pictures in Jesse's office.

"*¡Tío! ¡Tío Jesús está aquí!*" they shouted in unison. Tori smiled to herself. Jesse was the usual translation for Jesus, a name never used in English, though common in Spanish.

Jesse jumped out of the truck. "Teresita!" he

shouted joyfully, gathering up the little girl of perhaps five in his arms and smothering her with loud kisses.

Meanwhile the boy had run to the shiny red Corvette and stopped. He stood staring at it in awe and was about to touch it when a woman's command stopped him.

"Miguelito," she called in Spanish, "keep your hands off the lady's car."

The boy, about seven, pulled back his fingers, gave a longing glance at the vehicle and moved to Jesse's side. His expression as he looked up at his sister suggested he thought himself too old to be cuddled and kissed. But, Tori noticed with a smile, he seemed perfectly willing to hold the wide, callused hand of his big uncle.

"Lupe," Jesse called out to the woman on the porch as Tori climbed out of her vehicle and walked up beside him. "This is Tori Carr. This is my sister-in-law, Guadelupe Hernandez Viuda de Amorado."

"Buenos días," the woman said with a reserved smile. Since Jesse had addressed her in English, Tori wondered if Lupe's speaking Spanish now was intended to put distance between them.

"Mucho gusto," Tori replied. She caught the little grin of amusement on Jesse's face at her using the polite Spanish phrase that many Anglos in the Southwest knew.

Tori extended her hand. Lupe took it. She was dressed in frayed jeans and a much-washed man's coarse white cotton shirt. It emphasized the youthful freshness of her tan complexion. Tori guessed she was in her mid-twenties, but there was a melancholy expression in her large brown eyes that made her look older, or perhaps ageless.

Viuda de Amorado, Tori thought as she accepted the other woman's hand. Widow of Amorado. Miguel's widow.

An older woman in a dark blue Mexican peasant dress trimmed with vividly colored embroidery stepped out the back door. As she approached she put a hand up to the black hair that was salted with gray and gathered in a soft bun.

"Hello, Victoria," Elena Amorado said pleasantly.

A shiver careened down Tori's spine, followed by a wave of nostalgia, a poignant sensation of affection and caring and *familia*. So long ago, yet barely yesterday. Victoria. Her mother was the only one who ever called her by her full name. Tori was the pet name her father had given her.

"You probably don't remember me," Elena said in a pronounced but clear Spanish accent. "I used to visit Mrs. Gutierrez, your sitter. And I knew your dear mother. She was a lovely woman."

"Tía Elena. The lady from the bakery," she replied in Spanish, trying hard to swallow the lump growing in her throat and to shed the pain that suddenly gripped her heart. "I'm very happy to see you again."

Elena opened her arms and Tori impulsively fell into her warm embrace. Nearly twenty years had changed them both. Tori didn't see the joviality she remembered in the woman's face, but the glow of affection was still in her dark eyes, Jesse's eyes.

"Come sit down and have something cold to drink," Elena said. Tori smiled at the puzzlement on Jesse's face and the shocked gleam that said, *You speak Spanish!*

"Not for me yet." He bent and kissed his mother

affectionately on the cheek. "I've got to unload this stuff first."

"I can help," the boy insisted, looking up at his uncle eagerly and pulling on his brawny arm.

Jesse ruffled Miguelito's dark hair and winked at Teresita. "Let's go, *muchachos*."

The three of them trudged off together, the children stretching out their shorter steps in a vain attempt to match their big uncle's long stride.

Lupe went over to a gallon jug of tea steeping in the hot sun and carried it into the house. Jesse's mother smiled fondly at the retreating parade and ushered Tori to a wooden bench at a picnic table under the biggest of the sprawling oaks.

"You have become *una señorita muy linda*," Elena said quietly.

Tori had been called beautiful before, but she was unaccountably touched by the sincerity of this woman's compliment. *"Muchas gracias,"* she replied.

"I've seen your picture in the newspapers. Did you like it in the army?"

"I was in the air force," she said, amused that after fifty years there were still people who didn't realize the army and air force were separate. "Yes, I enjoyed it very much."

"My late husband was in the army," Elena went on, apparently still unaware of the distinction. "That was during the war, of course. Are you home to stay now?"

"I hope so. I'm trying to get a job here flying for one of the airlines."

She watched Jesse unload the truck and pile the lumber against the side of the garage. He looked so comfortable in this place, so at ease. She tried to picture him in some of the places she'd been—sitting at a sidewalk café in Paris eating *bifteck au poivre*. Or using chopsticks on Indonesian riijsttafel in Amsterdam. Spreading Gorgonzola on fresh fruit in a trattoria in Florence. Or sampling tapas at a bodega in Madrid.

Jesse's eyes made a quick, flashing contact and she felt as if a spotlight had been beamed at her. She smiled back and was rewarded with a wink. He resumed his work, but her smile remained, this time not for him but for herself.

Yes, she decided, she could see him very easily in those exotic places. But he would definitely not be just another face in the crowd.

Tori and Elena sat side by side at the picnic table watching the children as they scampered happily around Tío Jesús. Miguelito's little hand hung on the trailing edge of a two-by-four "helping" Jesse carry it, while Teresita marched determinedly in front. She would then turn, her small arms widespread, and show them where to deposit it.

Lupe came out of the house carrying a wicker tray with a pitcher of sun tea, a dish of lime wedges, a large sugar bowl and four oversize blue plastic glasses filled with ice. After carefully negotiating the three porch steps, she set the tray on the picnic table and poured a glass, handing it to her mother-in-law. Elena passed it to Tori, then accepted another one for herself. Lupe was pouring a third glass just as Jesse returned.

He reached out and took it from her hands. "Thanks," he grunted, and swallowed half of the cold liquid in one gulp, then ran the frosty glass across his forehead. The two children bounced up and down on either side of him, eagerly begging him to play ball. Joy, pure and sweet, welled up in Tori at the smile he gave them.

"Come up to the house," Lupe told them in Spanish, "and I'll give you some lemonade."

Reluctantly, the youngsters left their uncle, the little girl's backward glance and outstretched hand imploring him not to leave. For them, at this moment, Tori mused, life was good. They had lost one of their parents, but not their home, not the love of their family. Jesse filled the role of father figure with such natural ease, she wondered if he yearned for kids of his own.

He pulled a red bandanna from his hip pocket, sat on the other end of the bench and wiped his sweaty brow.

The children returned, carrying small red plastic glasses with both hands. Lupe hovered behind them, offering encouragement.

The little girl was a delight, even more captivating than in her picture. Round face, sparkling dark eyes, a perfect cupid's-bow mouth, long shiny black hair and a translucent olive complexion. One day she would be a beautiful woman.

When the drinks were safely on the table, Jesse reached over and pulled the girl to his chest.

"Have you said hello to Señorita Carr?" he asked.

Teresita looked doubtfully at him and shook her head shyly.

"Go on then, say hello," he prompted gently.

"Hello," came the soft greeting.

"I'm very pleased to meet you, Teresita," Tori said in Spanish.

The little girl giggled. Still clinging to her uncle, she said more confidently, *"Buenos días, señorita."*

Tori was also rewarded by the sight of Jesse grinning ear to ear as he placed a large hand on the boy's shoulder and coaxed him forward.

"And this is her big brother, Miguelito." Jesse leaned over and stage-whispered in the boy's ear, "As the man of the house, you should welcome our guest."

The boy stood stock-still and said nothing.

Tori offered her hand. "Hello, Miguelito."

Disconcerted at first by the unfamiliar gesture, the boy's bravery quickly reclaimed itself. He took her hand and pumped it up and down vigorously and said a little too loudly, *"Buenos días, señorita. Mi casa es su casa.* My house is your house."

"Muchas gracias, señor. I'm very glad to be here," Tori answered, touched by the boy's proud stance and courtesy. Just like his uncle, she thought.

Miguelito waved overhead and motioned to the sky. "Are you the lady who flies the plane?"

"Yes, I am."

Dropping his arm, he looked at her. "Someday I'm going to fly a plane," he said, chest thrust out. "A big plane."

Tori's heart swelled. "I hope you do."

"We're going to Sea World," Teresita announced excitedly.

"Sea World, huh?" The twinkle in Jesse's eyes matched the child's.

"And Fiesta Texas," Miguelito added just as eagerly. "We're going to be there a whole week. Grandma is taking us."

"I got some discount tickets," Elena explained to her son.

"We'll stay with my sister Anita," Lupe informed him.

"And we're going to see Shamu," Teresita bubbled to Tori. "He's a big whale!"

"Oh, my!" Tori exclaimed, charmed by the vivacious child. "I've never seen a whale before. Have you?"

"This will be my first time," the little girl said, turning very serious.

Tori could hardly resist the temptation to reach out and hug the child. "That'll be exciting, won't it?"

"Why don't you kids go play by yourselves for a few minutes now," Lupe prompted, "while we visit with Miss Carr?"

The children paused for a moment, disappointed at being excluded, then skipped across the shaded lawn.

"They're lovely children," Tori told Elena. "You're very fortunate."

"They look like their father," the doting grandmother replied.

"I heard what happened to Miguel. I'm sorry," Tori said in Spanish to the two women. Sensing Jesse watching her, she turned. The brittleness in his smile was relieved by the softness in his dark eyes. Touched, Tori continued to look at him.

"He was a good son and father," Elena declared. The statement jolted Tori. Jesse, a father? Then she realized his mother was referring to Miguel.

Lupe's nutmeg brown eyes were downcast, her fingers toying with the beads of sweat on the glass. How lonely it must be, Tori thought, to love someone deeply and passionately and then lose him. She'd never loved like that, never given herself completely to a man, never allowed one to become an inseparable part of her life. Not Burton. Not any of the few men she'd thought she might be falling in love with since him.

Jesse reached across and slipped the glass she was holding from her grasp and set it on the table. He extended his hand a second time. She was helpless to resist the power he exerted. There was a shiver of excitement as they stood facing each other, barely inches apart. In those fleeting seconds, she stopped breathing.

Their eyes were locked when he mumbled, "Please excuse us, ladies." But the others had already faded into abstraction. For now, there were just the two of them.

CHAPTER TEN

THEY STROLLED ALONG the path skirting a single-car garage, past the sloping roof of an old storm cellar. The children were trying to hang upside down from tires suspended from a sturdy limb of an ancient oak tree. Jesse called out to them, "Hey, you guys. Be careful."

"It's beautiful here," Tori said. "What a wonderful place to bring up children."

"Sure beats the barrio," he agreed. "There's room to roam. Things thrive and bloom here because it's their nature."

Together they watched the boy hoist his sister into the opening of the tire, then give her a mighty push.

"Ten cuidado," Jesse cautioned again. "Be careful. Don't swing your sister too high. You don't want her to fall. Miguelito, it is your duty to protect your little sister. Make sure she doesn't get hurt."

In that instant Tori understood the anguish Jesse must have felt when his brother was killed. As the older of the two, it had been his duty to protect Miguel. That he was in no way responsible for his death made no difference. In some inscrutable way, he'd failed his brother, let his family down.

Just like her father, she thought, blaming himself for her mother's murder, for something he couldn't have anticipated, couldn't control. The two men might be

surprised at how much they had in common, how much
they thought alike.

Tori watched Teresita dangling contentedly from the
rubber tire, apparently at peace with the world. She
envied the little girl's sense of security even in the face
of the death of a parent. She hoped that feeling of security would last for her lifetime.

She turned to Jesse. "You said you grew up in Santa
Marta. How long have you owned this place?"

"A couple of years. Most of the down payment
came from the insurance money my father left Mom.
Papa always wanted us to have a place in the country."

She remembered the bedroom in his house, the antiques, his sense of history and continuity.

"This was his final gift to you, Jesse."

"And to my children to come."

"You want to have kids?"

"A house full of them."

"That would be nice." She knew the words sounded
a little dreamy. But that was the way she felt here, in
this place, with this man—as if she were in a dream.
"Each of my parents was an only child," she went on
a moment later. "Like me."

"So you don't have any aunts or uncles," he noted,
"no cousins to play with. You missed a lot." He
seemed lost in thought for a moment, then added,
"Mom only had Miguel and me, but both my parents
came from big families. I've got relatives all over the
place."

Tendrils of summer sunlight spiraled through the
trees, but it was the touch of his hand that produced
the warmth Tori felt.

"Thank you for bringing me out here to see your
family."

He swung his arm, swinging hers with it, as if they were two schoolchildren on an adventure. "Mama wanted to meet you. She didn't tell me you already knew each other."

"It's good to see her again."

The shallow woods were alive with songbirds. Tori followed the flutelike gurgling of a meadowlark, then pointed when she spied its bright yellow breast bobbing on a low oak branch.

"I have fond memories of your mother from when I was a girl."

They passed a wild juniper. She reached out and plucked one of the silvery violet berries. When she crushed it between her fingers, it filled the air with the perfume scent of gin.

"I stayed with Mrs. Gutierrez every day after school," she continued, her other hand still buried in Jesse's. "Mom or Dad would pick me up on their way home from work." She slanted a sidelong glance at him. Sunbeams were playing hopscotch on his clean-shaven face. "I never knew your mother's last name. Everybody called her Tía Elena. She used to stop by in the afternoon with sweet cakes and candies from the Mexican bakery."

He coaxed her deeper into the woods with a gentle tug. "She worked there. Those were the leftovers from the day's sales."

Tori smiled nostalgically. "Well, it was very kind of her."

The buzzing of cicadas continued unabated.

"So you know what the barrio is like," Jesse said, releasing her hand, "and the people who live there."

Did she hear an undertone of accusation. Did he think she was betraying his community? This probably wasn't the time to tell him she was joining her father's firm as his partner.

"Funny," she responded lightly, trying to quell the tiny ripple of tension she felt building between them, "I don't remember ever seeing you there." I would have noticed, too, she told herself, even then.

He fanned long blunt fingers carelessly through his thick black hair. "I ran track before I got into football, so I was always busy. Besides, we didn't live close to Mrs. Gutierrez."

Behind them a red-winged blackbird made its characteristic clicking sound, followed by a high, slurred *tee-err*.

"How old were you when your mother died?"

He stole her tranquillity with his question. Tori had to fight the tightness in her throat. "Ten," she said huskily.

Jesse reclaimed her hand and squeezed it gently.

"I'm sorry," he said, his deep voice solicitous. "I didn't mean to upset you. I thought after all these years—"

"That it wouldn't still hurt?" she challenged more harshly than she intended. "Do you think a child ever gets over losing a mother?"

He closed his eyes for a moment. "We never completely lose the ones we love. There's always a part of them left inside us."

It was her turn to squeeze his hand. He'd lost a brother only a year ago. The recollection made her ashamed for lashing out at him. They walked on a little way in silence, her thoughts jumbled, her feelings chaotic.

"You didn't tell me you spoke Spanish."

She looked up at him, relieved to hear the dark mood

of a minute earlier turning playful. "I don't remember your asking." Laughter tumbled out with her words. "I guess you just assumed that as an Anglo, I vud not speak your langvich." Her mock accent sounded like something out of a bad horror movie.

He cocked an eyebrow, gave her an awkward grin, then burst into a self-deprecating chortle.

"Everyone spoke Spanish at Mrs. Gutierrez's house," she explained. "I learned it easily. Besides, Mom wanted me to."

"And your father? How did he feel about it?"

Damn, she thought. *Why do you keep sniping like this?* But she wasn't going to let him break the spell. "Do you think my father's prejudiced against the language as well as the people?" She could smile at his discomfort now. "He agreed, too," she told him. "Dad's never been any good at languages. Maybe it's something to do with right brain, left brain. I'm not sure. He tried to at least learn a few polite phrases in Spanish, but he could never master the trilled *r*. I used to help him practice saying words like *gracias.* Or we'd count together."

One of her clearest and fondest recollections of home and family was sitting on her father's lap, playing games, telling stories while her mother prepared dinner—and laughing together. There had been an innocent quality in their merriment that was missing after her mother died.

"Of course we never got beyond three. *Uno, dos, tr-r-res.*" She rolled her tongue around the word grotesquely.

Even as Jesse chuckled with her, she was aware of his simmering gaze. She stared out into the broad sun-filled spaces between the huge old trees. How different this spot was from the scrubby little backyard at Mrs. Gutierrez's tiny house.

"So you understood the things people were saying about you the other day," he commented.

"Enough to figure out I wasn't very welcome."

"I'm sorry."

She shrugged off the memory, unwilling to let him see how much the insults had stung. "I guess I understand. People react differently to the same stimuli, Jesse. I love Santa Marta because, for me, it basically holds happy memories of kind, warm people like your mother. But for my father, it's got a completely different association. His wife's death. That's why he turned the properties in Santa Marta over to Burton to manage. But, Jesse, he doesn't hate or look down on the people there."

He led her through the trees to the banks of the Coyote River. It was little more than a narrow stream at this point, slipping lazily between high, seemingly impregnable banks. Until the rains came. Then it would be a torrent, spilling over, Tori mused, like unwanted emotions into human lives.

"How about you? What are your dreams for the future?"

She didn't answer immediately, and he didn't push her.

"I left the air force," she finally said, "because I wanted to fly and they wouldn't let me."

"So now you're looking for a commercial airline job."

"Flying's important to me," she insisted, not sure why she felt defensive about it.

"You're obviously good at it. But why did you come

back here? There must be more and better opportunities elsewhere.''

She laughed. ''Much better.'' They strolled along for another minute. ''I love flying, but it's not all there is. The vagabond life of the military was fun. I got to see and do more things than most people do in a lifetime.''

They lingered in silence for a minute, the children's laughs and giggles remote, the loud drone of cicadas closer. She waited. His hand again reached out. She took it willingly. Turning to him, she brought a finger up to trace the cleft of his chin, the lines and planes of his face. She sketched the black slashes of brows while she looked into his eyes. They could be as hard as ebony or as soft and sweet as hot fudge.

''More than anything, Jesse, I want a home base. I want to unpack my bags.''

They walked on in somber silence for several minutes. He stopped and they listened to the stream gurgling at their feet while childish laughter filtered through the trees like half-forgotten memories.

''Tori,'' he said, and the gentleness in the way he pronounced her name had her heart floating, her pulse quickening. She looked expectantly at him. The grainy skin of his thumbs worked a tender massage on the backs of her hands. ''I owe you another apology.''

''For what?'' she asked raggedly.

''For misjudging you. I painted you with the same brush as your father. That wasn't fair.''

''You've misjudged my father, too.''

''Yes,'' he conceded. ''Perhaps I have.''

They drew closer. His mouth covered hers. The kiss deepened, became fierce. She snuggled into his arms, intoxicated by the spicy scent of juniper and pine lumber and man.

When finally their lips parted, he held her chin with the edge of a finger. "I've wanted to do that from the first moment I saw you," he confessed in an intimate whisper.

The muffled giggles of two little children finally brought them back to time and place. Tori felt her face flush for a moment at the realization that their kiss had been witnessed. Jesse just smiled and watched the youngsters scamper out of the woods. Hand in hand, Tori and Jesse followed them back to the little house.

His mother was waiting on the steps of the front porch, her round face bright with pleasure at their approach. Behind her, Lupe leaned against the doorway, the hint of a grin on her lips. It took Tori only a moment to realize the two little urchins had told them about seeing her and Jesse kiss. She felt her face warm and smiled contentedly.

Elena handed Tori a glass with shavings of ice in what looked like milk. "I thought you might like some of this."

Tori accepted it tentatively, not sure what it was until she raised it to her lips. The aroma of tapioca assailed her senses like a slash of pain ripping across her consciousness.

"*Orchada!*" she mumbled, then forced a grin.

"You remember it!" Elena exclaimed in Spanish. "We used to give it to you sometimes with the cookies in the afternoon."

"Yes," Tori whispered as tears welled up. She had been drinking *orchada* at Mrs. Gutierrez's house the day the madman murdered her mother. She squeezed out the memory, concentrated on the sweet drink she had enjoyed as a child but hadn't tasted since that terrible day. "It's made from rice, isn't it?" She sipped its sugary sweetness. *"Muchas gracias, señora."*

Elena smiled, unaware of the nature of the emotions the rich beverage was conjuring up. She took the glass when Tori was finished and left them.

Jesse had said things looked different out here in the country, Tori thought. Had he known the world would change—for both of them? He walked her to her car.

"I know who had my father arrested."

"I didn't think it would take you long to figure it out."

She stopped and faced him. Sunbeams sneaked through the breeze-blown trees and danced across his suntanned features. God, he was beautiful. "You knew? Why didn't you tell me?"

"When?" he countered lightly. "You accused me, if you'll recall. You weren't exactly in a mood to listen."

She winced at the recollection.

"But I knew once I gave you a hint, you'd work it out."

Tori nodded, not in the least consoled by her own brilliance. "It's so obvious. Martin has the most to lose if Santa Marta is torn down. The residents there are basically good, law-abiding people, but they're politically passive. If Riverbend becomes a reality, they'll be replaced by rich, powerful and presumably more politically active Anglos."

"Exactly. He runs unopposed in District Seven. In the rest of the town he's Henry Martin. In the barrio he's still Enrique Martinez, one of us. Years ago he *was.*"

"But without his Hispanic constituency, he's out of office," she said. "And out of power."

They stood beside each other in the bright summer sun. She didn't feel its heat. She was aware only of his hands on her shoulders turning her toward him, the slow sweep of his eyes over her face, his lips meeting hers. This kiss wasn't passionate so much as affectionate. It lasted only seconds. Long enough to leave her breathless.

He opened the car door for her and handed her in, then stood and watched as she drove away.

Tori barely remembered to close the gate when she left the Amorado ranch a few minutes later. Her mind was caught in a maelstrom. A flood of facts, ideas and emotions was swirling inside her with a turbulence that was overwhelming. The political implications were complex, but...

Jesse's kisses. She'd wanted him to kiss her. She wanted to kiss him again. Beyond that, what?

TWO HOURS LATER, Tori drove up to the Spanish Arms apartments on South Travis Street.

"What are you doing here?" Espy groaned when she opened the door, her tightly jeaned legs slightly apart in the classic stance of the defender.

"I came," Tori said firmly, "to talk to you."

"About what?"

Tori let the question hang for a moment. "About your relationship with Henry Martin."

Espy looked quickly over her shoulder. Tori became alarmed when she saw a shadow cross the doorway. Could Martin himself be with her?

"You might as well come in," said Espy with a fatalistic shrug, "and join the party."

Tori hesitated. What was she walking into? Just then, beyond the hall, a black silhouette appeared, the outline

of a man etched against the orange-and-purple glow of
the setting sun. Tori's heart skipped a beat.

"I didn't expect to see you here."

"Nor I you," she replied, and stepped into the en-
tryway. Espy closed the door behind her. Tori moved
into the living room. "If I'm interrupting anything…"

The flash of a smile quickened the edges of Jesse's
mouth. "Just a little question-and-answer session," he
replied. "About Martin and Espy."

"I don't know what you two are talking about."
Espy's long metallic earrings clinked as she stomped
around her guests.

Jesse followed her with his eyes. "I think you do,"
he declared, all hint of the levity he'd shared with Tori
gone from his tone. He leaned against the back of the
couch, his hands splayed on the upright cushions.
"You've been feeding Martin information about
what's going on in the barrio. In exchange for what?
This?"

He twisted around, picked up a Bennett scholarship
application that had been lying on the end table and
thrust it under her nose.

Espy glowered at him, bloodred lips compressed,
hands on hips. Fury seemed to battle with fear as she
seethed.

Tori broke in. "Espy, you were in the office the
other day when Jesse made his demands. You heard
my father say he'd consider and try to accommodate
them. You passed that on to Martin."

"What if I did?" Espy snarled back at her. Tori
wasn't looking forward to a shouting match, especially
in a small apartment with paper-thin walls.

"Jesse was going to sell out. Somebody's got to protect the barrio," Espy proclaimed self-righteously.

Tori noticed Jesse seemed unfazed by either the accusation or the violence of the outburst.

"You think Martin is that somebody?" she questioned. "Come on, Espy, you're not a fool."

"Or are you?" Jesse asked with a stabbing undertone of ridicule. "You know damn well I wasn't selling out. Carr couldn't possibly meet my demands. That was the point."

Tori knew she should be shocked at Jesse's admission of duplicity, but the dance had been well choreographed—both parties knew their roles.

"Martin not only hasn't protected Santa Marta," Tori told Espy, "he's hurt it and the people in it."

"It isn't Carr who's kept the barrio depressed all these years," Jesse added. "It's your friend, Martin, by turning down our permit requests to improve conditions there."

Espy glared from Jesse to Tori and back again.

"Well, it's her father," Espy yelled at him, "who let the houses get so bad Santa Marta turned into a slum."

Tori took a steadying breath. "My father is partly responsible," she conceded in a milder tone. "But what's happened isn't totally his fault."

"Yeah, right," Espy muttered under her breath.

"Carr's a businessman." Jesse waved his hand in dismissal. "All he did was take advantage of the situation Martin created by keeping his greedy little palm out for bribes. Bribes most of the people there can't afford and shouldn't have to."

Tori looked at him, unable to believe her ears. Jesse was actually defending her father. It was difficult to resist the temptation to smile, hard to suppress the urge to throw her arms around his neck.

She pointed to the scholarship application in Jesse's hand. "Is that what you want, Espy? Martin's help, knowing you'll always be indebted to him—owe him?"

Espy looked away balefully.

"He's using you," Jesse declared, "and he'll continue to use you."

"You don't want me to go to school, to get an education!" Espy cried.

He flung the paper onto the coffee table. "You know damn well that isn't true." His voice was tight, angry, but he softened it. "I want you to do it, but on *your* terms, not Martin's. Otherwise, you'll never be happy."

Espy picked up the application form, scanned it, crumpled it and threw it onto the table, then retreated, stiff-necked, to the window. Tori didn't have to see her face to know the turmoil raging within the woman, the frustration and sense of defeat.

"Espy, I need your help," Tori said quietly after a minute.

Espy turned, grabbed a tissue from a box on a side table and wiped her nose. "What kind of help?"

Jesse lifted a brow, then added, "We need answers to questions that'll bring Martin down."

Tori didn't miss his use of the word *we*. Clearly Espy didn't, either, as she surveyed them both.

"You'll still help me find a scholarship for college?" she asked Tori.

"I said I would."

Tori meant it. But she also knew Espy was assuming it was a trade-off—information against Martin in exchange for a scholarship. Under other circumstances Tori would have made it clear the help wasn't conditional and that she couldn't guarantee Espy would ever receive her grant. But not this time. Not when her father's reputation and well-being were at stake.

"What do you want to know?" Espy asked suspiciously.

ESPY WASN'T ABLE TO TELL them much they didn't already know or suspect. She had reported Jesse's meeting with Tori's father. Martin knew Winslow couldn't possibly meet Jesse's demands for land and backing to build on Coyote Mesa. What worried the councilman was that they were talking to each other, that Jesse had sought out Winslow. If the two men reached an agreement, Riverbend could become a reality and Martin would lose his constituency. Until then he'd been able to stand by and let Jesse undermine Winslow's ambition in Santa Marta. This changed everything. Martin panicked. Espy overheard him tell one of his men it was time to talk with the D.A. about having Winslow charged with bribery.

Tori's mind was eased when she realized her father's arrest had nothing to do with Burton's aborted attempt to have Jesse's properties condemned. She didn't like the way Burton handled things in the barrio, but at least he'd kept his word.

She had also watched the dynamics between Jesse and his "business associate." If Jesse had ever been tempted by Esperanza Mendez, he definitely wasn't now. Espy had betrayed him, used him and the people of the barrio to gain her own ends. He might forgive her someday, but he'd never forget it.

It was close to midnight when Tori and Jesse left Espy's apartment and went down to the parking lot around the corner. Jesse's truck was parked on the far side of a motor home—which explained why Tori hadn't seen it when she drove up.

They stood beside her car in semidark shadows. He draped his arms casually across her shoulders. Looking up at him, at the stubble of beard, she put her hands on his hips, then wriggled her fingers into his back pockets. She enjoyed the surprised, uncomfortable expression on his face.

"Tight jeans," she murmured, and watched him squirm.

"They do seem to be getting a little snug. He raised a brow, completed the circle of his arms around her shoulders and gave her a hard, hungry kiss. Loosening his grip enough to lean back from the waist, he gazed playfully into her eyes.

"Gutsy lady," he murmured. "You took quite a chance up there. If Espy turns tail and reports back to her *padrino,* Martin will be in a position to make things even tougher on your father."

It wasn't easy concentrating on his words when her mind was tuned to his body. "I thought of that," she replied. "Martin's wily enough to make Dad's contributions to his campaign fund look like the bribes they were. But it seems to me it's a two-edged sword. Martin can't very well blow the whistle on years of bribery without acknowledging he's been receiving it."

Jesse chuckled softly. "Don't underestimate a politician's ability to manipulate facts as well as people. He probably used someone as a go-between, someone he'll tag as the fall guy. He'll acknowledge mistakes were made, then blame some overzealous subordinate who acted without his knowledge or authority." He stroked her back.

"Do you think Espy will go running to Martin this time?"

Jesse considered her question. "No. She knows now Martin is a dead end, and worse, a victimizer."

Tori raised her head and looked up at him. "Jesse, she's been a victim all her life."

He pondered her words. "After all she's done, you're still willing to help her?"

"Everybody needs help from time to time, Jesse. We all have our dreams."

"And what about Tori Carr?" he whispered, his tongue tickling her ear. "What are her dreams?"

CHAPTER ELEVEN

JESSE WATCHED TORI DRIVE away from the apartment complex. They had parted with an unspoken mutual understanding that the time wasn't yet right for either of them, not for the potential commitments he knew they were both contemplating.

He climbed into his pickup and drove slowly, thoughtfully to his home in the barrio. There was no use denying it anymore. He was falling in love with Tori Carr, the daughter of the man he had until today considered his nemesis.

He spent the weekend at the ranch, mending fences, chopping firewood for the coming winter and diligently whittling away at his mother's list of chores. Sunday night, however, he was back in his own bed in Santa Marta, family and physical labor no longer able to distract him from the person foremost in his mind.

It was a torturous night, torturous because he kept imagining what it would be like to have her there in his bed beside him, under him, over him....

He'd never wanted anyone the way he wanted Tori Carr. He'd never ached for a woman the way his body ached for her now.

She felt the same pull. He was sure of it. Hadn't their kisses demonstrated that, the way she touched him, the way they fitted together, reacted to each other?

By sunrise Monday morning he was exhausted from

lack of sleep, from fantasies that had kept him in a perpetual state of stimulation all night long.

He donned jogging shorts and a tank top. Maybe a good run would clear his mind, ease some of the tension tormenting his body.

As he ran past decaying houses, Jesse pondered Tori's recognition that it was Martin who'd had her father arrested. Jesse had never liked Martin. He'd known for a long time the man was greedy and corrupt. But he'd found it easier to indict Winslow Carr and Burton Hazlitt, rich Anglos, than the "humble Hispanic." In the heat of sudden anger, he broke into a hard sprint, trying to escape the sudden realization that maybe he was the one who was prejudiced.

But, of course, Martin wasn't one of them anymore, hadn't been for a long time. Changing Martinez to Martin wasn't exactly like changing Przybyszewski to Price. He wasn't simply making his name shorter or simpler, he was denying his heritage.

The more Jesse thought about it, the more incensed and deeply offended he became. He'd blamed Winslow Carr for most of the things that had gone wrong in Santa Marta, and while Carr was partly at fault, Tori had made it clear her father wasn't the only villain in the case. Jesse knew he, too, was guilty of willful blindness, for misguided, if not cowardly, silence. Acknowledgment left a stale taste in his mouth.

Jesse returned to his house, showered, shaved and put on clean Levi's, a new open-necked knit shirt and polished boots. He forced himself to obey traffic laws as he drove from his house to the city councilman's office downtown. A middle-aged Anglo woman greeted him amiably at the reception desk and asked him if he had an appointment.

"I didn't know I needed one to see my elected representative," Jesse replied lightly, suppressing his animosity.

"Of course you don't," the woman said sweetly. "But Mr. Martin is very busy, so it's sometimes easier to get a moment of his time if he's expecting you."

Jesse inhaled deeply, paused, then spoke as casually as he could. "Well, would you see if he can spare me a few moments now?"

"May I tell him the nature of the visit?"

"Just tell him it's Jesse Amorado."

The woman picked up the phone and announced him. Martin was out of his office in a flash.

"Jesse, it's good to see you," he said, practically bubbling over with bonhomie. He had his hand out as he approached, and before Jesse realized it, he was shaking it. "Come on into my office." He reached up and placed a friendly hand on Jesse's shoulder, then ushered him through the open doorway, closing the door quietly behind them.

Martin planted his generous rump against the front of his big, shiny mahogany desk and swept a hand toward an upholstered chair. "Now, what can I do for you?"

Jesse ignored the invitation to sit and came right to the point. "It was you who had Carr arrested, wasn't it?"

Martin seemed both surprised and pleased by the question, as though he had single-handedly saved Jesse's properties and expected him to be grateful. "As a matter of fact, I was instrumental in bringing the information to the district attorney's attention."

"Why?"

"Why?" Martin repeated, his bushy black brows

arching in surprise. "Isn't it obvious? The man was breaking the law, attempting to bribe a public servant." When Jesse failed to respond, the politician went on. "Besides, I should think you'd be pleased, since it was your property he was trying to get condemned."

So Martin did know about Hazlitt's attempt to have Jesse's property inspected. Had Espy lied? Why would she? Or had Martin found out about it only after Carr's arrest?

"It just strikes me as curious," Jesse commented, "considering all the money he's paid you—"

"Hold it right there, Amorado," Martin said sternly, standing up as tall as his five feet six inches would allow. The smile was gone. "I suggest you think very carefully before you make any statements you might regret."

"I just figured you owed him a little more loyalty. After all, he's been paying you for years—"

"Stop," Martin said forcefully, his flabby face taking on a menacing color, his eyes narrowing. "It's true Winslow Carr has contributed to my campaign fund from time to time. So have a lot of other people. That doesn't entitle him or anyone else to special privileges."

"Doesn't it?" Jesse replied. "Tell me, do you think an audit of your bank account might uncover a correlation between the amounts you garner from various construction enterprises and the numbers and types of permits and contracts the office grants?"

Jesse watched as Martin's already flushed face grew even darker with rage. He could smell the fear.

"I understand you're under a great deal of strain, Jesse." Martin's pudgy fingers trembled as he combed them through his bottle-dyed hair. "But I'd be very

careful if I were you about making statements like that
in public. They constitute defamation of character. I
cannot and will not allow my good name to be be-
smirched by scurrilous comments from you or anyone
else.''

Maybe if Martin hadn't made reference to his name,
a name and a heritage he was obviously ashamed of,
Jesse wouldn't have gotten so incensed by the hypo-
crite's rhetoric.

''We're not in public here,'' Jesse pointed out.
''We're in your private office.'' He turned away from
his representative, took a step, inhaled deeply, then
spun around to face him again. ''You've done everything you can to keep the people of Santa Marta down.
You've turned against your own.''

''That's it.'' Martin threw up his arms. ''I don't have
to listen to any more of this. Get out,'' he thundered,
then, lowering his voice, said between clenched teeth,
''and kiss your properties goodbye. Carr may not have
succeeded in getting them condemned, but by God, I
will. I'll have every neglected house in this district condemned to make way for public housing.''

Jesse was shocked. It would be a major turnaround
for the councilman and a dangerous one. Jesse might
not constitute a threat, but Winslow Carr still had a lot
of powerful friends. ''Are you going to take over Carr's
properties, too?''

Martin smirked. ''You're the last one I'd expect to
be worried about Carr. Or is it the skirt of his pretty
little daughter you're interested in? She's sure got you
by the hormones.''

Jesse's blood was pounding in his ears. He considered continuing the confrontation but rejected the idea
as unproductive.

Martin strode to the door and pulled it open. "Now get out," he ordered imperiously.

As Jesse moved past him, Martin said in an intimate undertone, "I heard she got tired of doing it by the numbers military-style and is looking for a macho Mexican stud. So how is she in bed, *amigo?*"

Jesse snapped. Before he realized he was doing it, before he even had a chance to stop himself, he brought up a tight fist and slammed it into Martin's face.

The receptionist let out a scream as Martin crumpled, unconscious, his broken nose bleeding onto the thick carpet.

Jesse stomped out of the office, his body shaking with rage both at Martin and at himself for letting the SOB get to him.

An hour later, the police were at Jesse Amorado's front door with handcuffs and a warrant for his arrest.

LESS THAN TWO MILES AWAY, Tori was in her office around the corner from Lydia's desk. She was having a hard time concentrating on Riverbend. She'd never told Jesse she was proposing they scale back on the project, make it a mixed community very much like the one he himself envisioned. The problem was so many distractions.

Like the recollection of his kisses and the way his body had felt pressing against hers.

Like the relief of knowing neither her father nor his partner was as much to blame for the barrio's deterioration as she had previously supposed.

Like shame that her father was still charged with bribing a public official. The specific instance that prompted his arrest was invalid, but the overall charge was true. If the D.A. wanted to push it hard enough, he could probably make it stick. Would her father have to go to jail? Spend time in prison? The possibility was unthinkable.

A light tapping snapped her attention away from the publicity photos she'd been shuffling blindly for the past ten minutes. Burton was leaning against the door frame.

"It was just on the radio," he announced. "Special bulletin. Jesse Amorado's been arrested."

"Arrested? What for?" There was no way she could control the tremor in her question.

"It seems he and Henry Martin had a slight disagreement. According to the news report, Amorado went over to Martin's office, argued with him and punched the good councilman out."

In spite of the sudden knot in her stomach, she wanted to laugh. "Really? Did they say why?"

"No. Martin's secretary told the reporter it was completely unprovoked, Amorado came storming in, demanded to see his elected representative, spoke to him briefly and then coldcocked him."

Tori suppressed the urge to shout *"Yes!"* She didn't usually approve of violence, but punching Martin's lights out somehow seemed absolutely fitting. Her satisfaction must have shown on her face, because when she glanced across the small room, Burton was smiling, too.

"Where is he now? Jesse, I mean."

"In jail, of course."

Tori pulled a telephone directory from her desk drawer, looked up a number and grabbed the phone.

"What are you doing?" Burton asked. "Who are you calling?"

Tori held up a hand to silence him, then spoke into

the receiver in Spanish. "Señora Amorado, this is Tori. What's going on? How is Jesse?"

"Oh, Victoria, they have arrested him."

"Yes, I know. Did he really hit Martin?"

"*Sí.* He's in the hospital. They say he might have a broken nose."

"What about Jesse? Are they going to release him?"

"Lupe is talking with Jesse's lawyer, trying to figure out a way to get the bail money. The judge set the bail at one hundred thousand dollars."

A hundred grand for a punch in the nose? Wow! Martin did have clout.

Tori knew a bond would cost ten percent—ten thousand dollars. Nonrefundable. "How are you going to raise the money?"

"We will have to borrow it. But where? There is already a mortgage on this ranch. Perhaps we will have to sell—"

"No," Tori told her. "Don't do that. Tell Lupe not to sign anything, *señora.* Let me see what I can do first."

She could hear the tears in the old woman's halting speech. "I cannot let you do that, Victoria. Jesse will be very angry with me. This is a family matter. It will bring dishonor for him if I let you—"

"No, it won't," Tori corrected her gently, hoping what she was saying was true. Damn machismo. "Please, let me take care of everything."

"Victoria," Elena pleaded, "he is my only son now. He is a good man. He does not belong in jail."

"I know that," Tori said consolingly. "I promise you, *señora,* I won't do anything to hurt him. What's the name of Jesse's lawyer?"

Elena passed on Benito Guzman's address and telephone number.

"Everything's going to be all right," Tori assured her.

"Muchas gracias," the old woman sobbed. "I will do as you say. Jesse trusts you."

The last words swam in her head. *Jesse trusts you.* Tori wanted to ask so many questions. When did he say that? What else did he say? But there was no time now. She hung up the phone, suddenly aware of Burton looking quizzically at her, waiting for an explanation—in English.

"I was talking to Jesse's mother." Tori brushed past him. "Come on, I need to talk to Dad."

Burton followed as she rounded the corner, making directly for her father's office.

"Wait," Lydia called out as Tori reached for the brightly polished brass doorknob. "He's got someone with him."

Tori turned the handle and barged in anyway.

Winslow Carr wasn't used to being interrupted when his door was closed. But his annoyance melted the moment he saw his daughter.

"I'm sorry for intruding, Dad, but—"

Nelson Spooner, her father's attorney, rose from his chair and faced her, his courtesy mixed with irritation. He apparently didn't like being disturbed when he was with a client, either. They exchanged polite greetings.

"I'm glad you're here, Mr. Spooner," she said, shaking his hand. She turned to her father. "Dad, Jesse's been arrested."

"Yes, I know. We were just talking about—"

"We need to get him released."

Carr's brows wrinkled in confusion. "We do?" He

looked past her to Burton, but his partner merely shrugged.

"Actually," Spooner said thoughtfully, "I think you've got Amorado right where you want him."

"Maybe you like the idea of people being thrown in jail on trumped-up charges, Mr. Spooner, but I don't."

Her father cocked an eyebrow.

"All I know," she said more calmly, "is that Jesse's in jail and doesn't deserve to be."

"Trumped-up charges?" Spooner echoed. "How do you know they're false?"

"I don't," Tori shot back, unwilling to retreat from a statement she knew she couldn't prove. "But I know Jesse, and I know he wouldn't strike someone without provocation."

She also knew she was saying too much, getting too emotional, but the idea of Jesse languishing in jail because of a corrupt politician made her blood boil.

"Dad," she said, "we've got to go post Jesse's bail. I've spoken with his mother. They could lose their ranch."

Winslow frowned. "Maybe he should have thought of that before he physically assaulted a public official." But there was no conviction in the indictment.

"Martin deserved it," Tori insisted.

"That's for a court to decide," the lawyer reminded her.

Tori wasn't interested in a legal-political-philosophical debate with a man who was trained to take the side of whoever paid him. Over a cocktail at the country club it might be fun, but not here, not now.

"Mr. Spooner," she said formally, "I'd like to retain your services to effect the release of Jesse Amorado and to represent him in court if and when this matter is brought to trial.''

Burton stared at her, clearly mystified by this strange turn of events. "How are you planning on paying his legal fees?" he asked, not unreasonably. "Do you have the cash?"

"Not at the moment. But I can get it." She folded an errant lock of hair behind her ear. "I'll sell my plane."

"That's pretty radical. Do you expect him to pay you back?"

She swallowed a curse and was about to say that this wasn't about money, when her father interrupted.

"He means a lot to you, doesn't he?" It was as much a statement as a question.

"Yes," she answered simply, then pressed her lips together against the sudden threat of tears.

"No need to sell your wings," Burton observed. "Besides, it'll take too long. If this is so important to you, I'll lend you the money for Amorado's bail."

Tori felt as if the air had just been let out of a great balloon in her chest. Impulsively she threw her arms around Burton's neck. The unexpected embrace startled him for a moment, but then he hugged her back.

"We could be so good together," he whispered in her ear. "You and me again. The way it used to be."

"That's in the past, Burton," she replied softly. "We both know it. But thanks for doing this for Jesse."

"I hope you know what you're doing," he said, releasing her. "I can tell you this—your macho hero isn't going to be very happy when he finds out he was bailed out by a woman, even a beautiful woman."

I'll cross that bridge when we come to it, she thought.

Winslow studied his fingernails for a moment, then spoke up. "Make the loan to Carr Enterprises."

Jesse didn't have to know the money for his release had come from Burton, only that Carr Enterprises had come through for him.

Burton looked uncertain, then a big smile lit up his face. "Of course. It's easier to negotiate with a friend than a rival. That ought to get him on our side. Good thinking, Win."

Tori didn't like the turn the discussion had taken. This wasn't about manipulation. It was about getting the man she cared for out of jail.

JESSE FELT DIRTY. The surroundings had something to do with it, but he felt dirty inside, too. He'd finally joined that very special brotherhood of the barrio— he'd been in jail.

How would he ever face Tori? How could he expect her to respect him when he'd disgraced himself? He couldn't tell her he'd landed in jail defending her name. He should have had more self-control. Instead, he'd been a chump, allowed himself to be suckered, lost his cool and now his dignity.

A uniformed jailer came to his cell. He didn't say anything, just put a key in the lock, swung the door open, then nodded to a man behind him. The man, probably in his forties, seemed to sniff the air as he entered the cage. The turnkey walked away without locking the gate.

"Who are you?" Jesse asked.

"My name is Nelson Spooner. I'm an attorney." He seemed a little reluctant at first to offer his hand, but he did, and Jesse made it a point to give him a good, hard handshake. He had no doubt one of the first things the lawyer would do when he left was wash it.

"Did Bennie Guzman send you?" he asked.

"I've been retained by Carr Enterprises," Spooner explained.

"Carr? I don't understand," Jesse said, puzzled. "What's Winslow Carr got to do—"

"Mr. Carr asked me to post bail and represent your legal interests. Mr. Guzman's been informed. You're free to go."

"I still don't understand," Jesse said. "Why would Carr—"

"There's not much to understand," Spooner said curtly.

Was this Winslow Carr's way of suckering him? Jesse wondered. Tit for tat? *I got you out of jail, now you turn over your properties to me?*

"Do you want to get out of here or not?" Spooner demanded impatiently.

"Sure, but—"

Spooner reached into his inside jacket pocket, extracted a small white card and handed it to Jesse. "I recommend you contact my office in a day or two so we can go over your case."

Ten minutes later Jesse was on the pay phone outside the jailhouse calling the ranch. His mother answered on the first ring. It was painful listening to her pleas for assurance that he was safe and sound.

"I'm perfectly fine. I promise you. Ma, I have a couple of questions…"

A few minutes later, Jesse said, "I love you, Ma. I'll see you tomorrow."

The gusty fresh air of the busy street refreshed him

a little. He didn't have his truck here, but they'd returned his pocket money, which was enough to get a cab back to his house. But it was only a couple of miles to his office. He had a change of clothes there. Besides, the walk would give him time to stretch his cramped muscles and think.

He'd just turned the last corner when he saw the shiny red 'vette parked in front of Amorado Construction. The woman he hadn't been able to get out of his thoughts for days was leaning casually against it in a pose similar to the one he'd assumed in her parking lot two days before. The fatigue of a minute ago vanished.

TORI WATCHED HIM APPROACH. His clothes, normally so crisp and clean, were rumpled and smudged. But instead of detracting from his appearance, they enhanced it. His eyes, hooded by weariness, had an enigmatic quality that made them even more fascinating. The heaviness of his tread spoke not of weakness or defeat, but of strength. He strode with his head held high, proud, defiant, determined. And sexy as hell.

"Taxi, mister?" she said when he came within a few feet of her. When he didn't immediately respond, she began to panic. "We signed a truce, remember?" she teased, although her heart was thudding. *Say something, damn it!* she wanted to shout. *Please.* "And kissed on it."

Only then did he smile. She threw her arms around him. There was a desperation in the way she held him, as if she were afraid he was a mirage.

They kissed, a long, slow, passionate kiss. Then she laid her head on his chest. He reeked of disinfectant and sweat. She didn't care.

"I'm dirty and smelly," he said as he held her.

She chuckled softly and raised a hand to the dense stubble of his beard. "Your house or the ranch?"

He covered her hand with his, brought her palm around to kiss it. "My house." It came out a hoarse whisper.

SHE COULD ONLY SNATCH glimpses of him as she drove along the potholed streets. Only glance distractedly at the sunlight playing on his wrinkled jeans. Only see the movement of his hand as it brushed unruly, shiny black hair back from his somber face.

"Penny for your thoughts." She maneuvered a deserted corner just as the light went yellow.

"I was wondering what the *muchachos* will think about me being rescued by a woman."

"Now, where did you get that idea?"

His laugh crackled. "I've got to warn you about Ma. She can't keep a secret. Especially when she's happy about something."

Another moment of truth, Tori thought. She looked straight ahead, her fingers tightening on the wheel. "What do you think they'll say?"

Her heart skipped a beat at the twinkle in his sidelong glance and the gusto in his answer. "They'll say, 'Lucky man.'"

She had an irresistible urge to stop the car right in the middle of the street and throw her arms around him. She had to content herself instead with reaching for his hand. His caress, so warm and coarse and tender and strong, made her skin tingle, her heart sing.

"I haven't said thank-you yet," Jesse said seriously.

She squeezed his hand. "You just did."

He wrapped his other hand around hers and rested it on his thigh. Heat radiated from him. No words were necessary—or possible—as they drove the few remaining blocks to his house.

"I NEED A SHOWER," Jesse announced after he'd closed the front door behind them. "That place made me feel even dirtier than I am."

She gave him a quick kiss on the lips. "You go ahead. I'll make some coffee. Are you hungry?"

He thought a moment. "No, I don't think so."

"You will be," she promised him.

"Hmm," was his only reply as he went to the bedroom. A moment later, she caught a glimpse of him as he stepped into the bathroom down the hall.

She found the shower ridiculously distracting. It wasn't the sound of the running water that had her nerves on edge so much as the image it elicited, an image of Jesse, naked, standing in its cascading stream.

She searched for and found coffee beans. At least the noise of the grinder drowned out the sound of the shower. But not the images crowding her mind. Or the sensations creeping through her flesh.

She was opening the pantry door by the hallway to look for something to fix as a snack when she saw him emerge from the bathroom, bare-chested, wearing only his briefs. She stopped in midmotion, her pulse beating erratically. He smiled self-consciously at her and quickly retreated into the bedroom, closing the door softly behind him. Only then did she begin to breathe again.

He reappeared a few minutes later, barefoot, in faded blue Dockers shorts and a red knit shirt that showed off his olive skin to pure distraction.

"How are you doing?" he asked, surveying her, not the work in progress.

She could smell the tangy aroma of bath soap and aftershave. Her knees felt like jelly.

"Fine. I found some corn tortillas, frijoles and cheddar. I thought I'd make some *chalupas*."

"Sounds good. I'll get the salsa."

"Great." She turned toward the refrigerator just as he did, and they collided. Her rubbery legs gave out, and he grabbed her arms to steady her.

"Sorry," he murmured softly, his eyes on hers, his hands firmly clasping her arms just below the shoulders, his thumbs rhythmically massaging her bare skin.

"It was my fault," she muttered. Then, for no discernible reason, tears welled in her eyes.

He caught her chin with the side of a forefinger and lifted her face to his. Thank God he didn't ask what was wrong.

"It's going to be okay," he assured her, and pulled her against his chest. She could hear his heart beating in syncopation with hers. "Things will work out," he whispered. "Just you wait and see."

She lifted her face to him. He brought his mouth down to hers. The kiss was gentle at first, then grew in intensity. His hands stroked her back, settled on her hips for a brief moment, then reached down and pulled her to him. There was no doubting his need. No denying hers.

She clutched the firm muscles of his broad shoulders, pressed herself against his persistent hardness.

"Yes," she murmured to the silent question his subtle movements were posing.

He nibbled the delicate skin below her ear. "Are you sure?" He trailed his open mouth along the base of her throat.

"Mmm."

He led her by the hand. The evening light cast the bedroom into delicate shadow, but they could see clearly what they were doing.

His hands gently fondled the fullness of her breasts before they unbuttoned her blouse. The delicate touch of his fingers set her aflame. He nuzzled her neck with lips and teeth and tongue as he released her bra, melting away any desire to resist. His mouth played hungrily with her erect nipples. She threw back her head and bit her lip, breathing heavily.

She pulled his shirt over his head and ran her fingers across his thick pectoral muscles. He groaned as she released his buckle, tugged on the zipper and slipped her hand against his bulge before easing the pants down his narrow hips.

"I want you," he whispered as he settled her on the bed. "I've always wanted you." Together they removed the last barriers of clothing.

CHAPTER TWELVE

TORI WENT HOME to change clothes before going into the office. Her father was in the large country kitchen, eating a breakfast of fried eggs and sausage. He smiled when he saw her, then looked sheepish when she scrutinized the food on his plate.

"Don't tattle on me to Lydia, please," he begged, sounding like a little boy caught with his hand in the cookie jar.

"Lydia isn't the only one who's concerned about you, Dad," she said sternly.

"I know all that rabbit food is good for me, but once in a while I get hungry for the real stuff."

"Is that what this is, real stuff?" she mocked.

"Okay, okay, I won't lecture. Just promise you won't do this too often."

"Promise," he said, holding up the middle fingers of his right hand like a good Boy Scout.

This time she laughed and gave him a hug. She poured a cup of coffee and removed a slice of cantaloupe from the refrigerator. She and Jesse had taken so long in the shower they'd barely had time to gulp down a glass of orange juice.

"You didn't come home last night," her father commented as she took her place across from him and scooped a piece of the sweet Pecos melon onto a spoon.

"I was perfectly safe," she replied casually.

"I know," he said. She noticed he didn't ask where she'd been. "I drove around last night, saw your car at his house."

Had he been checking up on her? "I'm not a little girl anymore, Dad."

Winslow smiled. "I know you're not, sweetheart. I wasn't spying on you, and I didn't mean to sound as if I thought you had to ask my permission."

She watched him take a bite of toast. Then it struck her—he'd driven through the barrio.

"Do you love him?" her father asked after a sip of coffee.

A multitude of reactions raced through her at once, thoughts and feelings she needed time to sort out.

"I think I do, but it's happened so fast," she replied honestly. "This feels so different from anything I've experienced before."

Her father spread marmalade on another piece of buttered toast. "Does he love you?"

She thought about the way Jesse touched her. "I think so."

"But you're not sure?"

"Can any of us ever be sure about another person?"

Winslow regarded her with a gentleness she wasn't expecting or perhaps had never noticed before. For just a fleeting moment, she thought she saw sorrow, as well.

"Yes, I think so," he said. "About love we can. I loved your mother with the absolute certainty she loved me. I hope she never doubted my feelings for her."

Her father rarely talked about her mother, never on such a personal level. Maybe that was what she'd missed all these years, the sharing of intimate emotions.

"Listen to your heart," he advised. "You'll know.

If he does love you, love him back with everything you've got."

It was wise counsel, but the passion was hardly what she expected from her father.

"What about you and Lydia, Dad? Are you going to marry her?"

His face softened for an instant, then took on the detached facade she'd seen too often when delicate subjects were broached.

"When the time's right." He got up quickly, removed his half-eaten breakfast and took it to the sink, effectively cutting off any further discussion. He returned a moment later and refilled his coffee cup.

"Spooner sent the paperwork over for your partnership," he announced. "I thought I'd invite the mayor and some other dignitaries to the office today at high noon and get the newspaper and TV folks to record this historic event. Maybe we can distract attention from some of the less pleasant things going on. It isn't every day a man has the privilege of welcoming his daughter into his business as a full partner."

"Sounds great, Dad. But it's awfully short notice. Will anyone show up?" *Will Jesse?*

"This is Coyote Springs," he said with a chuckle, "not Washington. Don't need a week's notice here. Besides, I'll call people personally. Gives me a chance to brag about my little girl."

She liked the sparkle in his eyes. She got up and kissed him on the forehead. "I'm a pretty lucky girl to have a dad like you."

He gave a broad, self-conscious smile. "I'm very proud of you. Have I told you that lately?"

"Yep," she said quietly. They exchanged little grins. "Is there anything you want me to do?"

"No. Lydia and I will handle everything."

"Would you mind if I call Jesse and invite him?"

"Certainly, if you like."

A wave of affection washed over her, quickly followed by an undertow of regret. She wanted to fly airplanes, feel the exhilarating rush of adrenaline when she lifted off, the serenity of gliding through puffy white clouds, the thrill of danger when they snarled and bucked. She didn't want to give it up.

What about Carr Enterprises? Was she joining it on its dying gasp? Was she letting her growing feelings for Jesse kill the Riverbend project? How could she work in the best interest of the company her father had built over twenty years when she was falling in love with the man who held the key to its destruction?

"Regrets?" her father asked, his brows raised in concern.

"About the partnership? Absolutely not."

"I'm blessed, Tori, to have you." He paused, then said very seriously, "I know you're having second thoughts about Riverbend. I can't say I blame you after seeing the way the people in the barrio have been treated. I want you to know I trust you implicitly. If you feel we should abandon the project, for whatever reason, I'll accept your judgment."

She wrapped her arm around him. "We're going to make this thing work. Riverbend is a good idea. You wouldn't have undertaken it and you couldn't have gotten the kind of financial backing you have if it weren't. Sure, we've run into a few glitches, but isn't that to be expected with a project this size?" Who was she trying to convince? Her father or herself?

She studied his face. He suddenly looked discouraged, worn-out.

"Dad," she said, "I know Riverbend isn't working out the way you and Burton envisioned it, but I think by scaling back it can still work. Give me a little more time and I'm sure I can bring Jesse around."

"You know," he said too cheerfully, "I believe you will." He took her hand. "Now, let's get to that partnership business."

"I'VE GOT JUST ONE question," Lydia said as Tori and her father came through the front door. She smiled directly at Tori. "How did someone find out about your partnership even before we announced it?" She pointed to a huge bouquet of red roses sitting on a side table. "Just arrived ten minutes ago. They're addressed to you."

Tori felt her pulse quicken as she drank in their heady scent. She removed the still-sealed white card pinned to the crinkly green tissue paper. "May there be more love-filled nights and days." It was signed Jesse.

"Who are they from?" her father called out on his way to his office.

She kept her back to Lydia to hide the smile she couldn't suppress. "Jesse Amorado." She turned, trying to sound calm and impersonal. "I'm always amazed at how small this town is. You just can't keep anything secret."

Lydia didn't seem completely convinced by the display of casualness. "Is he coming to the signing, then?"

"He doesn't say," Tori told her, all too aware of her deception.

Right after breakfast, she tried calling him at home. She left a message on his answering machine to call her. He wasn't at his office, either, so she left another message. Then she dialed his cell phone number. No answer. Finally she called the ranch, thinking he might have stopped by there, but Elena said she hadn't seen or heard from him since the afternoon before.

"If he contacts you before noon," Tori told her, "ask him to give me a call, please."

"Of course, Victoria. Is something wrong?"

"No, no," Tori assured her. "But we're having a little ceremony to celebrate my joining my father's company, and I thought he might like to come."

"Congratulations, Victoria. Yes, I will tell him."

Noon approached but there wasn't any return call.

THE FORMAL SIGNING of the piece of paper marking Tori's official status as a partner of Carr Enterprises was attended by far more people than Tori had expected. The mayor was there, as well as several city councilmen. Notably absent was Henry Martin. So was Jesse.

At the appointed time, Tori took her position at the center of a long table facing the assembly. A tooled maroon leather portfolio containing a single piece of parchment paper was signed, first by her father on her right, then Burton on her left, and finally by Tori herself. Then Winslow Carr, grinning from ear to ear, held the folder with its red ribbon and gold seal over his head for everyone to see. Cameras clicked and buzzed and camcorders whirred.

Applause broke out. Burton popped the cork on a bottle of champagne and the three partners toasted one another and Carr Enterprises.

Caterers had set up a cold buffet of meat and cheese, fruit and relish trays, chips and dips. Champagne spouted in sparkling rivulets from a fountain in the center of the long table.

Tori felt light-headed by the excitement as guests shook her hand, many taking time to reminisce about her years growing up in Coyote Springs. If anyone noticed her frequent glances at the door to see if Jesse had arrived, no one mentioned it.

He finally showed up just before two o'clock, after everyone else had gone.

"Where were you?" she asked, warmth suffusing her at the memory of the night before. She looked up, gazed at his mouth, remembered the way his lips had touched her.

"I was in Oakdale," he said, his eyes fixed on hers. "On a job site." He smelled of summer and sawdust.

"I tried to reach you on your cell phone," she said, resisting a maddening urge to reach up and stroke his cheek.

"I thought I'd only be gone for a minute, so I left it in the truck," he explained. "It took me longer than I expected."

He grasped her hand, rubbed its smoothness with a coarse thumb. "Mom finally got hold of me after lunch and told me about your partnership," he said, taking her other hand in his.

"Dad's been talking about it for some time…but the actual paperwork only came through yesterday. I didn't know until this morning…"

She was babbling. Did he understand her ambivalence, the loyalties tearing at her? Her father needed her, yet…

"Congratulations are in order." His smile was as warm as his hands. "I'm sorry I didn't get here sooner."

"May I get you something to drink?" she asked him. Why was she sounding so formal? This wasn't some stranger she was talking to. This was Jesse, the man she made love with last night. "I'm afraid there's no champagne left."

He shook his head and bent close to her ear. "Seeing you is intoxicating enough."

The comment flustered her. "Coffee, then? Or would you prefer something cold?"

Amusement twinkled in his eyes, twitched at the corner of his mouth. "I definitely think I need something cold." He leaned toward her, his voice low and seductive. "I may need a cold shower if you don't—"

Winslow Carr chose that moment to come out of his office. "Mr. Amorado, it's good to see you. I'm sorry you weren't able to get here sooner. All the food's gone, I'm afraid."

Jesse accepted the outstretched hand. "Please call me Jesse. I want to thank you for what you did for me yesterday—"

"Glad I could help." They shook hands heartily. "It's an unpleasant experience we seem to have in common, Jesse."

"As well as a common enemy."

Burton emerged quietly from his office and joined them. He'd been interviewed by the press earlier in the day and praised the talents Tori was going to bring to their growing enterprise. He was, to Tori's mind, very much the old Burton, the charmer, the sophisticate, the corporate team member. If he had any lingering reservations about her becoming a partner, or resentment over her turning down his romantic overture, he hid them very well.

"Too bad about your problem yesterday," he said to Jesse.

Jesse shrugged. "Congratulations on acquiring a new partner."

"Isn't she great?" Burton enthused, and draped his arm around her shoulders, making the hairs on the back of her neck rise. She tried to smile to cover her discomfort, but the scowl on Jesse's face only intensified it.

"Since we're all together," Winslow said, "why don't we sit down and talk?"

He ushered them into his office, started toward his desk, then changed course and pointed them to the less formal sitting area by the window. Tori and Jesse sat next to each other on the couch, barely resisting the temptation to hold hands. Winslow and Burton took chairs across the coffee table from them.

"Mr. Amorado," Winslow started. "Jesse. I know we haven't seen eye to eye on the issue of Riverbend. For that I'm truly sorry. I can understand and, I might add, I share your concern for Santa Marta and the people who live there."

Jesse nodded.

"Now," Winslow continued, "I'm faced with a dilemma. As you know, I've invested heavily in the barrio and have convinced others to do so, as well. If I fail with Riverbend, I stand to lose everything I've built over the past twenty years—including what's left of my reputation. If I succeed, I dislocate and make unhappy a lot of people who've spent a lifetime there."

"Change is inevitable," Burton pointed out.

"Yes," Winslow agreed. "But it should be for the better."

No one disputed him.

"Now, about your proposal to build at Coyote Mesa—"

"There's something I think you need to know," Jesse interrupted. "Things may be taken out of our hands."

"What do you mean?" asked Burton, alarmed.

"In my last discussion with Martin, he said he was going to have neglected properties in Santa Marta condemned to make way for public housing."

"Public—public housing?" Burton stammered.

"All the properties?" Tori asked. "Ours, too?"

"That's what he implied. It makes sense if you think about it," Jesse told them. "We both own properties that are in pretty bad shape. It would be hard to discriminate between them."

Tori looked at him. The term slumlord burned in her throat.

"But public housing?" Burton repeated, appalled. Tori could practically see the cold shiver running down his spine.

"Can he do that?" she asked the group at large.

Her father sat with his elbows resting on the arms of his chair, his hands steepled as in prayer, his index fingers tapping against his lips.

Burton kept shaking his head in disbelief. "The city council has been discussing the need for additional public housing in Coyote Springs for years," he explained. "But they've never been able to settle on a site. Whenever somebody proposes building in an established neighborhood, the people who live there complain that it will devalue their properties. When a completely new site outside town is suggested, the potential residents complain it's too far from their jobs.

The city shudders at the idea of having to expand public transportation.''

"That's one reason why your suggestion of building new low-cost housing at Coyote Mesa has serious problems," Winslow pointed out to Jesse.

"Martin," said Burton, "has always been one of the loudest opponents of public housing. I wonder what's made him change his mind."

"He wasn't figured into the equation," Winslow said thoughtfully. "I should have considered the effect this project was going to have on him."

"But getting the council to agree to public housing's going to take more than his endorsement, isn't it?" asked Tori.

"Oh, he can't do it by decree or by himself," her father assured her. "So it isn't going to happen overnight. But he can certainly bring Riverbend to a screeching halt if he comes out strongly in favor of public housing in Santa Marta."

"As far as I can see," Jesse commented, "if Martin succeeds in pulling off this latest stunt, everybody loses. Even if we get reasonable compensation for our properties, which I doubt, we'll both take a licking financially." He looked at the senior man. "Especially Carr Enterprises. But Santa Marta loses, too. There's a world of difference between public housing and low-income housing. I want people to have access to affordable homes, something they can own and take pride in, not feel themselves the wards of some bureaucratic system, indebted to some rotten politician."

"What are we going to do?" Tori asked, voicing the question on everybody's mind.

"Bargain with him," Winslow said. "Find out what he really wants. I agree with Jesse. This is just a ploy.

Let's not forget Martin's a businessman as well as a politician."

"Exactly," Burton agreed. "We'll just have to deal with him on that level. I'll handle it."

"What would you use to convince him to change his mind?" Tori asked.

"The only two things that matter. Money and power. Whether he gets Riverbend or public housing, his constituency is going to change. It's to his advantage to go with the Riverbend crowd. They can contribute a hell of a lot more to his coffers than a bunch of paupers on the public dole."

Tori shook her head. "That approach might have worked a week ago, but not now. He burned some bridges when he had Dad arrested. He knows he's not going to get any more fees out of us. Chances are other outfits are rethinking their arrangements with him, too."

She got up and paced the floor. "No, Martin's right. He's blown his chance to gain support from the upper-income bracket in Riverbend. Power is more important to him than money. If he really believes Santa Marta is past saving, his only other option is public housing. I think he's a crafty enough politician to convince whatever low-income groups move into his district that he's their champion."

"So what have you got in mind?" Burton asked.

"Nothing yet," she replied. "But I am sure of one thing. The answer's not in compromising with Martin. It's in defeating him."

"WE NEVER DID HAVE those *chalupas* last night," Jesse commented to Tori a short while later as they stood in the parking lot between their two vehicles. "Are you hungry?"

She smiled at the recollection of their time together. "No breakfast, either." The smoldering fire in Jesse's eyes suggested his thoughts were running along the same lines.

"Yeah, I'm hungry. In all the glad-handing and talking, I never even got a taste of the food on the buffet."

His eyes were devouring her. "I know just the place to get the best *chalupas* in Spring County."

That could only mean one place, Tori decided. What bachelor didn't think his mother's cooking was the best in the world?

"Sounds like an offer I can't refuse."

He skimmed a finger up her arm. "Good."

"Do we need reservations?"

"I have no reservations." His finger reached her shoulder and began to skitter across her collarbone.

"Me, neither." Her heart was racing. "Sounds like we'll just have to take our chances."

"Together," Jesse whispered, his lips a breath away from hers.

"Togeth—" But she had to swallow the rest of the word when his mouth closed over hers.

TORI LEFT HER CAR in the parking lot and went with Jesse in his truck to the Amorado ranch. She breathed in the winter wood scent of his aftershave and admired his regal profile. She detected boyish embarrassment in the curve of his lips as he sensed her scrutiny.

He glanced over. "Is something the matter?"

"Just looking."

An eight-year-old red Ford Escort was parked beside

Lupe's even older Chevy when they arrived at the little house.

"Espy's car," Jesse commented.

"What's she doing here?"

"I guess we'll find out," he said, annoyance ringing in his words.

Elena was teary-eyed when she saw Jesse. She pressed his cheeks between her hands the way she would with a small child. But then, Tori reflected, he would always be her little boy.

"I was so afraid!" she cried.

"It's okay, Mom," Jesse said, uncomfortable with his mother's anxiety. He drew her hands away gently and held them between his own. "I'm fine."

Elena nodded, and a new tear cascaded down her cheek. Jesse brushed it away and kissed the top of her head. Elena hugged him tightly. A minute later she threw her arms around Tori, as well. Tori hugged her back, moved by the woman's caress. It had been years since she'd experienced that kind of maternal contact. It brought unexpected tears to her eyes. She caught a glimpse of Jesse smiling at their embrace, a smile of approval and contentment.

"Hey, Mom," he interrupted lightly, "whatcha got to eat around here? We haven't had lunch yet and we're starved."

Elena wiped her face with the back of her hand. "Just like a man," she said to Tori. "Always thinking about his stomach."

Tori looked quickly at Jesse and had to stifle a chuckle. The brief eye contact they shared, however, wasn't fast enough to get by Mrs. Amorado.

"Come on, you two," she said with a lilt, "I think

what you both need is some of my *menudo. Muy caliente.*''

The three of them walked up to the house, Jesse between the two most important women in his life, each tucked lovingly under a protective arm.

Lupe and Espy were standing on the small porch as they approached. ''How are you?'' Lupe asked Jesse.

''I'm fine. Thanks for your help yesterday.''

''That's what families are for.'' Lupe turned to Tori. ''You're the one who really deserves the thanks. *Muchas gracias.*'' Lupe kissed her softly on the cheek. The sincerity of the emotion and the sense of family overwhelmed Tori.

''What brings you out here?'' Jesse asked Espy, who was standing back a few feet from the group.

''I...I just wanted to say I hope you got your...misunderstanding with Martin worked out.''

''There was no misunderstanding about it,'' he told her. ''He insulted Tori and I punched him out.''

Espy stared at him, tight-lipped.

A rush of heat warmed Tori's cheeks. She shouldn't feel smug. Being the cause of Jesse's legal trouble ought to make her feel guilty, but there was a primitive satisfaction in being the object of such impetuosity. She looked up to see Lupe smiling at her.

''Just so you know I had nothing to do with it,'' Espy responded, apparently oblivious to the other women's reactions.

''I never supposed you did,'' Jesse told her.

''Has Martin dropped the charges?''

''No. I'm just lucky to have friends willing to help me.''

Espy lowered her eyes and said nothing.

The children came over from playing along the side

of the garage. Miguelito's greeting was considerably less exuberant than it had been on their last visit. Even Teresita seemed reserved.

"What's the matter, *amigo?*" Jesse asked his nephew. "You look like you just lost your best friend."

"We're not going to Sea World or Fiesta Texas."

"How come?" Jesse asked very seriously.

"Because of you!" The boy's eyes blazed.

"Me?"

"Grandma said we couldn't go because you were in—"

"We couldn't go and leave you," Elena hastened to point out.

"That was yesterday. There's no reason why you can't go now."

Miguelito brightened instantly. "We can? Really?" He dragged Teresita by the hands and they began to dance around in circles. "We're going to Sea World. We're going to Sea World."

"But, Jesse—" Elena began to object.

"Everything's okay, Ma. Don't disappoint the kids. They've been looking forward to the trip for so long."

"We're going to Sea World," Teresita chimed in as she skipped around with her brother.

Jesse grinned happily. "And to see Shamu. You can't forget Shamu."

"But, Jesse—"

"No buts about it," he insisted. "Go. It'll do you good. Lupe hasn't seen her sister in months."

"You can go with the children," Elena said to her daughter-in-law. "I will stay."

"No, you won't," Jesse said with loving intransigence. "You need a break, to get away from here."

"Do you think I will not worry in San Antonio?"

"It's hard to worry," he told her with an easy grin, "when you're watching Shamu the whale." He sat on the porch step and lifted Teresita onto his knee. "Or feeding dolphins out of your hand," he told the child playfully. He tickled her on the side of her rib cage, eliciting a squirming giggle that drove her deeper against his chest.

"*Muy bien.*" Elena finally conceded, to the children's delight. "But you can reach us at Anita's if something happens."

"Nothing's going to happen," Jesse assured her. "Now, go get packed."

"We already are," Lupe pointed out. "I never got around to unpacking yesterday."

"Well, then, I'll load the car for you, and you can be on your way."

"Can I help?" Miguelito asked his uncle.

"You bet, *amigo.*" Jesse rumpled the boy's straight black hair.

"Not until you two have eaten," Elena insisted to her son and Tori.

Espy had been silent, motionless, an outsider during the exchange. Now she looked around, trying to find something to say. "How long are you going to be away?"

"About a week," Lupe replied.

"Should be fun."

"Come sit down and eat with us," Elena invited Espy. "I have a pot of *menudo*—"

"No, thanks. I have to get going." She hurried away, only belatedly turning to wave and call out, "Have a good time in San Antonio."

She was gone before they could say goodbye.

"What was that all about?" Tori asked.

"Damned if I know," Jesse replied.

CHAPTER THIRTEEN

THOUGHTS OF ESPY soon faded. Elena bustled around serving generous bowls of spicy hot tripe stew with flour tortillas. She offered to make *chalupas* or nachos, as well, but Jesse and Tori gave in only to the offer of puffy light sopapillas smothered with wild sage honey. They smiled lustfully at each other as they licked the sweet syrup from their fingers.

Half an hour later Jesse loaded the luggage, checked the oil and tires and instructed his sister-in-law to call him at home as soon as they arrived. With arms around each other's waists, Tori and Jesse watched Lupe's Chevy pull out of the driveway, heading south toward San Antonio, Sea World and Fiesta Texas. Grandma and grandkids were singing happily in anticipation of their coming adventure.

"It'll take me just a few minutes to close up the place," Jesse told Tori. "Then we can be on our way, too."

Over his objections, she volunteered to wash the dishes while he picked up a few toys that had been left outside. She enjoyed observing him through the open window as he meandered across the yard to the garage to check on the door's lock and hasp and the windows on the sides. He bent over and checked the two-by-four wedged under the handles of the storm cellar door. Jesse Amorado was very much at home here, comfortable in his role as head of the family. She could imagine him growing older—very gracefully—his black hair becoming salted with gray, then turning alabaster white. She pictured him, strong even in old age, surrounded with children and grandchildren, nieces and nephews, the benevolent patriarch of a happy, protected clan.

They said little on the trip back to the city until they approached Carr Enterprises. Her discussion with her father that morning kept niggling at the corners of her mind. The Riverbend project wasn't just a matter of saving Carr Enterprises at the expense of Santa Marta anymore. It meant promoting a company that had failed in its moral responsibility to the people there. It meant losing Jesse.

The best compromise appeared to be the scaled-down Riverbend she'd suggested. But she couldn't ignore the counterarguments: they didn't have either the time to modify their plans before options ran out or the money to start over again. A refocused Riverbend seemed as fatal to Carr Enterprises as no Riverbend at all.

Jesse pulled up alongside her Corvette, shut off the engine and turned to her. "Are you coming over to my place later?" He released his seat belt and slid toward her.

"I don't know," she said. "I want to, but—"

"But what?" he mumbled, his lips featherlight against hers, tempting, promising.

She pressed her palms against his hard chest and felt his heartbeat. "I've got a lot of thinking to do—"

"We can do it together."

She grinned. "I'm afraid what we'll do together won't be thinking. Certainly not very objectively."

"To hell with objectivity," he said in a deep bass.

Lifting a hand to his face, she absorbed the warmth of his skin beneath the five o'clock stubble. "Objectivity might be the best thing for us right now."

"The best thing for me," he said, burying a kiss in the crook of her neck, "is you. You're all I need." He lifted her hand and kissed the palm. "But if you're not sure…"

Was she sure? She thought she was. She climbed out of the truck, slammed the door, then stuck her head through the window. "I'll be over later."

"I'll be waiting," he said, and watched her walk to her car.

AFTER CHECKING IN at the office, Tori decided it was her turn to supply the food for dinner—whether they ate it or not. How did Jesse like his steaks? she wondered. For no logical reason, she decided he was a medium-rare sort of guy. Wine. Did he like wine? Tradition said red wine with red meat. She doubted he felt bound by such conventions, but she couldn't picture him holding a glass of white, much less pink, wine.

She drove to the liquor store at the far end of North Travis and chose a cabernet sauvignon from one of the oldest wineries in Texas. She took the salesman's word that it was a prizewinner.

Next stop, the custom meat section of the supermarket. She ordered two well-marbled sirloin steaks, thickly cut and carefully trimmed. Then she picked out a couple of large baking potatoes and a variety of salad makings. On an impulse, she selected an avocado as an appetizer.

I WONDER HOW SHE LIKES her steaks, Jesse mused as he drove away from Carr Enterprises. Medium rare, he decided. Just like he did. Wine. He liked a hearty red, but she might prefer white. In his experience, most women did.

Since only beer could be bought in town, he went to the liquor store on South Travis just outside city limits, where he pondered the vast variety of fancy-sounding wines they offered. He chose a chardonnay he'd thought particularly good when he sampled it several months before at a wine tasting. In her world travels Tori had undoubtedly drunk all kinds of exotic wines. Probably none from East Texas, though.

He also stopped off at a small butcher shop in Santa Marta not far from his house, where the family had been doing business for as long as he could remember. The proprietor was a small, pear-shaped man in his seventies, with snow-white hair and a face of timeworn leather.

"Ah," he intoned when Jesse told him what he wanted. He twirled his majestically curled mustache. "Your friend is visiting this evening." He used the feminine form of the Spanish word for friend.

Jesse smiled, not surprised by the man's perspicacity. The barrio was a small community, and as Jesse was an eligible bachelor, the neighbors were inclined to keep track of his female visitors. Of course Tori's bright red sports car wasn't exactly inconspicuous.

"That's why this has to be a very good steak."

"You think I would give you a bad one otherwise?" the old man chided.

Jesse laughed. "Of course not. That's why I came here."

The butcher chuckled, a conspiratorial grin under

generous snowy brows. "I have something just a little special for you and the pretty *señorita*."

He trimmed a thick beef tenderloin. "Juanita Perez is moving this weekend," he commented. "She's lived here all her life and in the same house for nearly thirty-five years. Her husband built it himself right after they were married."

A familiar tale, Jesse thought. "Where's she going?"

"To live with her daughter in Oakdale. A few other members of the family have moved there over the years."

"How about you? Are you holding out against Riverbend?"

The old man shrugged. "I thought about it, but so many of our people are moving away. One of my sons has a restaurant near the courthouse. He does a good lunchtime business and has asked me to come help him out. It will be a kind of semiretirement."

Jesse knew the place well. It had started as a typical storefront restaurant, expanded into the shop next door and now boasted an outdoor patio, as well.

"I can spend more time with my grandchildren that way," he said with fondness.

"I'm glad things are working out for you," Jesse said, relieved the old man didn't seem depressed at the prospect of leaving the neighborhood he'd lived in his entire life. Was this the popular view, that the barrio was obsolete?

"Did you get a good price for this place?"

The old man laughed. "Very good. I expected one day to close the door and just walk away. None of my sons or grandsons is interested in cutting meat and standing behind a counter all day like me. One of my nephews negotiated for me. He's a good business-man.''

The butcher weighed two filets mignons on a balancing scale that might have been as old as he was, then carefully wrapped them in white butcher paper.

''They have some nice fresh shrimp next door today,'' he told Jesse as he made change from the sale. ''The ladies sometimes like a little shrimp cocktail before the main course.'' His eyes sparkled with mischief.

Jesse grinned. ''Good idea. *Muchas gracias, señor.*''

When he got home, Jesse spent a few minutes tidying up. He and Tori had left in such haste that morning, the place looked like a teenager's room instead of the neat house he took pride in. He was arranging a charcoal pyramid in the barbecue out back when the doorbell rang.

''Hi,'' Tori said when he opened the front door. She brought with her a subtle scent of freshly cut flowers. He wanted to throw his arms around her. Instead, he got an armload of packages.

''What's all this?'' he asked as he followed her to the kitchen and placed the groceries on the kitchen table.

''Dinner,'' she announced. ''Sirloin and sauvignon.''

''Oh.'' Disappointment lurked in his voice.

She turned around, an eyebrow arched.

''I got us filets and chardonnay,'' he explained.

She ran the tip of her tongue along her upper lip. ''Great minds think alike.''

He snaked his arms around her waist, his lips a fraction of an inch from hers. ''How about an appetizer?''

''I bought an avocado.''

His lips toyed with hers. "Not exactly what I had in mind."

The kiss was slow and deep. When at last they paused long enough to catch their breath, she muttered, "Are you hungry?"

"Hmm, yes, very." He slid his hands up her back, his upper arms brushing the sides of her breasts. "And you?"

"Ravenous," she murmured, and touched her mouth to his.

IT WAS AFTER EIGHT o'clock by the time Tori arrived home the next morning, once again to change clothes. Her father wasn't there this time and, looking in his bedroom, she noticed his bed hadn't been slept in. He must have spent the night with Lydia, she concluded with a grin.

"Where's Dad?" Tori asked when she reached the office. Lydia, usually so calm and efficient, looked downright harried this morning.

"He's meeting with investors. Apparently word's out that Martin's threatening to condemn our properties as well as Amorado's so he can build public housing."

"Oh, Lord."

Lydia compressed her lips. "Your father's decided to officially kick off Riverbend tomorrow at noon. He's got me working on setting up a signing ceremony with major contractors and builders. He wants the mayor and the city council here like they were when we announced your partnership."

Tori poured herself coffee, wishing it was caffeinated. "Isn't this rushing things? Why so fast?"

"He's afraid any delay will give Martin more time and ammunition to get his agenda approved." Lydia declined an offer to refill her cup. "I don't know what we're going to do if this Amorado property business hasn't been settled by then."

Neither did Tori. Thinking she still had time, she hadn't actually discussed her Riverbend modification idea with Jesse the night before. But while they were preparing dinner, he'd made several allusions to Santa Marta, how it was changing and people were moving out. If she capitalized on his awareness that the barrio was inevitably evolving, perhaps she could convince him to sell.

"When do you expect Dad back?"

"Probably not until lunchtime."

"Is Burton with him?"

"No. He had another meeting to go to. I'm not sure who with, but he said he expected to be back by ten."

"I'm going to call Jesse and ask him to come over here. I want a conference with him and Burton. Just the three of us. Let's plan on ten-thirty. Hopefully, we can get this thing resolved by the time Dad returns."

"I hope so."

Tori thought a moment. Her newly improvised office was too small and cluttered for a comfortable meeting.

"I'm going to use Dad's office, so would you—"

"Of course," Lydia replied before Tori could finish. "I'll have the conference table cleared off and a fresh pot of coffee made. Do you want me to call out for sandwiches?"

"No. Just coffee. And make it strong. Very strong."

JESSE WAS THE FIRST to arrive. He'd been surprised by the invitation but hardly mystified. He knew sooner or later they'd have to deal with the issue of Santa Marta.

His predicament was preposterous. First Carr threat-

ened condemnation, then Martin. Either way his properties seemed doomed. The irony was that in any other
situation he'd be in an enviable position with two competing interests vying for properties that were virtually
worthless except for their locations. The way things
were stacking up now, he would be on the losing side
no matter who won. So would the people of Santa
Marta.

Hazlitt was standing by Lydia's desk, handing her a
sheaf of papers, when Jesse walked in.

"Oh, Mr. Amorado," she greeted him nervously.
"Right on time. I'm afraid there's going to be a slight
delay. Tori had to run over to the newspaper office—"

"She's trying to straighten out some screwup on her
advertising campaign." Hazlitt looked over at Jesse.
"This might be an opportune time for us to talk privately."

Jesse wasn't interested in talking one-on-one with
Hazlitt, but didn't see how he could politely refuse. He
followed the stocky weightlifter to his office. Looking
at the stark black-and-white art on the walls, Jesse concluded the room was as cold as the man. Hazlitt waved
to a black-leather-and-chrome chair, then sat in an
oversize version behind the glass-topped desk.

Hazlitt swiveled toward him and leaned back, lacing
his fingers across his stomach.

"You think you're in a position to kill the Riverbend
project," he began, "and that you can save Santa
Marta. I'm sorry, but you're wrong on both counts,
Amorado."

"You mean because of Henry Martin's plan to build
public housing there?"

"I just had a long talk with Henry," Hazlitt replied.
"He's come to realize the barrio's beyond hope. He

also knows the success of our development is in his own best interest. So he's agreed to support it.''

Jesse couldn't hide his surprise. "He's changed his mind again? He's supporting Riverbend now?"

Hazlitt nodded, pleased with himself. "As I see it, Amorado, you still have two choices—you can sell to us before the construction contracts get signed…or you can be obstinate and get those shacks of yours condemned by the city."

Jesse cursed silently to himself but refused to give this muscle-bound twerp with the Napoleon complex the satisfaction of hearing the expletives.

"We've already made our offer," Hazlitt reminded him. "Frankly, I don't see that you have much choice. You'd do well to get this thing over and done with." He eyed Jesse for a reaction but got none. Showing his first bit of impatience, he added, "Lydia has the paperwork made out. All you have to do is sign."

Tori appeared in the doorway. One look at Jesse was enough for her to sense something was wrong. "What's going on?"

Jesse rose to his feet.

Hazlitt remained seated. "I was just trying to convince your friend here to sign on the dotted line."

"What about Martin's plan to put in public housing?" Jesse asked.

"Actually, I think it was just a tactic to get us talking." Hazlitt looked self-satisfied. "We discussed your situation, too, Amorado. He's not very happy with you at the moment, as you can imagine. But he's willing to put personal feelings aside today, just as I was a couple of days ago."

"I don't understand."

"Didn't Tori tell you? I put up your bail money."

"I thought Carr—"

"Spooner works for Carr Enterprises, but it was my money that bought the bond."

Jesse felt as if he'd just been rammed in the solar plexus. He looked at Tori. "Is that true?"

"Well...a little cash-flow problem. He loaned the money..."

"Look," Hazlitt said as he got up, "why don't I leave you two alone to work out the details. Tori's a partner now. She can speak for the company. There's really no reason we can't get this settled today." Smiling, he left the room.

"I'm sorry," Tori managed to say, then froze at the expression of outrage and disappointment on Jesse's face. "I should have told you."

Jesse rose to his feet. "I came here willing to make concessions, Tori, fully aware my position is that of a spoiler, a role I don't relish." She watched a vein in his temple throb. "I don't take easily to threats and bullying," he continued, "or being played with. Maybe I can't save Santa Marta, but by God, I won't let you get rich at its expense."

"Jesse, wait. You don't understand—" But it was no use.

Dragging in a lungful of air, he glowered at her and walked out of the room.

TORI REMAINED AT THE conference table for several minutes trying to fathom what had just transpired. Confusion soon gave way to anger. Anger at herself for not having been completely honest with Jesse, at Burton...well, for being Burton, and at Jesse for having so little faith in her.

She stepped into the reception area. "When's Dad due back?"

"He called when you were in your meeting. He's having lunch at the country club with Bill Rosenkrantz from the bank. Apparently one of the builders declared bankruptcy. Your father and Bill are reviewing their options."

"Damn, what else can go wrong?" Tori fumed. "Who's gone under?"

"Slater-Grasse."

Tori recognized the name from contracts she'd reviewed as one of several out-of-state custom-home builders. "Well, if there's a silver lining in this dark cloud, it's that they folded now rather than in the middle of construction."

JESSE WENT BACK to the building site he had been overseeing the day before. Hard work, dealing with construction crews and making decisions was what he needed to feel in control again.

The location was a cul-de-sac on the west side of town. His father had bought the lots cheap seven years earlier, confident the city's development was moving in that direction. He was right.

Jesse inspected the workmanship carefully, reviewing progress. But even while he discussed details with the site foreman, he kept seeing the shocked—no, hurt—expression on Tori's face when he walked out of Hazlitt's office that morning.

"Hey, Tony, that's the wrong wallpaper in the master bathroom," he called out as he surveyed the job. "It's supposed to be different from the guest bath. Get it changed."

When that stuffed shirt of a lawyer got him released

from jail, Jesse figured Carr would expect some sort of repayment. But the subject had never been brought up and Jesse had begun to wonder if Tori was right, that Winslow Carr was not the mercenary Jesse thought him to be. Now he knew differently. Carr hadn't demanded his pound of flesh because he wasn't in the position to—he hadn't been the one who paid the bail.

"Tony, whoever did the raised paneling in the family room did a nice job. Let him know I said so. Good work."

But something still didn't sit right. Hazlitt's style was strictly in-your-face, like this morning's meeting. Why had Hazlitt waited so long to use the bail as leverage? The time to make a deal for Jesse to turn over his Santa Marta properties would have been when he was still behind bars.

CHAPTER FOURTEEN

TORI FOLLOWED HER FATHER into the office when he returned from lunch. "Dad, we need to talk."

Winslow moved hurriedly to his desk and started riffling through papers. "I agree. We've got to get this last property issue with Jesse Amorado settled. Today."

"Have you heard the news? Burton's persuaded Martin to support Riverbend."

Her father stood hunched over his desk and looked up at her. "Henry's on our side now?"

Tori wondered why her father didn't seem to be overjoyed by the politician's change of heart.

"That man does more twists and turns than a python. Okay, let's take advantage of it. I want as much media coverage as we can get—with Martin a prominent part of it so he can't change his mind later."

"Everything's all set," she told him. "I've arranged for newspaper articles and ads, and I have calls in to schedule interviews on radio and TV. All I have to do now is get hold of Martin. Lydia said you wanted to kick it off here tomorrow."

Winslow looked up again. "Getting Martin's support is a big plus, but we need to have Jesse on board, too—" he picked up a piece of paper, scanned it and threw it back down "—to show there's no controversy in the community, that everyone's a player. The question now is, can you get him on our side by tomorrow?"

"I think I can. That's what—"

Burton appeared in the doorway, a huge grin on his face.

Winslow stopped what he was doing long enough to address him. "I understand you talked Martin into supporting us. Good work."

"I told you I would." Burton strutted over to a wing chair by the conference area, winking at Tori as he passed. He sat down and crossed one knee over the other. "I heard a rumor that one of our contractors dropped out of the project."

Winslow sank into his chair, exhausted. "Slater-Grasse declared bankruptcy this morning."

"Damn!" Burton said, pounding his fist on the chair arm. "We don't have anyone lined up to replace them, either." He looked at Tori. "Slater-Grasse is a multimillion-dollar corporation. I had no idea they were in any kind of financial trouble."

"Apparently," Winslow said, "they were counting on Riverbend to keep their heads above water." He slanted Tori a grin. "No pun intended."

Tori smiled back, taking it as a good sign that her father still had his sense of humor. She considered a moment, then asked, "Suppose we offer their building contract to Jesse?"

Burton's brows rose. "Give it to Amorado Construction?"

"It's got a couple of advantages," Tori explained. "If we go with Riverbend as currently designed, he'll be in a position to make a lot of money so he can follow through on his Coyote Mesa plans. If we go with the scaled-down version I suggested, he's ideally suited for the lower- and middle-income houses we'd want to build.''

"I always prefer dealing with local companies when I can," Winslow said slowly. He picked up his mechanical pencil and started drumming it on the folders in front of him as he stared blankly at his daughter. "Amorado does good work, Tori, but his outfit's pretty small. I'm not sure he can handle a project this size."

Tori felt a flutter of hope. Neither of them had rejected her suggestion outright. "I don't know if he can, either, Dad. What I do know is that if he accepts the contract, he'll do everything in his power to live up to its provisions."

Her father continued to tap his pencil.

"Give him a chance," she urged. "When Jesse made his Coyote Mesa proposal, he asked us for what amounted to several million dollars in subsidies. It was a bluff, but I'm positive he felt he could handle it if by some remote chance he got it."

"So he was blowing smoke," Burton said, but with a note of admiration rather than censure.

"Let him prove himself."

Burton knitted his brows in thought. "We could start him off small, see how he does and then increase his involvement as he grows. The other advantage is that we will have a full complement of builders present when we sign the contracts tomorrow."

"Knowing Jesse's reputation for hard work and integrity, he might even like this approach better," Winslow said with an approving nod. He turned to his daughter. "Will he go for it?"

"A week ago he probably would have, but after all this talk about condemning his property, getting arrested, and now Burton throwing in his face that he paid the bail…''

"He's still a businessman," Burton observed mildly.

"He's a proud man first," she reminded him. The image of him in his jail-rumpled clothes came instantly to mind. Strange, she thought, that it should be that picture that came to mind when she thought of male pride, a man undaunted by social conventions.

Winslow smiled. "Discuss it with him, Tori. You're both right. He's a businessman and a realist, and at the moment he's in a no-win situation. This might be his way out.''

IT WASN'T UNTIL nearly two hours later, as she was gathering her notes, that Tori finally figured it out.

Lydia and her father had already left for the day. She tapped on Burton's door and, without waiting for a response, walked in. Planting herself comfortably in the chair across from him, she asked, "When did you say you talked Martin into sanctioning the Riverbend project?''

Burton smiled. "I don't think I said.''

"You didn't talk to him at all, did you?''

The smirk on Burton's face answered her question. "I called Martin's office to invite him to the ceremony tomorrow and found out he isn't in town and isn't expected back for at least two more days. They wouldn't say where he was, but Evie Crump over at the Chamber told me he's been hiding out on a friend's ranch until his broken nose heals.''

Tori straightened out the hem of her yellow cotton skirt. "If I can find out Martin hasn't been in town since the day before yesterday, don't you think Jesse can, too?''

"The question is, will he? Are you going to tell him?"

"I'm not going to lie to him, Burton. I'm no good at telling lies. They always come back to haunt me. Besides, I have neither the need nor desire to lie to him."

Burton's features softened, reminding her of the man she'd once thought she loved, a man who could be tender and solicitous. "I know that, Tori. That's why I've played the heavy on this one. You're in love with him. Anyone can see that. I'm glad for you. I really am. Unfortunately, that's not very good for business." He chuckled. "Well, for some people it is. But I know you too well to think you would use it as a weapon."

He arched back in his chair, took a deep breath and exhaled, obviously content.

"Business isn't like chess, Tori. In chess all the moves are out in the open and you have only to recognize them. Business is more like poker, where you only see some of the cards and you win mostly by ruse. My tactics may seem underhanded to you. But remember, the other side has the same weapons available. It's a matter of who uses them better."

He'd used the same analogy years before, when he was aglow from having just been made her father's partner. At the time, they'd seemed like words of wisdom.

"You admitted yourself that Amorado didn't really expect us to go along with his Coyote Mesa demands," Burton noted. "It was a tactic, Tori, and a good one. I'm willing to bet he goes for your general contractor offer. He'd be a fool not to."

"So you were bluffing about Martin supporting Riverbend and threatening to condemn Jesse's properties if he doesn't cooperate with us." Tori frowned.

Burton spread his hands, palms up. "I don't know if Martin really meant what he said to Amorado about condemning our properties to build public housing or if Jesse made that up, too. I do know two things. Martin's power is in the Mexican community. He'd think twice about taking on Carr Enterprises if he didn't have Amorado to use as a wedge."

Burton reached out and toyed with the sterling silver letter opener on his desk, his words confident and sincere. "Whether Martin puts in public housing or we develop Riverbend, Tori, the barrio is gone. Amorado is smart enough to realize that. Once he comes to his senses and acknowledges that, I'm sure he'll join us. You see, I think he's as interested in making money as the rest of us. If he wants to develop Coyote Mesa, fine. I certainly have no objection. Who knows, we might even be able to make a deal with him on that project, too."

Tori left shaking her head. All this male posturing seemed such a waste of time and energy.

She went back to her office and called Jesse at home. His answering machine picked up. She hesitated about leaving a message, not quite sure what to say. "Jesse, I'm sorry about the way things went this morning. I'll explain it all when I see you." She paused and was about to add, "I love you," when the machine clicked off.

Burton stuck his head in her office doorway a few minutes later. "Go to him, Tori," he said with the encouragement of a sympathetic friend. "Tell him whatever you think is best for both of us. But don't take too long." He smiled. "I'll see you in the morning."

She wished him a good-night, promised she'd lock up and returned to her office. There was plenty of work to do and even more thinking. Had she misjudged Burton? Was she naive about the business world? There was no doubt Burton had been using her. Was Jesse? She pulled several files from Lydia's filing cabinet.

Her mind was again on Jesse as she finished the last bitter cup of hours-old coffee, washed out the pot, turned the key in the front door and strolled to her car. The sun was setting, and the air, still warm from the day's heat, gathered around her like Jesse's caress.

The Corvette, locked in the sun all day, would be stifling. Luckily it was only a short drive to Jesse's house.

No steak tonight, she decided as she approached the vehicle in the private parking space behind the building. *I wonder if great minds will think alike again. I'll stop off at the deli and pick up a roast chicken and salad.*

She was just leaning over to unlock the door when she caught the glimpse of a shadow behind her. She started to turn when an arm came down and struck her on the head.

JESSE FOUND TWO MESSAGES on his answering machine when he arrived home. The first was from Lupe, calling from San Antonio to say they'd arrived without mishap. He could hear the children laughing and yelling in the background and his mother, closer to Lupe, reminding her to make sure Jesse had Anita's telephone number. "Relax, Ma," he said to the tiny speaker. "Nothing's going to happen."

The second was the message from Tori. He knew

she couldn't have been part of that stupid charade this morning. They would get the whole ridiculous business straightened out this evening and then they'd make love...? Or maybe they should make love first.

He'd almost proposed to her in bed that morning, but something in her eyes told him it wasn't time yet. He knew she loved him. She'd whispered it in his ear often enough, and no woman could give herself to a man the way she did without loving him.

As he moved through the house, setting things out for the barbecued chicken dinner he'd brought home, his mind kept reliving the night before. While his hands were putting out soft, fresh bath towels, his mind fantasized about the supple texture of her skin, the full, firm warmth of her breasts. His body responded even now to the memory of her caressing him, of her soft, wet mouth enflaming him.

He spent some of the time waiting for her on the back porch refinishing a piece of old furniture he'd picked up in a junk store several months earlier. The small writing table would fit perfectly in the hallway.

The work took concentration, but by ten o'clock he was hovering over the telephone, getting ready to call her house to ask where she was, why she wasn't in his arms, in his bed. First, needing the reassurance of hearing her voice, he replayed the tape. With a sinking feeling in the pit of his stomach, he replayed it a second time. *Fool*, he chastised himself. *She never said she was coming tonight, only that she would explain things when she saw you.* She'd said it might be better if they spent some time away from each other and reevaluated their relationship objectively. Dispassion was the last thing he was feeling, however, when he finally crawled into bed well after midnight.

TORI'S FIRST CONSCIOUS thought was that she had a
hangover. She'd only had one in her life, back when
she was in high school. A friend had gotten hold of a
bottle of sweet cherry schnapps. The cheerfully red liquor was delicious with 7UP, but the aftereffects had
been so miserable she swore off alcohol completely
throughout the rest of high school and had never been
more than a light social drinker since.

Now she felt even worse. Her head throbbed as if a
pile driver were doing a slow tattoo on the back of her
skull. Her cramped muscles ached and her mouth tasted
like a dirty rag. It took another minute to realize the
cottony taste was just that—a piece of cloth. Awareness
made her retch. Instinctively she tried to remove it,
only to discover her hands were tied behind her.

Then it all came tumbling back. The walk out to the
car. Bending to unlock it. The arm coming down. She'd
caught a glimpse of it just before it struck her. There
was something about that arm. But what was it?

She blinked. *I'm not blindfolded.* Total darkness was
extremely rare, yet she could see absolutely nothing.
Not an outline, not a shadow. A new terror gripped
her. Had the blow on the head rendered her blind?

In near panic, she struggled to orient herself. The
room, or wherever she was, smelled dank and musty.
Something light and feathery skittered in short spurts
along the length of her bare arm. In the blackness she
could only picture a large Texas tarantula. The cry that
welled up inside her was stifled only by the soggy gag
in her mouth. Tears slithered across the bridge of her
nose and down the side of her face.

She forced herself to regain control, to breathe
slowly, willed her heart to stop its vicious pounding.
She listened...and heard nothing. At first. Gradually

tiny sounds began to eke their way into her consciousness. Night sounds. Delicate scratching noises. Crickets. The muffled hoot of an owl. A distant low rumble. But the cool earthy darkness was impenetrable.

My God, I've been buried alive!

JESSE DRAGGED HIMSELF out of bed the next morning before the alarm went off, showered, shaved, dressed and fixed a bowl of cold cereal with a banana. It didn't make up for the dinner he hadn't eaten the night before, but that didn't matter. He didn't have much of an appetite.

He picked up the phone to dial Carr Enterprises, then reconsidered. If he was going to be the one to say uncle, he wasn't going to be satisfied with only hearing her voice. He needed to see her. He locked the house and went to his truck.

As he drove past the front of Amorado Construction he looked for a bright red Corvette. It wasn't there.

Did you expect her to be waiting? She wanted time away from you, so why would you think she'd be here now? Because I need her. Because I love her.

He pulled down the narrow alley to his private parking spot in back.

Does she have any idea how much I need her? Doesn't she know the nights we've spent together have been the most wonderful I've ever experienced, that I want to spend every waking and sleeping moment of my life with her?

He fixed himself a cup of coffee, trying not to remember their first meeting and the allure of her perfect body as she sat across from him. He tried to ignore the image of her delft blue eyes gazing at him, challenging him, tantalizing him. The doorbell jingled, and he jumped out of his chair so quickly he almost tipped over the steaming hot drink.

He bounded through the narrow passage to the front reception area, ready to throw his arms around her, taste her lips, feel her body pressed against his. It wasn't Tori.

"You sold out to them!" Espy accused before he could even say hello.

"What?" he challenged, making no effort to hide his impatience. He wasn't in the mood for games this morning, especially with Esperanza Mendez.

"It's on the local radio and TV stations. Carr Enterprises is making a special announcement today at noon. It's very mysterious, but from the sounds of it, they're going ahead with Riverbend. You sold out to them," she repeated.

"I don't think you have any right to question my decisions, Espy," he snapped. "But no, I didn't sell. On the contrary, it seems your patron is the one who's sold out."

Her chin snapped up. "What are you talking about?"

"Martin is backing Riverbend now."

"I don't believe it."

"Believe what you like."

"Henry would never do that."

Jesse laughed. "I hate to disillusion you about your benefactor, Espy, but he's been using you, too."

Confusion and anger tightened her features. She looked as if she were about to fire off some biting remark, so he beat her to the punch with a question. "You say they're making this announcement about Riverbend at noon today. Where? At Carr's offices?"

"That's what the radio said."

"Then that's where I'm going." He strode to the front door and opened it for her.

She gawked at the brusque dismissal, started across the threshold, then stopped, looked him in the eye, raised her hand and stroked his smooth cheek. *"Pobre muchacho,"* she said, her tone not so much mocking as pitying. "You're being suckered bad and you don't even know it."

He stood there, dumbstruck, and watched her slither gracefully into her aging sedan and drive away.

TORI DIDN'T KNOW how long she'd been asleep. Passed out was probably more like it, considering how her head still ached. Whichever it was, she woke with a feeling of gloom and an awareness of the smell of fresh earth and the sour stench of decaying vegetation.

Jesse, where are you? I need you!

If only she could see something. Maybe it would give her a hint of where she was. Tears of utter frustration welled again in her eyes. She was a prisoner and she couldn't do anything about it.

But you can, said a little inner voice. *Keep your head. That's one of the key lessons you were taught in the military. Don't panic.*

Methodically she stretched her constricted muscles. Her legs were bound just above the ankles and below the knees, but she could still flex them. She managed to turn herself over to relieve the pressure on her right side.

Now, how extensive is my cell? Judging from the dampness and smells, I'm definitely underground, but not exactly buried. If I can sit up, I can explore my space, maybe find something useful.

The thought of falling off a ledge or platform, not

to mention meeting other creeping, crawling creatures, made her cautious.

The rag in her mouth was beginning to make her sick again, soaked as it was with the stale taste of her own saliva. She tried to catch the strip of cloth that was tied behind her head with her shoulder, but it did no good. She had to concentrate on other things—get her mind off it.

She thrashed around, attempting to get into a sitting position. Her joints were stiff and achy from the damp cold. She shifted and strained clumsily and was almost in a sitting position when she overbalanced and toppled backward, striking her head on the stone wall.

WINSLOW PACED the oriental carpet in the middle of his office. "Where is she?" he demanded of Lydia, who was standing at the edge of his desk, phone in hand. She'd been answering calls all morning from the curious and making outgoing calls trying to find Tori.

"Calm down, Win, we'll find her."

"Something has happened to her. I know it. She's been in an accident somewhere."

"I've checked with the police and the hospitals. There's no record of her being in an accident. She's fine, I'm sure," Lydia said, though she wasn't nearly as convinced as she tried to sound.

"Where's Burton?"

"He's over at the mayor's office. He should be back in a few minutes. We've got time, Win," she said, looking at the ornate, brass-faced mantel clock on the credenza. "Nearly two hours before we go on the air. Tori did a great job of setting everything up. She gave the caterers very specific instructions about what she wanted," Lydia rambled on. "I don't have to do a thing. A very organized young lady, your daughter." She smiled at him, but he didn't smile back. "Relax, Win, everything's running smoothly."

"Except that Tori's not here. Something must be terribly wrong for her to stay away. Have you checked the radio station?"

"And the TV stations," Lydia told him again. "She hasn't been there yet today, but they've got the spots she worked out with them all set for broadcast. We can go on without her if we have to."

"I don't want to go on without her."

He continued to interrogate Lydia while she made more phone calls. Burton came in a few minutes later and Winslow practically pounced on him. "Have you seem Tori?"

"No. Not today. She's probably at the TV station. Wasn't she going to do an interview on 'Coyote Springs in the Morning'?"

"That was over hours ago and she wasn't on it."

"Maybe she's taping it for tomorrow."

"I've checked," Lydia interjected. "The interview is scheduled for tomorrow, but live, not taped. They haven't seen her today."

"Did you check Amorado's place?"

There was a slight hesitation on Lydia's part, but she quickly realized there was no point in denying the obvious. "Yes," she said. "No one's there."

"Or maybe they're just too busy to answer the phone," Burton quipped lightly.

"That's enough!" Winslow exploded. "What my daughter does in her private life is none of your concern."

Burton looked startled, but he answered calmly, "I

never said it was. Hey, take it easy, Win. What's the big deal?''

"We're about to publicly announce a multimillion-dollar contract and my daughter is nowhere to be found. That bothers me, and it seems to me it should bother you. She's your partner, too.''

"That was your doing, Win, not mine.''

Burton slid into one of the visitor's chairs and stretched out his legs in a casual lounging posture. Winslow's mouth fell open.

"I tried to tell you she wasn't ready for this. The business world isn't like the military. You can't order compliance. I don't like saying I told you so, but this whole project was going along just fine when I was handling it. I had it down to one property owner who didn't have a snowball's chance in hell of holding out against us. Then Tori comes along and tries to play the wheeler-dealer. Sorry, Win, but she's out of her league. I know how to handle these people. She doesn't.''

He straightened up, pulled his legs back under him and leaned slightly forward on his elbows. "I can tell you why she's not here. Because she was supposed to get Amorado to sign with Riverbend and she's failed. Instead of dealing with him on a professional basis, she's chosen to sleep with the competition.''

Winslow sprang from his chair. "How dare you?'' he sputtered, his hands visibly shaking. "You have no right to talk about Tori that way.''

Burton rose slowly to his feet. "I'm sorry, my friend, but I think it's time you woke up and smelled the coffee. Riverbend hinges on our having all the property in the barrio. If you'd left it to me, like you've always done, we'd have Amorado's signature on a sales contract by now. But you chose to give the job to your daughter. Well, it hasn't worked, and now she's afraid to face you because of it. That's why she's not here.''

Winslow's face grew red, even redder than it had been, but it was Lydia who erupted.

"Burt Hazlitt, you're despicable! It was you who screwed up the deal. You're the one who turned Jesse—and everyone else in Santa Marta—against us by being such a penny-pincher on maintenance. If you were as smart a businessman as you think you are, you would have approached Jesse first, not last.''

"Mrs. Anderson," Burton said sharply, "stay out of this. You may be sleeping with your boss, but you're still an employee. You don't give me orders.''

"Stop!" Winslow bellowed, stunning them both. The veins in his neck bulged purple. "Burton, you owe Lydia an apology. Now.''

Burton clamped his jaw and spun around toward the conference table and the big map with the little colored pins on it. He stood motionless, the back of his neck crimson. A few moments passed. He took a deep breath, then turned slowly and faced them, his expression calm, closed. "You're right," he said contritely. "I apologize to both of you. My remarks were out of line. I guess the past few weeks have me on edge, too. I'm sorry.''

Winslow was not appeased. "Tori is neither a failure nor a coward, Burton. You know that as well as I do. She's not here because something has happened to her.''

Burton shook his head slowly, apparently still not convinced. "Have you checked with the cops and the hospitals?''

"Yes," Winslow snarled as he massaged his left forearm with his right hand.

"Well, I'm sure she's perfectly okay. Probably just needs some time to sort things out. This is her show. She'll turn up when she's ready."

CHAPTER FIFTEEN

A CADET LEADER WAS giving a lecture. Except it wasn't a cadet. It was Jesse Amorado, resplendent in military mess dress. Medals blazoned his chest; he was briefing a class. His even white teeth glowed and matched the spotless gloves covering his hands. His intense brown eyes were focused exclusively on her.

"The mind can play tricks on a hostage. Sometimes it's because of fear, sensory deprivation, boredom. Sometimes it's a coping technique, an escape valve from the horrors of the situation."

He paced in front of a giant military map of Coyote Springs, the sharp creases of his formal uniform pants—she noticed they were starched jeans—emphasized the muscularity of his long legs.

"The big question," he continued, "is, of course, who is responsible for this and what does that person hope to gain. Are you being held for ransom? By whom? And why? Logic tells you it has to have something to do with Riverbend. That could only mean one person.

"Is that person contacting your father at this very moment, telling him the price of his daughter's safe return is to abandon his venture? Your father will comply without a fight because he loves you, and that will mean his ruin. The end of Carr Enterprises."

It took several seconds for Tori to regain full consciousness and remember where she was.

But why was she here? Who was doing this to her? What did they hope to gain? If they were going to kill her, why hadn't they done so already? If they were going to let her go, didn't they know she and her father and Jesse wouldn't rest until they found out who had done this?

IT WAS A FEW MINUTES before twelve when Jesse pulled up at Carr Enterprises. The parking lot was crowded with cars, trucks and at least one limousine. Jesse squeezed his truck into a space between two media minivans.

The reception area of the real estate firm was even more congested. A long table was set up just inside the doorway with a variety of fancy finger foods, a champagne fountain and two bowls of colorful nonalcoholic punch. People were packed into the confined space, the festive cacophony of voices overwhelming. Jesse recognized many of the faces, dignitaries from the city council, county officials and prominent businessmen, some of whom greeted him by name.

"Jesse Amorado? I didn't expect to see you here." He felt a hearty slap on the back and turned to see Garnet Price grinning at him. Garnet was a feature reporter on the local TV station and was being touted as the heir apparent to the retiring news director. Despite his diminutive stature, he was reputed to be quite a ladies' man and was always the life of the party. His Bambi brown eyes suggested he'd already tasted liberally of the champagne.

"Why not?" Jesse asked, trying to be as friendly as

he could. He didn't dislike Garnet, but at the moment he found him tiresome.

"Didn't think you were an advocate of Riverbend."

"Times are changing," Jesse said diplomatically.

"So you sold to Carr after all?"

"I didn't say that."

Garnet laughed. "Ah, holding out for better money. I don't blame you. There's a bunch to be made on this deal."

"Have you seen Miss Carr?"

"The lovely Tori? She's not in my corral." Garnet laughed again. "Unfortunately. I wish she were. But from what I've heard, you've roped her into yours."

Jesse cast a withering look at the little man.

"Hey, chill out, Jess. I didn't mean any offense. Tori Carr is beautiful, charming and sophisticated." He sipped his champagne. "Obviously not my type."

Jesse smiled in apology and agreement. "Obviously."

"I'd say you're a lucky man." Garnet winked and moved off to mix with some of the other guests.

Jesse didn't see Tori anywhere, but he did see bright lights and cameras being set up in Carr's office. She was probably in there with her father and Burton, he thought, going over final details for their presentation, though he would have expected to see her out here meeting and greeting people. Maybe things weren't going as smoothly as they appeared.

He edged his way over to the reception desk, where Lydia was trying to talk to someone on the phone. The woman looked unhappy. Her face brightened perceptibly, however, when she saw him. She motioned him closer and hung up the phone.

"I'm glad you've shown up. Where's Tori?" she asked in anxious relief.

"I haven't seen her. Isn't she with her father?"

"We thought she was with you."

Winslow Carr poked his head out of his office. "Thank God you're here!" he exclaimed, and blindly offered Jesse his hand, clammy with perspiration, while he craned his neck, searching the crowd. "Where's Tori?"

"I was just going to ask you the same thing."

"She hasn't been in this morning. She was with you last night, wasn't she?"

Jesse's insides felt suddenly hollow. "I haven't seen her since our meeting here yesterday."

Winslow Carr's already pale complexion went gray. He flexed his left hand. "I assumed she'd gone to your house again."

Jesse didn't miss the word *again*, nor did he sense disapproval, only profound worry. Then the full implication of what Carr said hit him. "She didn't come home last night?"

Carr shook his head. "When I left here last evening, she was going over the final details of a business proposal she was going to make to you. When she didn't come home, I assumed—"

"That was the last time you saw her?"

Carr was more flustered now, his right hand trembling as he ran it through his hair. "Well, if she didn't stay with you, and she didn't come home—"

"Where the hell is she?"

"What's up?"

They both turned to see Hazlitt approach. Carr signaled them into his partner's office, closing the door behind them.

"We still can't find Tori," he told Burton. "She wasn't with Jesse and he doesn't know where she is. I'm really worried about her now. She seems to have disappeared."

Hazlitt's brow furrowed. "Could she have spent the night with someone else?" He looked at Jesse. "How about with your friend Esperanza?"

Jesse shook his head. "I saw Espy this morning. She didn't say anything." He remembered her taunt about him selling out. "She would have if Tori had been with her."

"So where is she?" Carr shouted.

Hazlitt raised his shoulders in a shrug, then filled himself a glass of water from the carafe on the corner of his desk. "Did she have someplace she needed to go?"

"Where?" Carr demanded angrily, losing the last vestige of patience with his partner. "We even checked the airport to see if she went flying. She didn't. Besides, what could possibly be more important than being here? This is the biggest thing that's ever happened to Carr Enterprises."

The anguish in the man's entreaty disturbed Jesse even more than the words themselves. Carr was scared.

HAVING HER HANDS TIED behind her back was becoming excruciatingly painful. Cramped muscles screamed, not only in her arms, but in her back, as well.

Then she realized something. Her hands weren't tied with rope. It was something less bulky, less abrasive. She struggled against it, but to no avail. It twisted with her movements, stayed stuck to her, so that even when she spread her wrists a little, as soon as she took the pressure off, it rebounded. Tape! What kind? Masking tape would tear easily. Duct tape. Flexible and stronger.

The chilly stillness of stale air was making her shiver. She dreaded activity, yet yearned for it. *I've got to keep moving, keep active.* Once her muscles began to warm, she found it exhilarating, a new act of defiance.

She strained against the tape binding her wrists. Again there was the sensation of it stretching. *Maybe if I do it often enough, it'll lose its elasticity. Or will I run out of energy before it does?*

Aside from being bound hand and foot, she wasn't restrained in any other way. Time to further explore her space. How much was there? How wide, how tall was this "grave"? An icy shaft of pain shot up her spine as she writhed to get her bound legs under her to get into a kneeling position.

It was when she shifted around again to relieve some of the pressure on her elbow that she thought she heard it. A distant sound, one that was easily lost in the dead acoustics of her own personal black hole. She couldn't even be sure she'd heard it. She struggled all the more, if only to keep her body active, her circulation moving.

There it is again, closer, more distinct. Thunder. A storm moving in.

IT WASN'T TILL HE REACHED the parking lot and didn't see Martin's Cadillac that Jesse began to put the pieces together and comprehend the meaning of Espy's parting gibe. He was being toyed with, manipulated, but maybe not by Martin.

He went back inside and found Garnet Price.

"Is Martin here?"

Garnet chuckled. "I'm not even sure he's recovered

from the pounding you gave him. He's certainly not showing himself in public. Not with two black eyes from a broken nose. Word has it he's holed up on a friend's ranch in another county. Anyway, he's still adamantly opposed to Riverbend.''

"Hasn't changed his mind, huh?"

Garnet threw back the last swallow of his champagne. "His staff would probably like him to." He laughed as he moved toward the buffet table. "But then they don't have to run for reelection."

So they didn't have Martin in their pocket. Burton had only said that to force Jesse's hand. Did Tori know the truth? Was she part of the scheme to bring him onside?

The words on the taped message echoed though his head. "I'll explain everything when I see you." Explain what? That his bullheadedness had put her in an untenable position, forcing her to choose between her father and him, and that she was going to stand by her father? The pity, he mused sadly, was that he understood and respected that decision. Family loyalty came first.

TORI WOKE to a sharp crash, a clap of doom. It frightened her that she had fallen asleep again. *Am I so weak that a few minutes of struggle exhausts me? And my vision. I still can't see anything. Am I really blind?*

Then she heard it. Drip. Drip. Drip. Faster. Faster.

It was raining. Water was coming in, filling her prison.

Thunder grumbled continuously now, deep reverberations that shook the ground and compressed the air, turning her cell into a drum.

She forced herself to think logically. Summer rains

didn't last long. But that didn't mean the flow of water wouldn't. Flash floods were often at their most devastating when it wasn't even raining.

Tori's skin burned where she kept pulling on the sticky tape binding her wrists. *It doesn't matter. I'm going to get myself out of here.* Slowly, very slowly, the spread between her hands was increasing. *Yes, damn it. I'll get myself free. I just have to keep working at it.*

But the strain on her restricted muscles was becoming more and more torturous. *I need to rest, need to regain my stamina.* She let her tensed posture slump. The momentary relief felt wonderful. *I'll just give myself a few minutes' respite.*

BURTON SAT UPRIGHT in his high-backed executive chair opposite his senior partner and spoke with a firmness usually reserved for negotiations with contractors and competitors. He often achieved his goals not by compromise, but by being tough and unbending. Winslow had always considered his obstinacy an asset. He'd never expected to be at the receiving end of it.

"I don't know where Tori is, Win. But I know one thing. Unless we announce the plans for Riverbend in a couple of minutes, whether she's here or not, the project's going to be lost, this business is going to be ruined and we're going to go bust. Everything you and I have been working for will go down the drain."

He got up and leaned across the desk. "If that happens, Win, I'm going to sue you for breach of faith for whatever you might have left. I haven't worked my ass off for fifteen years, doing your bidding, taking care of your properties, working the deals and details, to have you throw it away because you can't find your precious daughter. Now, I think we'd better get out there and do our job. Our public is waiting."

Burton moved toward the door and opened it, only to find Jesse standing there, his knuckles raised to knock. Burton stepped back dramatically, allowing Jesse a chance to slip into the room. He closed the heavy paneled door behind him to block out the hubbub outside.

Jesse faced Hazlitt. "You never convinced Martin to join you on Riverbend. He isn't even in Coyote Springs."

Hazlitt's smirk was all the answer Jesse needed. The temptation to punch out the bastard the way he had Martin was overwhelming. There would be a moment of blessed satisfaction in doing it, but experience proved it would be unproductive. He'd humiliated himself and his family once already by lack of self-control. He wouldn't do it again.

"Tori knew all about it," Hazlitt replied smugly, to reinforce any suspicion Jesse might have had that he was the victim of a conspiracy to get his property. "In fact, it was her idea. Now, if you'll excuse me." He bulldozed past Jesse.

"No!" Carr called after Hazlitt as he bumped into Lydia, almost knocking her down. She caught her balance and looked after him, then turned her attention back to her boss.

"Win," she said, "it's nearly twelve o'clock and Tori still isn't here. Do we go on without her? What do we tell all those people. Win? What's the matter? *Win!*" she screamed.

Winslow Carr was slumped crookedly in his chair, his left arm dangling over its edge, his right arm thrown across his chest. His face was beet red, his features contorted in pain. Thick beads of sweat were poised on his forehead.

Jesse ran to his side. He'd seen this happen before. "Call 911," he shouted to Lydia. "He's having a heart attack. Hurry."

"Oh, God," Lydia cried, and raced to the phone on the desk.

Jesse loosened Carr's tie and prayed—he wasn't sure how silently—that this time the man could be saved. Three years before, Jesse's father had died of a heart attack, died in his arms. "Win, try to relax. Breathe slowly. Hang on. We'll have an ambulance here in a minute."

In the background, though it was barely a few feet away, Jesse heard Lydia fighting to keep calm as she relayed information back and forth between him and the emergency dispatcher. With every exchange, she added, "Please hurry." Stretching the stricken man out on the oriental carpet, Jesse wondered for the millionth time if his father might have survived if he could have gotten him medical help more quickly.

"You've got to find her," Winslow cried in painful gasps that reminded Jesse of his father's dying injunction to take care of his mother and the family.

"I'll find her," Jesse promised. "I swear to you, I'll find her."

THE RAIN WAS making puddles now, and pooling around her. The water rippled when she moved, splashed against her waist. If she fell asleep again and slumped over, she might not have the strength or dexterity to get her head above the rising tide. Awareness brought new terror. She couldn't rest now, couldn't give in to the seduction of sweet repose and dreams of

Jesse holding her in his arms, stroking her skin, murmuring love's inspiring words in her ear. To sleep now might mean drowning in a foot of water.

Jesse, are you looking for me? Do you even know I'm missing? Surely he had expected her last evening after the nights they'd spent together. *What are you doing now? Did you call me at home to see if I was there? Have you spoken to my dad?*

She pulled violently against the tape on her wrists. How long had she been unconscious? Or…was this a trick her mind was playing on her? But the bands that held her weren't imaginary. She tugged harder and might have given up if she hadn't felt the slight tear.

The bonds gave a little more, and she knew she was making progress. It was slow but enough to spur her on. Just a few more tugs and twists. Despite the damp coolness around her, she could feel the sweat on her face stinging her eyes. *No matter. I'm going to get out of this hellhole…if I don't drown first.*

"I'M GOING WITH YOU," Lydia announced to the paramedics who'd come in response to the 911 call.

"It would be better if you didn't, ma'am," the young man said over his shoulder as he adjusted an oxygen mask on his patient.

"I have to," she insisted, her voice nearly breaking.

Jesse moved behind her and placed his hands lightly on her shoulders. She leaned against him. He could feel her trembling.

"Let them take him," he said quietly. "They'll need all the room in the ambulance they can get. You'd be in the way. I'll drive you to the hospital."

She turned toward him, tears coursing down her cheeks. "But I—"

"Shh," he intoned sympathetically, and wrapped an arm around her to quell her shaking. "He's in good hands. Give them space to do their jobs."

"Ready?" the paramedic asked his burly assistant. "On my count. One, two, three." With one sure and steady motion they lifted their charge onto a portable gurney, placed the small oxygen tank between his knees, strapped him down, then raised the gurney on its accordion legs.

The only way out was through the reception area, which was bursting with people. The deafening hubbub of a few minutes earlier had diminished to a tense murmur when the paramedics arrived. Now, as the deathly pale figure of Winslow Carr was being moved along the corridor, the only sounds were of cameras clicking and camcorders whirring. Flashbulbs blinked like streaks of jagged lightning.

"Is he dead?" Jesse heard someone whisper as they passed by.

"Nah," someone else responded in the same hushed tone. "They'd have his face covered if he was dead."

"Where's his daughter?" another person asked. "I thought she was supposed to be here."

TORI STRUGGLED against the last sinew of tape lashing her wrists. A spasm of pain, sharp as a knife blade, burned into her shoulder when her left arm sprang away from her body. Her hands were free! The muscles in her arms shrieked as she flexed them. Painfully, for her bones and ligaments seemed fossilized by the enforced inactivity, she untied the foul gag in her mouth. Removing it made her retch. She worked her jaw, then took a long, deep breath, exhaling more slowly. *Control. Keep under control.*

She set about freeing herself from the rest of her bindings. Her hands were reluctant to work. It took several minutes to tear the tape holding her legs together. She tried to stand. Her head swam. The darkness compounded her dizziness, bringing on a sudden jolt of nausea.

The only sound was of rain pelting the wood above. She moved slowly, stretching her arms to gauge the dimensions of this horrible place. Four walls of smooth round stones. River rocks? In a chamber perhaps six feet by twelve. There was a narrow wooden staircase at one end. *So I'm not in a grave but some kind of cellar. A cellar near a river.* She knew of only one such place. The Amorado ranch.

JESSE AND LYDIA RACED into the hospital emergency room.

"He's been taken to a treatment room," was all the harried nurse behind the counter could tell them.

"Where will he go from there?" Jesse asked.

"They're evaluating his EKG," she said, "the one that was transmitted from the ambulance. Based on that, they'll probably take him to the cardiac care unit. We'll let you know as soon as we can," she said as she handed a chart to another nurse and ordered a paramedic to put the latest arrival in room number six. "There's a waiting area just over there," she informed them. "Someone will be with you in a few minutes." Then she charged off down the corridor.

At least he wasn't dead, Jesse thought, and from the expression on Lydia's face guessed she was thinking the same thing. He escorted her to a small square room. Several people were scattered around it, some paging mechanically through magazines, others staring blankly into space.

No one was paying attention to the television mounted on an overhead platform in the corner of the room. The sound was turned down, but the picture was clear, a news shot of the outside of Carr Enterprises. Jesse reached up and adjusted the volume.

"...the most ambitious residential development in Coyote Springs in recent memory. Less than an hour ago, only minutes before they were scheduled to announce a multimillion-dollar contract with construction companies, suppliers and major investors, Winslow Carr, founder and senior partner of Carr Enterprises, suffered what is believed to have been a heart attack. He was taken by ambulance to Coyote Springs Memorial Hospital. At this time, hospital spokesmen are saying only that he is in stable but guarded condition...."

"Whatever that means," Lydia commented contemptuously.

"...conceived several years ago by Carr Enterprises when they began buying up vast holdings in Santa Marta. The old Mexican quarter, commonly known as the barrio, has been deteriorating for some time, and Carr and his partner began developing plans to replace it with a modern, carefully planned community...."

"No mention of Tori," Jesse noted.

"Strange, isn't it? I wonder if Burt asked them not to mention her."

"His partner for the last ten years, Burton Hazlitt, delayed the ceremony that would kick off the Riverbend project until he received word that Carr was stable and making progress. He then decided to exercise his partner's proxy and proceed with signing contracts with several major construction and building companies, saying his longtime business associate and good friend would want him to go on...."

"That son of a bitch," Lydia muttered softly. "That son of a bitch."

TORI MOVED OVER to the narrow wooden stairs. They seemed solid enough when she placed her foot on the first step. She put her hand above her head, felt rough-cut boards of what she supposed—hoped—was the trapdoor out of this dungeon. Pushing up, she felt a tiny bit of give, mostly from the resilience of the sodden wood, not its weakness.

She ran her hands along the edges of the door. On her left were four projections, which she quickly figured out were nuts on the ends of bolts. A hinge. Which meant the door opened on her right.

Summoning a reserve of strength, she applied pressure in the right corner and almost fell over. Light! She'd seen light. Its whiteness was painful and forced her to blink. *I'm not blind. I can see!* Her pulse quickened with a joy she would have thought unimaginable in this horrible place.

The pounding in her head wasn't important now. She pushed harder to get another glimpse of daylight. Glorious daylight.

Suddenly the step she was standing on made a splintering sound. Before she could react, the board under her snapped. Her knees slammed against the stair above. She tripped on the lower step and tumbled backward.

CHAPTER SIXTEEN

JESSE REDUCED THE VOLUME on the TV when the news bulletin was over and a soap opera resumed. He turned in time to see the sheriff come into the room and go directly to Lydia.

"How is he?" Rudy Kraus held out his hands, which she took greedily. "They said on the radio he had a heart attack."

She nodded, her eyes brimming. "No word yet, but I think it's pretty serious."

"Where's Tori? I heard you called down to the station asking about her."

"We can't find her, Rudy."

"Where have you checked?"

"Everywhere I could think of. The businesses we deal with. Her friends. Even the airport. Nobody's seen her."

Kraus looked skeptical. "Who saw her last and when?"

Lydia toyed with the rings on her fingers. "Win and I left the office a little after five yesterday. She said she had some details she wanted to work out before she quit for the day."

"Where was she going from there?"

"We assumed to see Jesse. She's been discussing some property issues with him and thought she'd worked out a solution."

Kraus looked at Jesse. "Did she go to your place?"

"No. I had a message from her on my answering machine. She said she wanted to talk to me, and I expected her to stop by, but she never did."

"Weren't you worried when she didn't show up?"

Let down, disappointed, Jesse thought. "Her message only said she wanted to discuss matters when she saw me. She didn't specify a time or place. When she didn't show up, I figured we'd see each other today."

Kraus nodded and turned back to Lydia. "So you and Win were the last ones to see her. Was she all right when you left her?"

"She was fine. But...no, we weren't the last ones out. Burt was still there. He must have left a few minutes later, though, because he called us from the country club to say they were auditioning a new dance band and wanted to know if we would have dinner with him. We declined," she added. "Win was too tired." She put a hankie to her nose.

"What were Tori's plans for today?"

"We had the Riverbend contract signing set up for noon. When she didn't show up at nine, I supervised the catering. I figured she'd gone over to see Henry Martin."

"Martin?" Jesse interrupted. "He's not even in town. Why would she go to see him?"

Lydia raised a delicate brow. "To invite him to the signing. She tried to call him yesterday, right after you came to the office. But he wasn't in. When she didn't show up this morning, I figured she'd stopped over to see him on her way into work. But by ten-thirty, I was getting worried, so I called Martin's office. They said they hadn't see her."

"What did you do then?" Kraus pressed.

"I asked Win if he knew where she was. We thought at first she was with Jesse, but then he showed up looking for her. That's when Win started getting really upset."

"There was no one else she might have gone to see?"

"Rudy," said Lydia, "Tori's a partner in the company now. She would have been at the contract signing. Riverbend is the biggest venture her father has ever undertaken. I tell you, she would have been there."

THE POOL of flooding water cushioned Tori's fall. Slightly dazed, her knees burning from the abrasions they'd received, she climbed back to her feet. The water was up to midcalf now and was colder than she would have expected a summer shower to be.

Soaking wet and beginning to shiver, she found her way back to the steps. If the stairs were so weak and rotten, how would she ever manage to get enough pressure on the door above to force it open?

With her escape hatch slammed shut again, pitch darkness had returned. *But it won't frighten me this time, not nearly as much as it did when I thought I might never see again.*

She groped along the inside of the stair riser for the broken step and found it when a splinter of jagged wood rammed itself under her fingernail. She winced with the pain, made a cursing sound and pulled it out. Once more she inched her hand carefully along the upright support and found a piece of the shattered step. Carefully she ripped off a sliver of wood about eighteen inches long and an inch square at the fat end.

The first step was completely under water now, the second one missing. She lifted her foot to the third rung and mounted it, this time spreading her feet so she was standing on the edges of the step. Putting her back against the overhead door, she pushed up enough to create a tiny chink of light, then forced the wedge of wood into the breach as far as it would go.

At least now I have fresh air and light.

What she saw when she turned around, however, made her wish she hadn't.

"SHE KNOWS HOW STRESSED out her father has been," Lydia went on. "She'd never stay away like this, not without an explanation."

"Sheriff," Jesse said, "if we could find her car—"

Kraus nodded. "Her Corvette shouldn't be too hard to spot, assuming, of course, it's not tucked away in a garage somewhere."

"So you think she's been kidnapped?"

"I'm not jumping to any conclusions yet. But it does seem strange she's not here. I've known Tori since she was a little girl. I agree with Lydia. This isn't like her."

"How about going on TV and radio and appealing for information?"

"Can't do any harm. It'll take me a few minutes to set it up. In the meantime, I'll put out an alert for her vehicle."

Jesse waited until the sheriff left before asking Lydia, "Did Tori know Martin never endorsed the Riverbend project?"

She was clearly confused. "But Burt said yesterday he had. Win didn't trust Martin to keep his word. He asked Tori to make sure it got highly publicized so Martin couldn't renege."

"It was a lie. Martin's been out of the county for the past three days. In fact, when I was talking with

Mr. Carr just before he had his heart attack, Burton admitted he'd made it up. He said Tori knew about it and went along as a means of pressuring me.''

"That's impossible," Lydia objected angrily. "Burt might do something that underhanded, but not Tori. Certainly not to you. She talked to her father about offering you a construction contract for the Riverbend project.''

"As a bribe?" he asked.

Lydia looked disappointed. "Do you really believe that?''

"No," he confessed, and shook his head apologetically.

"The three of them talked about it, Win, Tori and Burt. Win was all for it. Even Burt agreed to making you the offer.''

"Funny he never mentioned it to me this morning."

"Tori thought you could use the profits to finance your Coyote Mesa venture." Lydia gave him a hard stare. "She loves you, Jesse. You've got to find her.''

THE WATER WAS REVOLTING. Dead leaves and twigs covered its surface, though where they had come from she couldn't imagine. The side walls were festooned with crawling bugs. A black widow spiderweb was an inch from her left elbow. A dead field mouse bobbed in a corner. The head of a snake made a vee pattern as it rippled across the little pond. Instinctively Tori pulled back against the stairs, only to discover it was merely a water bug.

Heart pounding viciously, she took a series of long, deep breaths to help regain her composure. But she couldn't stop the trembling.

I'm trapped. I'm helpless. I'm going to die.

The rain was coming down hard, drumming on the door, splashing in pools around it, through the gap between the door frame and the rock wall underneath. Placing her hand in the fissure, she found the wood soft and porous. Rotten. *Can I tear enough of it away to crawl out the side of the cellar? What's beyond the wood frame? Earth? Concrete? Stouter wood?*

She began to chip away at the edges of the opening with her fingers. As soon as she dislodged a large piece of rotten wood, she realized she had made a tragic mistake.

Oh my God, I've broken a dam! The trickle filling her tomb had turned into a torrent.

"ARE YOU GOING TO BE all right?" Jesse asked Lydia.

"I'll feel better knowing you're out there looking for her."

He felt a pang of guilt, nevertheless, in leaving her alone to cope with the terrible ordeal of waiting to find out if the man she loved was going to survive. Winslow Carr, Jesse concluded, was a lucky man to have found this lady. Almost as lucky as he was to have found Tori.

When he went out to his truck, Jesse climbed behind the wheel and stopped. Where to look? What could he possibly do that the police, who were so much better equipped and trained for such searches, couldn't do? Still, he had to do something.

He checked back at Carr Enterprises, which was the closest place she might have gone. The parking lot, packed with vehicles just a couple of hours before, was now completely deserted.

He checked his own office. But it, too, was abandoned. On an impulse, he drove by Espy's apartment house. There were any number of reasons why Tori might have gone to see Espy—to help with a scholarship application, to challenge her on her association with Martin—but there was no sign of the Corvette or of Espy's Ford.

THE RAIN REFUSED to let up. Water kept pouring into the bunker. It was waist-high now, though Tori did her best to stay above it on the wooden steps. Bugs climbed up the insides of her clothing. She ignored them.

She searched desperately for an escape route. She'd salvaged another piece of wood from the splintered step and forced the corner of the door up another half an inch. It afforded a little more light and air, but nothing else.

She thought of her father. He deserved better than to lose everything he'd worked so hard for and for so many years. *To hell with the Riverbend project. To hell with Carr Enterprises, if it comes to that. We'll start over if we have to. Nothing's more important than being surrounded by family, the people I love. Dad. Lydia. Jesse.*

Oh, Jesse, please help me.

But there was no answer.

The storm not only showed no signs of letting up, it was gathering strength. Lightning strobed around her. Thunder boomed almost simultaneously. It was directly above her now and staying there.

Frustration and fear intensified as she pushed and pounded on the wooden door until she was drained of what seemed like the last shred of energy. *Can the noise I'm making be heard? Should I call out? Is anyone there? And if so, is it friend or foe?* Desperation fought with indecision and won. She beat with sore fists harder than ever against the wet wood and yelled her loudest. "*Help! Help!* Jesse, where are you?" But no one was there.

JESSE WAS TWO BLOCKS from Espy's house when he caught a flash of color down a narrow alley. Was it possible there were two red Corvettes in Coyote Springs? Maybe, but not with personalized license plates.

He pulled up behind it and got out. The storm that had been building to the northwest was moving in. Its dense cloud cover blocked the sun, but the cool respite it brought wasn't enough to explain the cold shiver that careened down his spine as he approached the vehicle.

Or what was left of it. The sports car had been stripped. The wheels were gone, the hood removed and parts of the engine torn out. The bucket seats were in tatters, head and taillights missing. It was a frightening sight, the maimed, broken skeleton of what had been a beautiful, well-functioning vehicle.

Where was its owner? What condition was she in?

Jesse bounded up the walk of the dilapidated house, little more than a shack, behind which the car was parked. An ancient woman, bent with arthritis, her wrinkled face framed with thin wisps of gray hair, came warily to the screen door.

"*Señora, por favor,* that car behind your house. What can you tell me about it?"

"*Nada.* I saw nothing."

Santa Marta had become the most run-down sector of the city, and this was the worst part of the barrio. Gang graffiti marred fences, walls and signs. Admitting to knowledge could sometimes be dangerous.

"Can you tell me where the young lady is who drove it?"

"No," she answered him in Spanish. "I never saw anyone."

"How long has it been there?"

"When I got up this morning it was parked there."

"It is very important that I find the owner," he continued. "Her father has had a heart attack and needs her."

The old woman's expression softened. "I am sorry to hear that. I would help you if I could, *señor*. But I really did not see anyone."

This time Jesse believed her. "Do you have a telephone? May I use it?"

She said nothing but stepped aside to let him in. The room was small, cramped and shabby. The cheap furniture would never qualify as antiques or collectibles. The phone, an old rotary dial, sat on a scarred wooden box that served as an end table. His hands shook as he picked up the dog-eared directory, found the number and dialed the police desk. The old woman turned away with a fatalistic shrug.

"This is Jesse Amorado. I've just found Tori Carr's Corvette..." He gave the desk sergeant the address and promised to wait for a patrol car to arrive. Perhaps he could serve as interpreter, since the old woman might suddenly forget her English in the stress of talking to the police.

While he waited, he called Lydia at the hospital. In all the panic and confusion when Winslow was stricken, she'd had the presence of mind to pick up Carr's cellular phone and put it in her purse. She'd given Jesse the unlisted number, making him promise to keep her informed.

"How is Mr. Carr?" he asked.

"Not good. I got tired of getting vague reports and finally had to threaten them with the wrath of Lydia if I didn't start getting some straight answers to my questions."

"The wrath of Lydia?" he asked, amused in spite of himself.

For a moment, her tone lightened, too. "I hope you never experience it, Jesse. It's not a pleasant thing. But there are a few old heads around here who remember when my husband was sick and they tried to patronize me."

He turned serious. "What did you find out?"

"He's suffered a major heart attack and may have to have surgery."

"At least he's alive. I've got some news, too, though I'm not sure if mine is any better. I found Tori's car, or what's left of it, in an alley behind Hidalgo Street."

"God, that's the worst part of town. What would it be doing there?"

"I don't know. The police are on their way now," he said. "Apparently the car was parked here during the night. I've talked to only one person so far, but she didn't see who drove it here. Does Tori have any friends around here?"

Lydia was silent for a moment. "As far as I know, the only person she knows in that part of town is Espy. But that's a couple of blocks away. Why would Tori park there to visit her?"

"It doesn't make sense," Jesse replied. "Leaving the car here would be asking for it to be trashed, and being in this neighborhood at night would be dangerous for a woman alone, especially a beautiful Anglo woman."

"It must have been stolen somewhere else and dumped there."

The notion had occurred to him too. It wasn't a happy thought. If someone had stolen the car, where was Tori? Had she been abducted? Was she lying in a ditch somewhere beaten, maybe raped, perhaps dead?

Impotent rage, fanned by terror, tensed every muscle in his body. He had to find her.

THERE'S NO ESCAPE. I've explored every inch of this hell-hole. The water's up to my chest now. Another eighteen inches and I'll drown. Three-quarters of an inch from freedom!

Suddenly there was an explosion of lightning so intense the air was rife with ozone. The simultaneous thunder shook the ground. Tori's heart jumped in terror as she pressed her hands to her ears. Slowly she removed them. They were still ringing when, ten seconds later, something crashed on the door above her. The shock wave jolted her off her perch on the slippery, wet stairs and tossed her like a rag doll into the putrid, muddy water.

JESSE HAD HARDLY HUNG UP the phone when two uniformed men arrived. Neither was Hispanic, nor did either of them speak Spanish, except, perhaps, for a few curt commands. As he expected, the old woman refused to divulge any information to the police. Jesse realized he'd made a serious tactical error. He should have spent the time questioning her instead of talking to Lydia. He felt sure she would have had more information to give if he had approached her right. He'd lost an opportunity to learn more about what had happened to Tori.

"What are you going to do?" he asked the senior policeman, a man in his mid-forties, whose name was Henshaw.

"We'll get some patrolmen here who speak Spanish and start questioning the neighbors. We probably won't learn anything. It's amazing how deaf, dumb and blind these people can be."

Jesse was tempted to ask who "these people" were but let it pass. The phrase would doubtless be used in any neighborhood. For the police, it was often a matter of "us" and "them."

"I don't imagine you'll get much from the car," he commented. "By now every kid and his big brother has probably pawed it."

"You'd be surprised what forensics can turn up. Trouble is, it takes time."

How much time was there? Jesse wondered. "The old woman said the car was parked there when she got up this morning."

"Ask her what condition it was in," Henshaw prompted.

Jesse did so.

The woman hesitated. "I don't know. It was just there."

"*Señora,*" Jesse said, unable to hide his impatience, "a man's daughter is missing, kidnapped. Now the man has had a heart attack in grief for her loss. If you can tell us anything that might help find her, I'm sure he will want to reward you for the information."

The woman's rheumy eyes sparked with contempt and he saw an old, deep-seated anger flare, an anger mixed with resignation and suffering. "Do you insult me, *señor?* Do you think I hold back information because I value money more than a daughter's life?"

She hobbled to a rickety table and picked up a small plastic frame containing a faded snapshot of a girl of perhaps fifteen. The teenager wasn't pretty, but there was life in her eyes, a rare kind of joy.

"They killed her," she said, "my granddaughter. They killed her because she would not do what they wanted. Because she would not disgrace herself."

"Who?"

"It does not matter. It was a long time ago."

Jesse felt a lump in his throat. "I'm sorry."

"I do not know what time the car was brought," the woman said. "But it was not there when I looked out the window at midnight. I got up at seven, when the sun was just rising, another bright, sunny, empty day. It was there then. Already boys were starting to take things off of it. Hubcaps, then wheels. They wanted to take the seats, too, but they could not figure out how. Maybe they did not have the right tools. I do not know. But one of them got mad and began slashing the leather. His companion shouted something and started punching him. They fought."

"Who?" Jesse prompted.

"Neighborhood boys. It does not matter which ones. They had nothing to do with bringing the car here. They just take things that do not belong to them. You cannot stop them. Even if the police put them in jail for a while, they do it again when they come out. While they are there they learn more ways to hurt people."

"You never saw the person who brought the car here?"

"No. But it was an Anglo."

"How do you know that?" he asked, startled by her certainty.

"One of our people would never leave such a rich

possession here, not unless he wanted it to be destroyed. Only an Anglo would be stupid enough to do such a thing.''

GASPING AND CHOKING, Tori managed to reach the stairs again. She couldn't touch the floor of the cellar anymore. The water was too high. There was barely a foot left between its filthy surface and the wooden ceiling above.

She checked through her little peephole. It took a moment to understand what she saw. Rescue was impossible now! A huge tree limb had fallen on top of the door, pinning it shut. There was no escape.

JESSE KEPT THINKING about Espy. She was involved, he was sure of it. Tori's Corvette being found only a few blocks from where Espy lived was too much of a coincidence. Could Tori have gone to see Espy—on her own volition or by invitation—and been waylaid there? Why? Obviously to keep her away from the contract signing. Espy was upset about Riverbend, but would she be a party to such a trick? Besides, Tori was helping Espy, which should make them friends. There was so much about this that didn't make sense.

The two policemen at the old woman's house were soon joined by another patrol, this time composed of a young man and a woman who both spoke Spanish. Jesse excused himself when they began to canvass the neighborhood for information. He hoped it wasn't a futile effort.

A few minutes later, as the first raindrops splattered across his windshield, he pulled up in front of Espy's apartment. Her car was in its usual spot. She wasn't very quick about answering the bell, however, so he began pounding on the door.

"What do you want?" Espy called out impatiently through the narrow crack allowed by the security chain.

"In," he replied harshly. "Open the damn door, Espy, or I swear I'll smash it in."

Her mouth fell open. "Jesse, what's the matter with you? Okay, okay. Hold your horses."

She closed the door long enough to release the chain. When she opened it again, he pushed it wide and stormed into the apartment.

"Where's Tori?" he demanded.

"Tori? How the hell should I know?"

The tiny kitchenette was too small for anyone to hide in, so he checked out the bathroom and finally went into the bedroom. Espy followed close behind him.

"Has she been here?"

"Not since the other day when you were here with her. What's going on?"

"She's missing."

"Missing?" It took a minute for the word to sink in. Then Espy exploded. "You think I'm holding her prisoner?" Her dark eyes blazed. "You bastard. I think you better leave now, before I call the police. Get out."

He ignored her. "You said this morning that I was being jerked around, but you didn't say who was pulling the chain."

She glared at him. He was about to demand an explanation when he saw something on the table beside the bed. He picked it up and examined it. A cold chill ran down his back, followed by a burning rage.

"Tell me everything," he commanded, holding out a gold monogrammed tie clasp.

CHAPTER SEVENTEEN

EXHAUSTION CREPT into Tori's bones. A pervading sense of hopelessness and futility wormed its way into her willpower. So many things left undone. So many dreams unrealized. She'd finally found the man she wanted to spend the rest of her life with...

Tears she didn't know she had left coursed down her already wet cheeks. *I can't give up without a fight. I won't.*

Her arms felt like lead as she reached out to the fist-size hole she'd created between wood frame and rock. Energy nearly spent, she overbalanced and tumbled again into the pool of swampy water.

When she tried to recapture her perch, it wasn't there. The staircase, jarred from its moorings by the vibration of the fallen tree limb, had broken loose. It bobbed uselessly beside her, further restricting her space and movement.

JESSE'S STOMACH MUSCLES were tight with fear and dread. Espy's visitor had been unusually inquisitive about her visit to the Amorado ranch and had asked several times if she was sure no one was staying there. Jesse was convinced now that was where Tori had been taken.

He rammed his foot to the floorboard of the aging pickup, but he had to back off as the full force of the storm that had been rumbling in from the northwest finally reached town. He couldn't help Tori if he got into an accident. But he knew he had to hurry. Rain was coming down again in horizontal streaks. His windshield wipers slapped violently back and forth, but not fast enough to clear the glass of the sheets of water striking it. An empty pickup was not the vehicle to be driving in such a storm. The rear wheels planed on the flooded roadway. He steered and countersteered with each gust of wind.

The going got even tougher when he left the paved highway. The bar ditches that lined the edges of the narrow, high-crowned road were running like spring streams, full of tumbling rocks and branches. Jesse forced himself to slow down lest he careen off the side and become hopelessly stuck.

The air coming through the vents in the dashboard was damp and chilly. At any other time he would have thought it refreshing. Not now. The purple-and-green tinge in the heavy charcoal gray clouds hanging low over the drenched land only added to his alarm.

He approached the turnoff to the ranch only to find the driveway blocked by a fallen ash. There was no way he could get around it. No way he could move it. Tiny pellets of hail bounced on the hood of the truck as he jumped out of the cab. In less than ten seconds he was soaked to the skin, hailstones stinging his bare arms and neck. He clawed his way around, through and over the huge tree's branches as they whipped at his face and arms.

Adrenaline pumping, he ran to the house, calling her name. *"Tori! Tori!"*

The house was dark. He fought furiously to get his key out of his wet jeans, then to hold his hand steady

enough to get it into the lock. All the time, he kept
calling to Tori.

He bounded into the kitchen, dodged from room to
room. She must be here. But where? There was no
cellar. Oh, God. Yes, there was.

He shot out the door into the backyard and ran
around the side of the old garage. His heart pounded.
His belly was clenched with dread. He slid around the
end of the listing wooden building and his heart
stopped. A huge branch of a mighty oak tree, its nub
scarred by lightning, lay sprawled across the entrance
to the underground shelter.

"Tori. Where are you?"

He heard nothing but the howl of the wind, the beating of hail on the tin roof of the garage. Pure terror
gripped his heart. He ran over to the fallen branch. He
tried to pull it, to push it. It wouldn't move. Maybe she
wasn't there. Maybe he'd gotten it wrong. Then he saw
it. The piece of wood jammed under the corner of the
door. From the inside.

"Tori!"

A finger appeared and his heart lurched.

He tried to pull the door up. No good. It was pinned
by the fallen limb. He bent down by the finger, trying
to see inside. "Are you all right?" He had to yell even
to hear himself.

The thin voice that answered him was muffled by
the shrieking wind. "Jesse. I'm…hanging on to the
side. Nothing to stand on… Water coming in. Help
me."

"I will, I will," he promised. "Hang on, Tori. I love
you."

He ran to the garage. The door was locked. The key
was in the house. No time to get it. The tall, old sash

window on the side was painted shut. He picked up a fallen stick and smashed all the glass, then climbed through the jagged opening. In the corner were tools. He picked up a crowbar and a long-handled ax, then crawled back out through the window again.

"Tori, I'm going to get you out of there."

"Hurry, Jesse." He could hear the weakness in her reply—and the hope.

He used the crowbar, but the tree limb was too close to the edge of the door and too heavy to move. He didn't have time to chop it up with the ax.

"Tori," he shouted close to the slip of an opening. "I've got to smash the door with an ax. Can you move away from it?"

"Yes. Hurry, Jesse. Hurry."

He watched her finger disappear and he almost panicked. Then he gave a mighty yell of warning and swung the ax with all his might between the forked branches. It struck the middle of the door and bounced off the water-slick surface.

"Tori, speak to me."

A muffled, "Jesse, I can't hold on much..."

Again he let out a mighty yell, and the ax rebounded once more off the planking of the blocked door.

Larger hailstones began to fall. They pinged like golf balls across the soggy rough ground. Several struck his shoulders and head. Instead of making him wince with pain, they only whipped his fury.

This time when he brought the ax down, it stuck in the wood. He yanked it out and hurled it down again into the rent he'd made. On the third swing, the board split.

TORI LOOKED UP at the dull metal sticking through the thick board overhead. Her arms were outstretched, her muscles burning as she grasped the frame of the doorway. She kicked her feet sluggishly to keep her head above the muddy water. Her arms ached. Her shoulders ached. Her neck felt stiff and sore.

The ax head disappeared, then reappeared with an earsplitting crack. It wriggled in the splintered gash like an infuriated snake. Tori started to relax, only to sink. Water invaded her nose and she began to sputter. Then the board split and she was looking up at Jesse's shadowed face. She watched with inexpressible relief as he grasped the shattered edges of the plank and wrenched them farther apart, then sat across them and used his feet and hands to widen the gap.

Suddenly his arm was reaching down. She put her hand forward, only to sink in water over her head. A strong hand grasped her right wrist and pulled her out of her slimy grave.

She crumpled, weak and trembling, against his wet, hard body. He scooped her up in his arms and carried her to the ranch house. Only when they were under the protective roof of the porch did he put her down. But he didn't let her go.

FOR SEVERAL MINUTES they held each other. Finally, reluctantly, Jesse released his crushing grip on her.

"*Querida*, darling, are you all right?" he asked, unaware he was speaking Spanish.

"I'm fine," she assured him, the words wobbling through a teary smile. "Now."

"You haven't been harmed?" He lifted her hands to his lips to kiss them and saw the bloody, jagged nails, the ugly marks on her wrists. "Oh, God!" he gasped. "You *are* hurt! There's a gash on your head, too!"

"I'll be fine." Tori took a deep breath.

"I'll get you to the emergency room."

"No," she said. "There's no need, really. But how did you know I was here?"

"I found your car a couple of blocks from Espy's apartment. It was stripped. Totaled. I'm sorry."

She stared at her hands. "It's not important now."

"From the things Espy told me, I figured you'd probably been brought here."

"You know then who—"

"Yes," he said, hugging her to him, wishing that was the worst he had to tell her. "But I've got some more bad news."

Even filthy and drenched, she was beautiful. He dreaded the pain he knew he was about to bring. "Your father's in the hospital. He's had a problem."

She clutched his arm, her tired blue eyes round with renewed fear. "What do you mean?"

He looped his hand around her neck, felt the bunched, quivering muscles. "Tori, he's had a heart attack. But he's doing fine. He's going to be okay."

She wilted, nearly tumbled over. But he grabbed her, took her in his arms again and stroked her back.

"He might need surgery. Lydia's with him."

She sobbed into his shoulder. "I want to see him, Jesse. Right away. Please."

He pressed her body close to his and led her to his truck.

"We'll stop by your house so you can get cleaned up. He shouldn't see you looking like this. I'll need to make some telephone calls, then we'll go to see him."

WINSLOW CARR'S pale cheeks were wet with tears as he held his daughter's hand. "Are you all right, sweetheart? I was so worried. I was sure somebody had kidnapped you."

"I'm fine, Dad. How about you?"

"Much better now that you're here. What happened?"

"It's a long story," Tori said. "I'll tell you about it tomorrow. You just rest now."

"You're not hurt?"

"No," she assured him. "I'm perfectly fine." She carefully avoided bringing attention to her scratched and nail-chipped fingers. Her eyes brimming, she said, "Dad, I love you," and put her cheek to his. "Tomorrow I'll answer all your questions," she told him, regaining her composure. "Right now I want you to get a good night's sleep."

"I will—now."

Jesse was behind her, his wrists resting gently on her shoulders.

"Take good care of my girl, you hear?" Winslow whispered.

"You have my promise, sir."

"Go home now," Winslow said. "And take Lydia with you before she drops." He smiled shakily at her. "I love you, woman."

Lydia made no attempt to hold back her tears. She bent and kissed him. "I love you, too."

SHERIFF KRAUS WAS WAITING outside the hospital room when they emerged. He immediately noted the abrasions on Tori's hands.

"Are you sure you don't want medical attention?" he asked her.

"I'm sure."

"Then I need you to come down to the station and give a formal statement."

"We have to drop Mrs. Anderson off first," Jesse said.

"I'm going with you," Lydia declared.

"It's really not necessary," Tori told her. "You must be exhausted."

Jesse looked at the older woman. "Beware the wrath of Lydia," he said laughingly.

Lydia smiled in appreciation. "Let's go."

Ten minutes later they were in the sheriff's office.

"Now, what happened?" asked Kraus.

"Where to begin?" Tori said, then told them about being attacked in the parking lot outside the office and waking up, bound and gagged in the storm cellar at the Amorado ranch. She smiled at Jesse, reached out and touched him on the arm. "But Jesse rescued me in time."

Lydia twirled her rings viciously. "Obviously Martin wanted to keep you from signing the Riverbend contract."

Tori shook her head. "The problem was not that I'd sign, but that I'd insist on Jesse being a part of it."

Lydia looked blankly at Tori. "I don't understand."

"Yesterday afternoon I proposed bringing Jesse into the Riverbend project as a contractor. Dad agreed. So did Burton. In fact, he was very supportive. The big question was whether Jesse would go along with it."

"I would have," Jesse acknowledged.

"But Burton couldn't allow that to happen," Tori declared.

"Burt?" Lydia exploded. "Are you saying it was Burt who kidnapped you and left you to die?"

Tori nodded sadly. "When Dad agreed to offer Jesse

a Riverbend construction contract, he said he preferred dealing with local businesses whenever possible. That made me wonder why more locals weren't part of the deal. So I researched. Burton closed all out-of-town contracts."

Lydia lifted her shoulders. "Win's never liked that kind of negotiating," she pointed out, "and Burt's good at it."

"I suspect he's also into kickbacks. Dad never caught him in a lie, so he trusted him. But even if Burton was honest in the past, Riverbend was too big a temptation. When one of the corporations he'd bargained with went bankrupt, he was forced to get signatures on current contracts quickly, before anyone else had a chance to pull out, and that left an opening for Jesse. Burton knew if Jesse became an active participant in the operation, he'd pick up on the corruption and blow the whistle. So he had to make sure Jesse couldn't do that."

"But why kidnap you?" Lydia questioned. "Why not Jesse?"

"I'm not the one Hazlitt's really afraid of," Jesse explained. "He's been sucking everything he could out of Santa Marta and I wasn't able to stop him. Then Tori shows up, and suddenly the chances of him getting nailed go up astronomically. So he's got to remove her from the equation."

Lydia wrinkled her brow. "But to leave her helpless in a cellar on your ranch... This is about more than just Riverbend and money, isn't it?"

Tori bowed her head, then looked up. "You've got to remember Burton comes from a very poor background. For him, Jesse and the people of the barrio represent the kind of social pride and self-confidence

Burton never found at home. What could...what *should* have developed into admiration turned into jealousy and hatred.''

Tori looked at the smooth tan complexion of the man holding her hand. ''My falling in love with Jesse may well have pushed Burton over the edge. I broke up with him a long time ago because... I couldn't define my reasons then, but I think I can now. I was a trophy for him, not the focus of real love.'' *Not the kind of love I see in Jesse's eyes at this very moment,* she said to herself. *The love I feel whenever we're together, every time I think about him.*

''But how was Burt so sure nobody was going to be at the Amorado place?'' Lydia asked.

''Espy Mendez,'' Jesse said.

Kraus shook his head in exasperation. ''What's she got to do with this?''

''After I found Tori's Corvette, I went to Espy's apartment, thinking Tori might be there. I found a tie clasp with BH on it--Burton Hazlitt. Espy came out to our place the other day to assure me she had nothing to do with Martin's tricks. While she was there, she learned the family was going to San Antonio for a week. She passed the information on to her new lover, Burton.''

''That makes her an accessory to kidnapping,'' Kraus noted.

''Not if she didn't know what the information was going to be used for. I don't think she did. It was probably something she let slip in a tirade about seeing Tori with my family.''

''I hope you're right,'' Kraus said. ''For her sake.''

''So,'' Jesse concluded, ''I put two and two together. Hazlitt knew no one would be at the ranch and had to get Tori out of the way. What could be better than to make it look like I'd taken her?"

"Okay," Kraus said. "You've made a pretty good case against Hazlitt, but it'll never stand up in court without some proof. Do you have any?"

Tori shook her head unhappily.

"Will fingerprints do?" Jesse asked.

"Fingerprints?" Tori and Lydia exclaimed together.

Jesse looked at Tori. "You were bound with tape."

"Yes," she said skeptically, then understood what he was driving at. She brightened, only to have her hopes dashed. "Oh, no. It got soaked."

Jesse addressed the sheriff. "One of your men said you can do wonders with forensics. Hazlitt probably wore gloves when he drove Tori away in her car and later when he dropped it off in the barrio. But I don't see how he could have taped her up with gloves on. Can you get prints off the sticky side of tape that's been underwater?"

IT TOOK ANOTHER HOUR for Tori's statement to be typed and signed. Lydia, finally giving in to her exhaustion, asked Rudy to call her a cab, but he insisted on one of his deputies driving her home and checking the place out before leaving her.

At last Jesse escorted Tori out of the sheriff's office.

"I don't want to be alone tonight," she said quietly as they walked with arms around each other to his truck.

"You didn't think I'd let you, did you? I gave your father my word I'd take care of you." He gathered her in an embrace and pulled her close.

"I love you," she said.

He opened the door on the passenger side. "The

only question is, whose bed do you want to sleep in, yours or mine?''

Her mouth curved at the edges. ''I want to sleep in your bed, Jesse.''

''Our bed,'' he replied, and took her home to Santa Marta.

She stood beside him as he unlocked the front door, aware of the magnetic pull of his dark silhouette on her mind and body.

He pushed the door open, stepped back and lifted her close to his chest. With a purr of anticipated pleasure, she snuggled her head against his shoulder, took in the scent of his hair and skin and ran her hand up to and around his neck.

Two steps into the house, he closed the door with his foot. He didn't bother to turn lights on as he carried her to the bedroom. Trembling, she unbuttoned his shirt and ran her palms across the wiry mat of coarse black hair. Her tongue tickled his neck, then coursed down the taut center of his body.

His fingers fumbled as they undid the buttons of her blouse. He unclasped her bra and gathered her breasts in a delicate caress. Clutching his shoulders, she threw back her head when he brought his mouth down and ran his tongue around their sensitive peaks. At her whimper, he looked up, framed her face between his hands and whispered, ''I love you, Tori.''

THEY LAY ABED UNTIL NOON the next day, sleeping in each other's arms, touching each other's bodies, making love. Afterward, Jesse drove her to the county jail. He parked in the lot in back and they walked arm in arm around the side. Tori could feel the tension in his grasp.

She looked up. His face was firm, set. "You okay?"

"It's not even a nice place to visit," he tried to joke.

Inside the front door, she asked to see the sheriff. Rudy Kraus appeared a minute later.

"Did you arrest Burton?"

"About an hour and a half ago," he answered as he rubbed a hand across yesterday's five o'clock stubble. "That was a smart call you made, Amorado." He turned to Tori. "Good thing you tore the tape instead of unwinding it. Got several sets of clear prints from two pieces."

"Has he made a statement yet?" she asked.

"Only to claim he's been set up. Insists he's completely innocent. His lawyer's with him now."

"I want to see him."

"He's not going to tell you anything," Kraus assured her.

"I have to ask him why he's done this to Dad and me."

Kraus thought a moment. "Let me see what I can do. His lawyer may not like it."

As they waited on an uncomfortable bench, Jesse took her bruised hands in his. "You don't have to do this, you know."

She bowed her head in disagreement. "Yes, I do. Sheriff Kraus is probably right, I won't get any answers. But this may be my last chance to talk to Burton face-to-face, instead of through lawyers and maybe prison bars."

"I don't want him to hurt you. Not ever again."

She looked into Jesse's dark, handsome face, at the full lips that could be so gentle and sweet. Her gaze settled on his deep, mysterious eyes, eyes that said so many things at different times. Her heart fluttered at the memory of the joy and excitement in those eyes when he made love to her.

"You can't promise me infinite safety," she told him gently. "Pain is a part of life. But I love you for wanting to protect me." She raised his hand to her lips and kissed it. "All I can offer you," she said softly, "is my promise that I will never intentionally hurt you. I love you too much."

They were about to seal this new bond with another kiss when they heard a muffled cough. Sheriff Kraus looked down, half amused, half apologetic, and told Tori she could see Burton.

"You'll be watched through a one-way glass for your protection," he said, "but your conversation won't be monitored."

Burton was sitting at a plain wooden table, his fingers moving nervously in front of him, one foot tapping on the floor. He looked like a recalcitrant teenager cooling his heels in the principal's office. He'd obviously been obliged to leave his apartment in a hurry. For once he wasn't wearing a well-pressed suit and tie, just a short-sleeved shirt and baggy pants. Even his hair was untidy. At work she'd paid no attention to the tattoo on his biceps. It had long ago lost its fascination. Now, as she stared at it, she decided the leopard had truly changed its spots. She also realized it was the tattoo she'd glimpsed when his arm came down and struck her.

She sat on the chair across the table from him. "Hello, Burton."

He looked at her with wary eyes. "What do you want?"

"I think you know. Why did you kidnap me and leave me to die?"

"I don't know what you're talking about. I didn't leave you to die."

"You mean you hadn't planned on my drowning in that cellar?"

He said nothing.

"No one is listening," she said evenly.

When he looked up at her this time, the venom and ferocity in his eyes shocked her. What was he so angry about? How long had that rage been eating away at him? She sat back, stunned, her hands dropping to her thighs. "Why do you hate me?" she asked quietly.

He twiddled his fingers in front of him on the table-top. "I don't."

She gazed at him in wonder. "Then what's this all about?"

He slammed his palms flat on the wooden surface. "It's about power, Tori. That's what life's about. You were in the military. Haven't you figured that out yet?"

She shook her head. "Life taught me that happiness is about love."

He laughed at her. "Love is about power, too." He stabbed a finger at her. "It's the power to get people to do what you want them to do because they want to do it for you."

She knew she should despise this man, but his words only brought sorrow. "That's not love, Burton. That's manipulation."

His patronizing contempt said she was a fool, but his eyes avoided hers.

She straightened up. "I almost drowned."

"If you had," he spit out, "I wouldn't be here. That damned Mexican would." He raised his head and snarled, "I wasn't refined enough for you..."

He trailed off, aware he'd said too much. Where she

had been imprisoned hadn't been made public, and she doubted the police volunteered that piece of information.

"What about Dad?" she asked. "He's always been good to you."

"Why shouldn't he be? I did all the work, came up with all the ideas. I had to push him into Woodhill Terrace. He made a lot of money on that venture."

"So did you. But it's not true that Dad didn't do anything. He built the company with hard work. He respected your ideas, your drive, your intelligence. He gave you the freedom to grow and prosper. He loved you like a son."

Burton waved the notion off dismissively. "He was ready to give up on Riverbend. Do you know how much money we could have raked in?"

She shook her head pityingly. "He didn't make you a partner because it would profit him. Yet you were willing to trade his love and your own honor for a few extra bucks. I feel sorry for you, Burton."

He jumped up from his chair, knocking it over behind him.

"Get out of here," Burton growled as a guard charged into the room.

CHAPTER EIGHTEEN

JESSE WAS OUTSIDE THE DOOR when Tori emerged. Until that moment she hadn't realized how cold the jail was. She welcomed his outstretched arms and the warmth of his embrace. Tipping his head, he planted a kiss in her hair. They held each other as the deputies and Burton's lawyer streamed by to attend to the prisoner.

Jesse drove them to a small restaurant on the outskirts of town, where they ate a quiet lunch. She told him about her talk with Burton.

"Actually, he's right," she said as she pushed aside a half-eaten quiche and fruit plate.

Jesse swallowed the last morsel of fried catfish and wiped his mouth with a napkin. "About what?"

She reached out and twined her fingers with his. "Love is power," she told him. "It's the power to share joy and happiness, the power to endure pain and disappointment. It's the power to like yourself for being who and what you are. I'm sorry he's never been able to experience that."

Jesse smiled softly. "I love you."

"TORI SHOULD BE HERE in a few minutes," Jesse said. "She and Lydia went shopping."

"No telling when they'll get back, then." Winslow chuckled. He was sitting in the chair by the window.

The hospital gown and coarse robe of a week earlier had been replaced by casual slacks and an open-necked shirt. He was due to be released in less than an hour. "That's okay. It'll give us a chance to talk."

"You're looking better every day," Jesse said. At Winslow's invitation, he settled into the other metal armchair. "How do you feel?"

"Better than I have in a long time." Winslow held up a current bestseller. "This is just camouflage. I've been doing a lot of thinking over the past few days. Lydia's right. I should have taken a holiday a long time ago. Maybe then things would have turned out differently."

"Water under the bridge," Jesse observed.

"Do you think we can overcome our mistakes of the past?"

"The future is hopeless if we can't."

Winslow poured himself a glass of water from a plastic pitcher. "I'm going to honor my commitments to the home owners in Santa Marta and to the other investors of Riverbend," he said. "I know we're being inundated with calls from people wanting to back out of the project."

"You can fight them," Jesse replied. "After all, the contracts were signed by a partner of the corporation."

Winslow smiled ironically. "Signed by a man who is about to be a convicted felon. Legally I might have a case, but morally I don't. Besides, lawyers' fees will eat up any gains. I may have to declare bankruptcy before this is all over, but I'm still going to honor my debts."

He took a sip of water. "Jesse, tell me honestly, do you think Santa Marta can be salvaged?"

Jesse crossed one booted foot over the other knee.

"The barrio? Some of it can be, and some of it needs to be torn down."

"What do you think of Tori's idea for a revised Riverbend?"

"I think it's probably the solution we were both looking for all along. She told me the reason you first invested in Santa Marta was because you wanted to improve living conditions there."

"I'm sorry I didn't have the courage of my dreams. Instead, I got caught up in Burton's illusion of making big profits. I forgot that money's a tool, not an end. Did you know Tori and I wanted to offer you a construction contract for Riverbend?"

Jesse nodded slowly. "I would have gone for it," he acknowledged.

"I'd like to—"

Tori and Lydia came through the open doorway, laughing and bragging about the shopping bargains they'd found. Tori gave Jesse a hug, and he rested an arm around her hips. Lydia went over to Winslow and kissed him softly on the cheek.

"I was just going to tell Jesse," Winslow continued, "that I want to reorganize Carr Enterprises into three divisions. I'll keep sales. I never have been very comfortable with big projects. I'm a salesman, not a developer."

"You were going to sell houses in Riverbend," Tori reminded him.

He smiled almost nostalgically. "It's not the same. Big fancy houses for rich people are financial investments. I'm not talking about that. I'm talking about homes—for newlyweds and growing families. For a man there's pride in providing shelter and comfort for his family. For a woman, I expect it's the gratification of a basic instinct to civilize and nurture kith and kin.''

She walked over to him and kissed him on the forehead. "Dad, you're a romantic."

Lydia's eyes glowed warmly as she looked at Winslow. "He's an incurable sentimentalist, a romantic to the bone."

"Gee, I hope that's a blush I see on your face and not your blood pressure going up again," Tori teased her father.

He blushed all the more and cleared his throat. "About this reorganization... Tori, I'd like you to handle our second division, investments and property management." He looked over at her. "Or at least set it up until you get a job with an airline."

She tightened her grip on her father's hand and smiled at Jesse.

"Jesse," Winslow said, looking straight at him, "I...we would like you to take over a new third division—construction and restoration."

"Me?" Jesse stared at him for a long moment, then rose and joined Tori at the side of her father's chair. She smiled up at him. "There are two or three little problems," he said.

Tori pulled back, but not away. "What kind of problems?"

"For one, I have no cash to invest—"

Carr held up his hand. "You have six houses worth half a million dollars."

Jesse laughed. "That was under slightly different circumstances—"

"I'm prepared to accept that valuation in trade for a third interest in Carr Enterprises. Which, by the way, may not be worth a plugged nickel if we go bankrupt. What's your second problem?''

"Money. You said you wanted to rebuild the barrio. So do I. But even using sweat equity, we're going to need capital. How—''

"Well, listen to this!'' Tori jumped in. "My advertising campaign on the new Riverbend project is beginning to pay off. Lydia told me we've been getting calls from residents and outside investors interested in the venture.''

Winslow smiled contentedly. "Well, that's taken care of.'' He looked at Jesse. "Think it over, son—''

"There is one other problem,'' Tori interrupted. Everyone stared at her. "The name.''

"The name?'' her father asked.

"I think we need a new image.''

"What would you suggest?''

"C and A Enterprises sounds terrible,'' Lydia noted. "Like a used-car lot.''

Jesse chuckled. "Carr and Amorado is a mouthful.''

Tori pursed her lips thoughtfully. "How about Carmorado, Inc.?''

Winslow's eyes twinkled. He looked at Jesse. "Will that do?''

"It does have a nice ring to it.'' He glanced from father to daughter. "I accept your offer, Mr. Carr.''

The older man rose and put out his hand. "In that case you better call me Win...partner.'' They shook hands, then, impulsively, Winslow put his arm around him.

Sheriff Kraus chose that moment to walk into the room. His face froze with surprise when he saw the two men embracing. "Ahem.''

The women, hidden behind the wide hospital door,

laughed. Tori stepped forward. "Pay them no mind, Sheriff. It's just one of those male-bonding things."

Rudy Kraus still didn't look very comfortable as he began his announcement. "I just thought you'd like to know, Win, the D.A. has dropped the charge of bribery against you. As a matter of fact, he's turned the tables on Martin and is now using your evidence and testimony from several other businesses in town to add the charge of extortion against the councilman."

Lydia giggled. "That's a twist even Henry ought to be able to admire."

"What's Martin's reaction?" Jesse asked.

"Denies it all, of course. Says it's a smoke screen by Carr Enterprises to hide their own criminal activities. But there've been enough complaints for the D.A.'s office to subpoena his records. Martin submitted his resignation to the city council a few minutes ago."

"Good riddance," Lydia snorted.

"I want to take you all out to dinner tonight," Winslow announced. "At the country club."

Lydia touched his arm. "Win, I really don't think—"

"Nonsense, dear. We've got a lot to celebrate." He patted her hand. "I promise not to order a big steak or ask for extra butter and sour cream on my baked potato—though after this hospital food, it sounds awfully tempting." He grinned. "Have you told them yet?"

She beamed at him.

"Told us what?" Tori asked.

Her father glanced at Lydia and received a smiling nod. "I've asked Lydia to marry me, and she's honored me by accepting."

Tori wrapped her arms around Lydia and her father.

Jesse offered his congratulations and kissed Lydia on the cheek.

"All that shopping we just did," Lydia explained to Tori as they wiped away joyful tears, "was for the Caribbean cruise your father's taking me on for our honeymoon."

AFTER DROPPING the newly engaged couple off at Lydia's house with a promise to pick them up for dinner, Jesse and Tori stopped off at Carr Enterprises. He surveyed the office layout while she checked the mail and messages stacked on the reception desk. One message was from Sam Hargis at the airport.

"Don't tell me something's happened to my plane," Tori mumbled as she dialed his number. She caught him just as he was leaving for the day.

"Look," he said after they'd exchanged pleasantries, "I know you said you weren't interested, but I thought I'd make the offer anyway. I need another pilot to work my charter service. It will only be part-time and the pay isn't as much as you can make with one of the big airlines, but you'd be able to set your own schedule."

Tori's heart began to pound.

"You interested?"

She looked over at Jesse, who was idly opening closet doors and peeking into file cabinets.

"Can I call you back later?"

"Sure thing. Take your time."

Jesse came over just as she was hanging up. "You'll definitely have to redecorate Hazlitt's office," he said. "Get some color in there. Ready to go?"

She picked up a legal-size envelope from the desk, tapped it on the tip of her thumb and stuck it unopened in her purse. The logo and return address indicated it came from the airline she'd interviewed with in Dallas. From its thickness, she knew it was a job offer with a contract for her to review. A rejection, she calculated, would be a one-page letter. Suddenly it didn't seem important anymore.

Her mind was filled with only thoughts of Jesse when she locked the office and climbed into his truck. She could hardly respond coherently to his enthusiastic plans for Carmorado, Inc. as they drove to his house on Otero Street.

He waited until they were in the living room before he took her in his arms. She looked up at him, eager for his touch.

He brought his mouth down to hers. Their breath mingled. The kiss was languorous, arousing. At last they separated long enough for him to speak.

"I love you, Tori." He nibbled the tender skin just below her ear. "I want to marry you."

Her heart stopped, then revived with a wild throbbing. Pulsing heat pounded in her chest, filling her with fever.

"Oh, yes," she murmured as he kissed her earlobe. "Yes!" she cried. "I love you so much."

They clung to each other in the middle of the living room, savoring the union that only a man and woman can share.

It was later, as they lay beside each other, that Jesse thought to ask, "What was that letter you brought from the office?"

So he *had* noticed. "It doesn't matter now," she said dreamily. "I've finally come home."

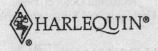

MEN at WORK

All work and no play?
Not these men!

October 1998
***SOUND OF SUMMER* by Annette Broadrick**
Secret agent Adam Conroy's seductive gaze
could hypnotize a woman's heart. But it was
Selena Stanford's body that needed saving—
when she stumbled into the middle of an
espionage ring and forced Adam out of
hiding....

November 1998
***GLASS HOUSES* by Anne Stuart**
Billionaire Michael Dubrovnik never lost a
negotiation—until Laura de Kelsey Winston
changed the boardroom rules. He might
acquire her business...but a kiss would cost
him his heart....

December 1998
***FIT TO BE TIED* by Joan Johnston**
Matthew Benson had a way with words
and women—but he refused to be tied
down. Could Jennifer Smith get him to
retract his scathing review of her art by
trying another tactic: tying him *up*?

Available at your favorite retail outlet!

MEN AT WORK™

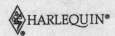 

HARLEQUIN SUPERROMANCE®

BUFFALO GAL

by Lisa McAllister

Welcome to White Thunder Ranch in North Dakota!

Andrea Moore learns on her wedding day that she's won a buffalo ranch. In less than twenty-four hours, Andrea's life changes completely. It goes from predictable to surprising…and exciting. Especially when she meets White Thunder's foreman, Mike Winterhawk—who's determined to protect his business from a city woman who knows squat about ranching!

Watch for *Buffalo Gal* in November 1998.
Available wherever Harlequin books are sold.

HARLEQUIN®

Makes any time special ™

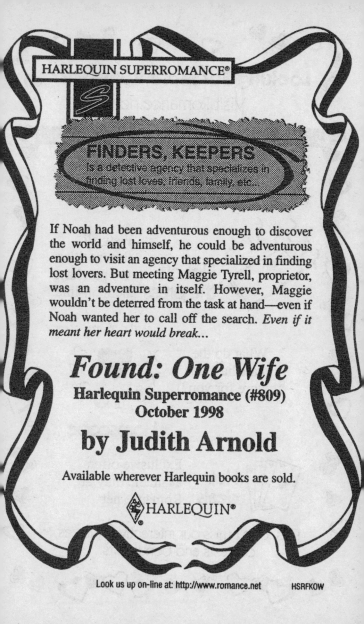

HARLEQUIN SUPERROMANCE®

FINDERS, KEEPERS
is a detective agency that specializes in
finding lost loves, friends, family, etc...

If Noah had been adventurous enough to discover
the world and himself, he could be adventurous
enough to visit an agency that specialized in finding
lost lovers. But meeting Maggie Tyrell, proprietor,
was an adventure in itself. However, Maggie
wouldn't be deterred from the task at hand—even if
Noah wanted her to call off the search. *Even if it
meant her heart would break...*

Found: One Wife
Harlequin Superromance (#809)
October 1998

by Judith Arnold

Available wherever Harlequin books are sold.

◆ HARLEQUIN®

CHRISTMAS Treats

PENNY JORDAN,

DAY LECLAIRE &
LINDSAY ARMSTRONG

bring you the best of Christmas romance
in this wonderful holiday collection where
friends and family gather to celebrate
the holidays and make romantic wishes
come true.

Christmas Treats is available in November 1998,
at your favorite retail store.

HARLEQUIN®
Makes any time special ™